D0240199

Susan Donovan attended Northwestern University's Medill School of Journalism and has worked as a newspaper reporter in Chicago, Albuquerque and Indianapolis. She lives in Maryland with her husband and children.

HE LOVES LUCY

Most women would *kill* to have access to personal trainer Theo Redmond. But Lucy Cunningham's starting to wish she'd never met him! Marketing exec Lucy's original idea for a reality TV show, in which Theo transformed someone from flabby to fabulous, hadn't featured *her* being the star . . . Balancing the need to lose weight against being watched by the whole of Miami, Lucy sweats her way into a new life. And as things also heat up between them, could chocoholic Lucy and Gym Bunny Theo be about to discover that true love lies somewhere between pizza and Pilates?

SUSAN DONOVAN

HE LOVES LUCY

Complete and Unabridged

ULVERSCROFT
Leicester

First published in Great Britain in 2006 by
Headline Book Publishing
London

First Large Print Edition
published 2007
by arrangement with
Headline Book Publishing
a division of Hodder Headline
London

The moral right of the author has been asserted

British Library CIP Data

Donovan, Susan
He loves Lucy.—Large print ed.—
Ulverscroft large print series: romance
1. Physical fitness centers—United States—Fiction
2. Personal trainers—United States—Fiction
3. Love stories 4. Large type books
I. Title
813.6 [F]

ISBN 978–1–84617–896–2

Published by
F. A. Thorpe (Publishing)
Anstey, Leicestershire

Set by Words & Graphics Ltd.
Anstey, Leicestershire
Printed and bound in Great Britain by
T. J. International Ltd., Padstow, Cornwall

This book is printed on acid-free paper

This book is dedicated to
every woman, everywhere,
who wants to be
at peace with her own body.

Acknowledgements

The author would like to thank the following people for their assistance in writing this book:

Thank you to Amie Dugan, Vice President for Public Relations for Special Olympics Florida; Mark E. Thompson, Executive Director of Special Olympics Miami-Dade County; and all the athletes and families who took time to talk with me at the 2004 Summer Games in Tampa, especially Anna Maria Miyamara, and the Leivas family — Felipe, German, and Camilo. A special thanks to Ruth, Jim, and Zachary Slagle of Tampa for use of their guest wing.

Thanks to Revonda Montoya, personal trainer to the beautiful people at the Hagerstown, Maryland YMCA, for her many helpful suggestions and her contagious positive attitude.

Thanks to my patient husband for taking the kids to Six Flags, the movies, the golfing range, the Mexican joint, and wherever else they went, so I could write. And thanks to my children for giving me the nickname Typerella during the writing of this book. Now *that* made me laugh.

Thanks to Kim Winkelman, marketing goddess at the Philly Pops, for answering questions about advertising, and to Ron Sulchek, CPA and generally cool dude, for answering questions about business and accounting practices.

Thanks to the real Doris Lehman, an insurance executive, not a therapist, for placing the winning bid at the Maryland Symphony Orchestra ball and silent auction to have her name used for one of my fictional characters.

Thanks to Celeste Bradley and Judi McCoy for brain-storming.

Thanks to the human milieu of Miami Beach, Florida, especially the crowd I hung with at the gay and top-optional beach (yes, I ended up there quite by accident), because knowing how to have a good time is so very important in this life.

And finally, thank you, Magic.

November 30

Lucy Cunningham's control tops were so tight that her inner thighs hissed like a swarm of cicadas with each step. The rhythm of nylon-on-nylon provided the soundtrack to what was becoming a long and humiliating stroll through the Palm Club's cardio studio, where she was scheduled to meet the man that fate — and her psycho boss — had selected to change her life.

Yes, people were staring. But that was because Lucy was wearing a business suit in a sea of spandex. That, and she was the only chubby chick in a room full of skinny people, which was always *funtastic*.

Lucy adjusted her laptop strap and pasted on a smile. So where was this guy? It was horrifying enough that she'd agreed to a public makeover as part of one of her own marketing campaigns, but now she had to go peeking behind treadmills in a game of find the über-trainer? According to the receptionist, he was a hard-to-miss man with short light brown hair, blue eyes, and a little gold hoop in his left ear. Yet so far, she'd managed to miss him and his hoop just fine.

1

Lucy felt ridiculous. Then she felt around inside her jacket pocket for the comfort of her edible worry beads and popped two Milk Duds into her mouth. It hadn't escaped her that the beloved Duds would have to go if she was going to lose a hundred pounds in a year. But for that blissful instant, perhaps the last she'd ever know, Lucy closed her eyes and felt the chocolate melt on her tongue until it was yielding and warm, just the right consistency to swirl around under her soft palate to position for the gratifying payoff — the lethal slam of her bite.

Ah, Milk Duds. The official candy of pissed-off fat women everywhere.

Lucy chewed, now much happier, and allowed her eyes to scan the rows of gleaming steel fitness machines displayed on acres of plush charcoal carpeting. She glanced down at the Post-it note in her damp palm. It said: *Theo Redmond*. Her boss had referred to him as 'personal trainer to the beautiful people of Miami Beach,' which made Lucy smile, seeing that he was about to become personal trainer to Lucy Cunningham, originally of Pittsburgh.

As she rounded the corner and entered a wide sunlit area full of high-tech machines, it occurred to Lucy that she might not have thought this through sufficiently. After all, who in her right mind decides to turn over a new leaf during the holidays? Talk about masochistic.

And she hadn't even considered how she'd introduce herself to this trainer, once she located him. She always preferred the blunt approach but wondered how he'd handle a quip like, *Howdy! I'm the out-of-shape babe you ordered!*

'Lucy Cunningham?'

Her head swiveled toward the deep voice. She stopped in her tracks as the bronzed God of Fitness arose from his knees. He'd been helping a vaguely familiar-looking woman with a machine that flapped her arms up and down like chicken wings, and the woman now seemed forlorn that he was leaving her side. The man began to walk toward Lucy, smiling.

Her stomach clenched with that near-sick anxiety she felt in the company of jocks, even though it had now been a whole decade since the Taco Bowl incident and there wasn't an ESPN reporter in sight.

She reminded herself to breathe. She reviewed to herself the truths one by one — the guy moving her way had nice eyes; he had a genuine smile; the guy looked like a life-size Ken doll, only hotter.

His big hand swallowed hers. His skin felt warm and a bit calloused. He squeezed her chubby little fingers. And Lucy knew she was staring, but the sheer physical beauty of this man had apparently left her mute and brain-dead.

He smiled at her and inclined his head to look her in the eye. 'I'm Theo. I'm running a little late, so would you mind having a seat in the conference room?' He gestured toward an area walled off in smoky glass. 'I'll only be a few minutes.'

Lucy nodded. She looked from the trainer's big white smile to the exotic woman on the exercise machine and it hit her. She'd just seen that perfect female face and that perfect female form on the front of that month's *Cosmo*! The woman on that bench was supermodel Gia Altamonte!

Lucy sucked in a breath of surprise, and the partially desiccated Milk Duds went along for the ride.

Theo Redmond peered at her, his brow now furrowed in concern. Then he patted Lucy's back in an area that would have been between her shoulder blades if she'd had shoulder blades, but there'd been nothing remotely blade-like on Lucy's body for years, as she well knew, and she was about to make some amusing comment along those lines when she realized she wasn't getting any air into her lungs.

'You OK, Miss Cunningham?'

Lucy smiled nonchalantly, confident she could will herself to breathe. Any second now it was bound to happen.

The trainer and the cover girl continued to stare at Lucy as the seconds ticked by.

The hell with this, she thought, clutching her throat in what she prayed was the universal sign for: *There seems to be a Milk Dud lodged in my airway.*

Trainer Ken leaped into action. He ripped Lucy's laptop strap from her shoulder, twirled her around so that her back was toward him, and brought his arms up under hers. In a hot flare of humiliation, Lucy realized several things at once: Gia Altamonte was on her cell phone, summoning the paramedics in a particularly annoying high-pitched Latin accent; the trainer had his hands dangerously close to Lucy's underwire-buoyed twins; and, in her last oxygen-fed thought, she realized she was too large for Theo Redmond to encircle in his arms in order to save her life.

* * *

Lucy was swimming, up, up into the bright world, surfacing from a heavy and sensual dream, where she was being kissed like nobody's business, kissed so hard her lungs burned. She tried to embrace her dream lover, but her arms felt too cumbersome to move, so she just angled her mouth to better accommodate his kiss.

'The ambulance is here, so you can stop making out with her, Theo.'

That voice sounded like fingernails on glass.

'Lucy? Miss Cunningham? Can you hear me?'

That voice was *sooo* much nicer.

Then it came back to her, and Lucy opened one eye to see the face of Theo Redmond hovering above. He had exquisite soft blue eyes framed in dark brown lashes and brows. He had smooth but strong lips. He was stroking her cheek.

'Welcome back.'

Lucy closed her eyes tight and tried to melt into the plush carpeting of the cardio room floor. The paramedics rushed in. Their voices were hurried as they took her blood pressure, asked her what medicines she was taking, and — could this possibly get any worse? — heaved her onto a stretcher, wheeled her out through the busy Palm Club, to the elevator, the model and the trainer hurrying along at her side.

'We're taking you to the hospital, where — '

'No.' Lucy's eyes snapped open. She glared at the paramedic.

'Just to be on the safe side,' he said.

'I'm fine.'

As Gia Altamonte signed autographs for the ambulance crew crammed in the elevator, Theo leaned down close to Lucy's face.

'Do it for me, OK, Lucy?' One side of his mouth hitched up, and he winked at her. 'When a woman loses consciousness on our first date, I have to wonder — is it my antiperspirant? My mouthwash?'

'It was my Milk Duds.'

'Those things will kill you, you know.' He let his little grin explode into a blazing smile.

Lucy couldn't help it — she smiled back, still feeling the astounding pleasure of that dream kiss. And in the heat of Theo Redmond's smile, something inside her ignited. It occurred to Lucy that dropping a hundred pounds had just become her second-biggest challenge.

1

December

'Nice to see you again, Lucy.'

She heaved herself up from the low white leather couch in the Palm Club's lobby and stood before Trainer Ken in all his glory, wondering how the man had managed to become better-looking in the last four days.

'I'm baaack,' Lucy said.

Theo laughed, and she scanned his crisp uniform of navy blue athletic shorts and white Palm Club polo shirt, then looked at those perfect bright teeth framed in those perfect man lips and thought if it weren't for the mouth-to-mouth-induced nirvana she'd experienced in his presence, she'd need to poke Theo to make sure he was real flesh and blood. The guy was way too perky for first thing in the morning.

'So how are you, Lucy?'

'I'm breathing on my own today. At least I got that going for me.'

'And I can assume you're not armed and dangerous?'

Lucy wasn't sure she'd heard right, and frowned.

'I'm asking if you're packin' any Milk Duds this morning, Miss Cunningham.'

Lucy's jaw fell open. It seemed that Buff Body Theo's sense of humor was a little edgier than she'd assumed. Maybe she'd been too preoccupied with her own mortification and near-death experience four days ago to appreciate it.

'No ammo today,' she said, letting go with a nervous laugh. Then, as if on cue, she patted her sweat-pants pocket in search of the comfort of a Milk Dud. She looked up in horror to see Theo smiling softly.

'It takes about six weeks to establish a habit or to break one,' he said, his voice kind.

'So I hear.'

'The good news is we've got fifty-one weeks left.' He reached for her hand, squeezing her fingers in a gentle grip. 'How about we start over? I'm Theo Redmond, your trainer for the next year.'

Lucy steadied herself with a deep breath, aware that passing out was passé. 'And I'm Lucy Cunningham, your worst nightmare.'

'Let's think positive, shall we, Miss Cunningham?'

She pulled her hand away and huffed. 'Call me Lucy. I'm not that much older than you, and when you call me 'Miss Cunningham' I feel like your spinster piano teacher or something.'

'I'm thirty-two.'

'I'm only twenty-nine.'

'I know.' He tapped his thigh with his clipboard and scowled a little, like he was thinking hard. 'This is where I usually ask my new clients to fill out a bunch of forms, but I don't feel like filling out forms this morning. How about you?'

'So we're going out for doughnuts instead?'

Theo tossed his clipboard on the reception counter and cupped Lucy's elbow, turning her toward the elevators as he chuckled. 'How about coffee and a sunrise? We can get to know each other a little, see what approach we're going to take, while we watch the sun come up.'

As they walked down the three flights of stairs to the lobby on Washington Avenue, Lucy checked out her trainer from the corner of her eye and, as she always did, wondered how much more she weighed than the person next to her. She knew it only made things worse, but she couldn't seem to stop her brain from doing the calculations. Maybe it was another one of those habits she could break with Theo's help.

'Are you originally from Miami, Lucy?' The

elevator doors opened and they headed for the street and into the pleasant, saltwater-scented city air.

'Pittsburgh. I moved here about a year ago to be closer to my parents. They retired to Fort Lauderdale.'

'Are you enjoying it?'

Lucy smiled to herself as they turned east along Fourth Street, heading toward the strip. The truth was that moving to Miami had made her feel like a foreign exchange student plopped down in an alien land. But her appreciation for the sun and heat and colorful array of humankind was slowly beginning to chip away at the culture shock. 'It's growing on me,' she said.

Theo gestured toward the front patio of the News Café on Ocean and motioned for her to go up the steps in front of him. He pulled out a wrought-iron chair for her, then sat down across the table under the market umbrella.

'I already know what approach I'd like to take to this whole business,' Lucy said.

Theo grinned. 'Oh? What approach is that?'

'I'd like to stroll through one of those magic chambers and come out a hundred pounds lighter, a hundred grand richer, and drop-dead gorgeous.'

Theo leaned back in his chair to leisurely study his newest client. Her brown hair was yanked into a tight and shiny ponytail. She had a sweet face, with smooth and clear skin, nicely shaped full lips, and adorable cheeks. Theo briefly scanned the rest of her. At about five-seven, she was a big woman but evenly proportioned. She carried herself well. It dawned on him that Lucy Cunningham might be the real deal if she lost the weight. *No.* When *she lost it*, he reminded himself.

It was true that Lucy had ended up in the ER before she'd even laced up her sneakers, but he still saw this year-long project as doable. He'd help the marketing executive lose up to one hundred pounds, documented in monthly TV appearances, magazine columns, and nonstop advertising, and they'd make a thousand dollars each for every pound she shed.

At the end of the year, Lucy would be thin and rich and he could afford to get his butt back to med school. Everybody wins.

Theo took note of the hefty-chick camouflage Lucy wore that morning — navy blue leggings that ended just below her knees and a large T-shirt that hit mid-thigh, an attempt to hide what couldn't be hidden. He returned his gaze to her face and encountered a set of big gray-blue eyes that were lit up with anger and defiance. Her pretty smile had transformed into a smirk.

13

The waitress appeared and Theo ordered decaf. Lucy followed suit. 'I'm assuming you know where we can find one of those magic chambers?' he asked.

'I was hoping *you* did.'

'There isn't one. So that leaves Plan B.' Theo waited for her to respond, but her gray eyes bored into his, unblinking. 'Aren't you curious what Plan B is, Lucy?'

The coffees came and Lucy swore she could smell cologne over the scent of java. She hoped it was only shampoo or soap, because she didn't trust jocks who wore cologne. Like most of her issues surrounding men, that little quirk could be traced right back to Brad Zirkle and the Taco Bowl incident. But for this thing to work with Theo, she was going to have to at least *try* to trust him, cologne or no.

'Plan B? Bring it on,' she said.

Lucy watched Theo hide a smile by sipping his coffee. Then his eyes wandered over her head toward the street. She followed his gaze to a beautiful redhead strolling confidently up the sidewalk, who waved and called out, 'Catch you Thursday, Theo-dorable!'

'Thursday it is!' Theo returned his gaze to Lucy, not missing a beat, and as he chatted about unrefined grains and positive thinking, Lucy wondered just how much of a ladies' man her trainer was. With those looks and liplocking skills, he had to be an A-lister among the single females of South Beach.

But *Theo-dorable*? Puh-leeze.

'Plan B is whatever works for you. We find it and we do it every day until it becomes a part of who you are.' Theo leaned across the small café table, lowered his chin, and looked directly into Lucy's eyes. She realized the most disarming thing about the guy was that he was masculine and exquisite at the same time. His face was perfectly balanced — a strong and straight nose, widely spaced and intelligent blue eyes, smooth lips, defined cheeks, ending in a slightly squared and cleanly shaven chin.

And his body was . . . well, Theo's body was solid and graceful and sun-kissed. He wasn't some bulging, muscle-bound hulk. The man simply *flowed*.

Lucy wiped perspiration from her forehead as her heart thudded, wondering if the redhead on the sidewalk or Theo's other girlfriends ever grew immune to his looks. Did they break out into a sweat just listening to him talk? She wondered if Gia Altamonte was one of those girlfriends and how many more of Miami's supermodels belonged to that club.

'And you'll follow Plan B until you can't

imagine life without it. Until you feel balanced and healthy, look fabulous, and have more energy than you ever thought possible. How does that sound?'

Lucy scrunched up her nose. 'I still want the magic chamber.'

Just then, a pretty blonde sat down a few tables away, chatting on her cell phone while she smiled at Theo. *Hey, you,* she mouthed silently. Theo nodded his head in the woman's direction and Lucy began to wonder if he was a trainer *and* a gigolo.

Theo described how he wanted her to keep a daily journal of her food, her feelings, and her goals. 'We'll tackle all the hard stuff tomorrow, after the TV studio, OK?'

'Yep.' Lucy eyed the blonde who eyed Theo.

'I'll have a detailed questionnaire for you about your fitness and health history, your current food choices and lifestyle. The more thorough your answers, the faster we can hit on exactly what will work. Sound good?'

Lucy froze, slowly understanding the implications of his last comment. She had to put in *writing* what she'd been eating lately? Was nothing sacred? 'Make sure to have extra sheets of paper handy,' Lucy said.

Theo lowered his voice. 'You'll need to bring your swimsuit tomorrow, too, OK?'

No, that wasn't *OK*! She'd rather die than let him see her in a bathing suit. 'Are we going snorkeling?'

Theo shook his head gently, knowing this part was going to be rough on Lucy. 'It's for the hydrostatic tank — '

'The whaaa — ?'

'We'll immerse you in water and get an accurate measure of your percentage of body fat.'

Lucy's eyes went huge.

'We have to know where we're starting. That's all it is — a place to start.'

'But do we have to start *there*?'

'I thought you agreed to a fitness evaluation.'

Lucy gulped. She blinked. She looked away for something to focus on while she got hold of herself. Her eyes landed on the blonde again, now crossing her zero-body-fat legs and batting her eyelashes at Theo.

'Couldn't we just make a guesstimate on my body fat? Like, say, ninety-eight percent, and go from there?'

Theo tried not to laugh. He watched Lucy Cunningham swallow hard and keep her eyes on anything but him. The embarrassment pulsed off her body in waves. He felt for her, he really did, but they couldn't start until he was sure she was a willing participant.

'Did you agree to this, Lucy? Are you aware that what we find out tomorrow and everything else we glean from lab tests, strength and cardiovascular evaluations — *everything* — is going to be made public?'

'I'm doing this for the cash; let's get that straight right from the start.' Lucy took a deep breath. 'I know I could stand to lose weight, but I plan to use the money to start my own company. And I do not plan to fail. It's just that getting started sounds so . . . ' Lucy looked down at her hands. '*Hard.*'

Theo pondered the slope of her neck and shoulders, how she overfilled the small café chair. Clearly, they'd be doing lots of cardio, adding machine and freestyle exercises over time. He was thinking Pilates for core strength. Yoga for flexibility.

He watched Lucy's jaw clench with frustration and figured she'd benefit from a few sessions where she could beat the living shit out of a kickboxing dummy. He made a mental note of it.

But as he continued to watch her, Theo was struck with the urge to hug this woman, tell her everything would be all right. That had never happened with a client before. Yes, it was about money for him, too, but he liked Lucy Cunningham. He wanted her to be happy. And there was something about her

— maybe the mix of brave girl and smart-assed woman — that tugged at him.

'I know it takes a lot of courage to do what you're doing.' She didn't respond, and he watched as she hid her face in her hands. Theo worried she'd choked again. 'Lucy?'

'I need a minute, please.' She jumped from the chair, laced her way through the tables, and ran out onto the sidewalk. Theo watched her go — she had decent running form and seemed pretty agile — then he saw that she was crying.

He sighed, threw a ten down on the table, and went after her. Lucy had stopped at the corner. She was red-faced and out of breath as she waited for a chance to cross at the curb.

'How long's it been since you took a nice run?' Theo stood at her side, following Lucy's blank stare toward the entrance to Eighth Street Beach and the rising sun beyond.

'What year is this again?' The light turned and Lucy walked across Ocean Boulevard, still breathing hard.

'That long, huh?'

'I used to run. I gained fifty pounds during college, but before then I used to play softball and racquetball. I rode horses, skied, and hiked, too.' She turned to him in direct challenge.

19

Theo couldn't prevent the surprise from showing on his face. He was sorry Lucy saw it, because she looked away, embarrassed. 'So why did you stop?'

Lucy whipped her head around so fast her ponytail brushed his shoulder. She looked up at him with what he could only describe as dread. 'No reason.'

Theo didn't push it. He knew that tomorrow she'd cover all the details in her client questionnaire. Today was for getting her to relax. Getting her psyched up for the long haul ahead. And so far, he'd failed miserably.

The timing couldn't be worse, but Theo saw a curvy little woman heading toward them who had once dated his best friend, Tyson. Theo couldn't remember the woman's name and was relieved when she strolled by with only a smile. Then he saw Lucy's openmouthed stare.

'Do you run an escort service on the side, Theo?'

He laughed. 'Naw. I just know a lot of people on South Beach.'

'A lot of female people.'

'And now I know you.' He smiled at her.

Lucy was not often tongue-tied, but she was a little rusty at engaging in small talk with gorgeous hunks. The truth was, she felt just plain defenseless against Theo Redmond and his enchanting smile.

'Where are we going, Lucy?'

She'd apparently been staring at him in a trance, walking aimlessly. It was a wonder she hadn't flattened a few pedestrians.

'Wherever you take me,' she said, flinching at the lovesick eighth grader she'd become, worrying she'd just officially blown her second chance at a first impression.

But Theo only laughed. He put his arm around her shoulder and gave her a squeeze. 'You're in good hands, Lucy Cunningham.'

★ ★ ★

Office of Doris Lehman, MSW, PhD

'Help. I have the hots for my trainer.'

Lucy had barely flopped down into the familiar peach damask love seat when she made that pronouncement. She let her eyes settle on the peaceful Japanese paper folding screen in front of the window, the focal point for her meditative stares the whole year she'd been in Miami. Her eyes scanned the familiar graceful sweep of bamboo leaves and transparent cherry blossoms, the little tiny female mouths of the little tiny women in tiny kimonos and tiny wooden platform sandals.

Tiny, tiny, tiny.

Lucy's therapist sat as she usually did,

21

serene, neat, notebook perched on a crossed thigh, eyeglasses tucked on top of her heavily sprayed salt-and-pepper pageboy like a headband.

'Have you told him you find him attractive?'

'I can't stop drooling long enough to form the words.'

'I see.'

'Besides, it's the Brad Zirkle thing all over again, you know?' Lucy leaned forward and balanced her elbows on her knees. 'Why do I always go for the ones who are out of my reach? Why do I set myself up like that?'

Doris smiled politely. 'From how you've described him, it would seem Theo is much nicer than Brad Zirkle.'

'Yeah, Mr Wonderful is still wonderful.' Lucy sighed, then snarled at the geisha girls, trying to picture how her size 22 hips would look in a kimono pulled that tight at the waist. If she had a waist. She used to have one, if she recalled correctly, but she couldn't remember how it felt to walk around with an indentation somewhere near the center of her body.

'I sense some anger in how you describe him.'

Lucy had to laugh. 'Not anger. I'm just kind of ashamed of myself for fantasizing about him the way I do — you know, him naked, feeding me Lorna Doone cookies while I watch Andy Griffith reruns.'

Doris began to scribble on her clipboard.

'Am I having a breakthrough?'

Doris grinned. 'I'm not sure yet. Please go on.'

'Theo seems pretty shallow, but God is he *hot*, Doris. I'm talking perfect. Theo Redmond is perfect. He's so perfect that it doesn't even matter that he's shallow. Did you know that most of his clients are models?'

'Shallow.'

'Yes.'

'And you know this how?'

Doris's tone of voice surprised Lucy. 'Look, he's very nice. All I'm saying is based on all that perfection, I'm thinking he must focus more on his appearance than his character. It must take all his time to have that perfect body. The perfect hair. That perfect smile.'

'I see,' Doris said. She put down her pen. 'Just as one might assume that an overweight person is a lazy slob?'

'*Doris!*' Lucy sat back in the love seat and blinked a few times.

'Just a little food for thought, Lucy.'

2

January

Journal Entry Jan 1

Breakfast: ¾ c oatmeal; 1 c skim milk; 1 c strawberries; half decaf/half regular coffee

Lunch: 3 oz chicken breast; 1 slice whole wheat bread; 1 tbsp light mayo; celery; lettuce; tomato; 1 med apple

Dinner: 3 oz corned beef; 1 c cooked cabbage; large salad w/ orange and red peppers, tomatoes, cucumbers, and 2 tbsp light ranch dressing

Snack: 1 c plain yogurt; ¼ c light granola; 1 orange

Affirmation for Today:
I am strong enough to refrain from killing any or all members of my family.

★ ★ ★

'Lucinda, honey, would you pass the soda bread?'

Lucy handed the still-warm Irish bread to her mother and tried not to let the heavenly scent enter her nostrils and pierce her primordial brain, which would force her to stick her face directly into the basket and growl like a starving alley dog as she ripped off giant hunks with her incisors.

'You're eating like a bird.' It was the fifth time her father had made that observation since they sat down to dinner. 'No potatoes. No bread. Are you sick?'

'Oh, for crying out loud, Bill. Leave her alone. You know she's on that diet.' Lucy watched with envy as her mother slathered butter all over a thick chunk of soda bread and savored a healthy bite.

Lucy reached for her glass of ice water and sipped demurely, looking around the New Year's Day table, wondering why she'd thought she could survive another visit to the Land o' Food when Christmas had been such an unmitigated disaster. She still hadn't come clean to Theo about the pecan pie from December 26 and the deception was gnawing a hole in her soul. She'd promised that everything that went into her mouth would go into her food journal, and she'd already blown it, not even a month into her new life.

And tomorrow was her first weigh-in! On live television!

She had no choice but to come clean. It's not like she could say she *forgot* she ate half a pie.

'What kind of diet is it again, honey?'

The kind where you sneak a half a pecan pie.

'It's not a diet, Mother. Lucy calls it a fitness and nutrition plan.' This clarification came from Lucy's older sister, Mary Fran, who was shoveling some kind of green bean paste from a jar into the open maw of her youngest.

Lucy watched her nephew spew most of it out and bang his fists on the high chair tray. She could relate. If she didn't get a piece of that soda bread in the next five seconds, she'd be banging her fists on the table as well. Somehow, she'd survived an entire month eating nothing but whole grains, fresh produce, and lean cuts of meat. What the hell kind of torture was *that*? Nothing fried. Nothing gooey. Nothing with icing on it. Nothing even vaguely cupcake-shaped. Lucy didn't think she'd make it through this dinner without shaming herself.

'She doesn't need to diet. She's beautiful.' Her father patted Lucy's hand. 'Have some potatoes, sweetheart. You won't have good luck this year unless you do.'

'Where do you get this stuff, Daddy? I swear!' Mary Fran wiped a green smear off little Holden's face while attempting to feed herself. Lucy decided it was no wonder Frannie was thin. She never had a second to eat. Maybe having three babies in five years was the secret to staying thin.

Lucy's eyes strayed to her mother. *Cancel that*.

'So how much poundage you dropped so far, Luce?' Dan could always be counted on to cut to the chase. That's what brothers were for, she supposed.

Her mother gasped. 'Danny! What a rude thing to ask! I hope to God that's not the way you speak to your patients!' Then, from across the table, she produced a sympathetic smile for Lucy. 'So how much *have* you lost, honey?'

Lucy was in the throes of a bad case of déjà vu and looked at her watch. It wasn't like she could feign a work emergency today and get in the car and drive the forty-five minutes to Miami. Even Stephan Sherrod, the world's worst boss, managed to avoid marketing and advertising emergencies on New Year's Day.

'I don't know how much weight I've lost, Dan, Mother, Daddy, Frannie. As I think I may have mentioned at Christmas, my trainer will weigh me just once a month, and tomorrow marks the end of my first full month. Right now, the numbers aren't as important as improving my fitness level.'

'So you haven't lost anything yet?'

Lucy gave Dan the look of disgust she reserved only for her baby brother. 'You'll be the first to know. The minute I'm weighed, I'll have them put out an all-points bulletin. It's unfortunate you're still in Pittsburgh, or you could just watch the *WakeUp Miami* show like everyone else.'

'I think you look great,' Mary Fran said, hauling Holden's wiggling body from the high chair. Lucy watched her hustle into the kitchen, where she held the baby over the kitchen sink and used a damp paper towel to scrape bean paste from his hair and clothing. Then she called out, 'Just don't try to lose too much too fast, Lucy! That's dangerous!'

'I'm doing my best to avoid that.'

Dan laughed.

'Well, I saw the ad in the *Herald* the other day,' her mother said. 'You should've worn your hair down, sweetheart. You look much better with it down. But your trainer looked like a movie star. Here. Have some more brisket.'

Lucy decided maybe she could lie about the work emergency. 'Thanks, Mom. I think.

I'll pass on the beef.'

'So let me see if I understand this, pumpkin.' Lucy's father offered her a slice of bread, which she managed to turn down. 'You and Jack La Lanne get to split a hundred grand if you pull this off?'

Lucy sighed, positive that she'd gone over the details with her father at least once. 'No. We each get a thousand dollars for each pound I lose, up to one hundred.'

'And that crazy boss of yours is paying for this? Was this his idea?'

'It was my idea to capitalize on the reality-show make-over craze and build a campaign around one person's success story. I just didn't know it would be me. That *was* my crazy boss's idea, and our client — the Palm Club — agreed to put up the cash.'

Dan cleared his throat. 'Uh, Luce? Aren't you afraid somebody will figure out that you're . . . well, you know . . . the girl who brought down the Pitt State football program? The famous slump buster?'

'*Daniel Murphy Cunningham!*' Her mother's fork crashed to her plate. 'How *could* you? You know we've agreed never to speak of the Taco Bowl incident in front of Lucy!'

'What in God's name did he just say?' Mary Fran yelled over the running faucet.

'Hey, it's not a big deal, really.' Lucy had

worried the same thing, so she couldn't blame Dan for asking. 'I'd never do this kind of thing back home, but it happened ten years ago in Pittsburgh. It probably didn't even make the news down here.'

Dan shot her a grateful look. 'I just wanted to make sure you'd thought this through.'

'I told Stephan I wouldn't do it at first, but then he dangled the money in front of me, and I saw it as my way to escape Sherrod & Thoms and start my own company. It was just too good to pass up.'

Her brother frowned. 'But what happens if you blow it?'

'*Dan!*' Mary Fran hustled back to the table and shoved Holden into her brother's lap. 'She's not going to blow it! Lucy can do anything she sets her mind to.'

Holden chose that moment to rake his little raggedy baby fingernails across Dan's cheek. 'Ow!'

'I think what we're asking is, are you sure you want to put yourself out there like this?' Lucy's mother reached across the table to stroke her fingers. 'It's a huge challenge, Lucy. I just don't want to see my sweet girl hurt or humiliated — not ever again.'

'Thanks, Mom. I think. But it's too late now. The Palm Club is paying our agency a lot of money to run this campaign, and *I'm* the campaign — monthly appearances on *WakeUp Miami*, a weekly column in *Miami Woman*, the biggest advertising blitz I've ever put together. I have no choice but to be successful.'

'That's an awful lot of pressure to put on yourself, Luce.' Mary Fran looked worried.

'By God, those reality TV shows are something, aren't they?' Her father served himself more potatoes. 'They make over your car, your house, your marriage, your filing cabinet, your face.' He went for the cabbage next. 'I think the only frontier left for TV is ritual human sacrifice and live copulation.'

Lucy's mother rolled her eyes. Mary Fran pursed her mouth in disgust. Then Dan said, 'You must not have direct satellite yet.'

The men took a cleaned-up Holden into the family room to watch football while the women cleared the table. Since her sister had traveled from Atlanta with just one kid, Lucy hoped they might have time to chat. But Frannie looked like she needed a nap more than a heart-to-heart.

'How's Keith doing?'

Mary Fran sighed at Lucy's question. 'The usual. He claimed the promotion would mean less time on the road, but I don't see it.'

Lucy put a stack of leftovers in the

31

refrigerator, concerned by the fatigue in her sister's voice.

'He said that's just temporary, right?'

Mary Fran looked up from the sink. 'I'm not falling for that again.'

'If you ask me, you look like you're just plain ready to fall over.' Lucy's mother hugged Mary Fran and suggested Lucy take her to the guest room for a rest.

'We'll have dessert a little later.' Her mother gave Lucy a wink. 'Pecan pie. Your favorite.'

⋆　⋆　⋆

Lucy sat on the edge of the guest bed and watched Mary Fran peel off her size 4 jeans and crawl under the hand-made quilt. She tried to remember what it felt like to be a size 4 and take up this little space on a double bed, but her memory of second grade was fuzzy.

'So tell me about this trainer, Luce.' Mary Fran took a deep breath and pulled the quilt up under her chin. She looked pale. 'Is she a weight-lifter chick? Or one of those aerobics instructor-cheerleader types?'

Lucy smiled a little, realizing that Fran hadn't been inundated by the image of Lucy and Theo at metro stops. She also realized she'd never been asked to describe Theo to anyone.

Four weeks had now passed, which meant she'd made it through twenty one-hour training sessions. He met her at the door every weekday before dawn, wearing his trainer getup, never a minute late, always in good spirits. He was accredited out the yin-yang in everything from sports nutrition to exercise physiology. He was patient but pushed her to go a little higher, do a little more, every day. As a bonus, he remained the most searingly hot man-babe she'd ever laid eyes on.

'My trainer is a he, and he's quite good at his job,' Lucy said.

Frannie looked at her suspiciously. 'That cute, huh?'

'Lord help me — I think I'm gonna die if I don't get me some of that.'

Frannie laughed. 'This sounds promising.'

It was Lucy's turn to laugh. 'Yeah, well, a girl can dream, but he's way out of my league, and besides, it seems he already dates half the premenopausal female population of South Beach.'

'Hmm. When was *your* last date, Luce?'

Lucy sighed, hating to admit the truth. 'Remember the Oktoberfest two years ago? Very good schnitzel, very bad date?'

'You mean that programmer dweeb Keith set you up with?'

'Yep.'

'The one who said you had childbearing hips?'

'That would be him.'

'My God, Lucy. You haven't gone out since?'

'I think that night cured me of my urge to date.'

Mary Fran patted Lucy's arm and laughed. 'We'll go out on the town together. Meet some people. I'll be running away from Atlanta soon anyway, so how about I move in with you? We can party every weekend. Won't that be fun?'

Lucy reared back and stared. 'What *are* you talking about?'

'Oh hell, Lucy.' Her sister's words came out soft and sad. 'He's never home — and I mean *never*. We're lucky to have two family dinners together a month.'

'Jeesh!'

'I think I've had it. I'm so tired some days I can't stay awake.'

'Oh, Frannie. Does Keith know how much you need him at home?'

Mary Fran laughed. 'The man knows. Trust me.' She got quiet. 'I think he's having an affair.'

34

'What?' Lucy sat up straight. 'I'm going to *kill* him!'

Fran yawned. 'Maybe I'm just imagining it, but when he's not on the road he can't wait to get out of the house, and it's such chaos all the time that I can't blame him. I just wonder if he's running to someone else — someone who doesn't have kid snot on the front of her blouse.'

'Oh, Fran.' Lucy stroked her sister's sassy little haircut. 'Talk to Keith. Confront him.'

Mary Fran leaned against her sister and shook her head. 'I'd rather just hang out with you and enjoy the single Miami girl lifestyle.'

Lucy chuckled. 'Yes, just day after day of nothing but sex, clubbing, sex, sex, sex.'

Mary Fran turned her sleepy gaze to Lucy. 'It might be for the best. Sex is what got me in this mess to begin with.'

'But it's such a good mess.' Lucy kissed her sister's cheek, seeing once again why people used to say Mary Fran was a miniature version of herself. Her sister was two years older, five inches shorter, and God knew how many pounds lighter, but with the same color hair and eyes and light pink complexion. Her petite cuteness didn't bother Lucy as much as it used to, and seeing her wrung out like this broke Lucy's heart.

'Anyway,' she said with a sigh, 'I only have a one-bedroom and we'd end up killing each other over bathroom countertop space.'

Mary Fran had no comeback for that, because she'd fallen asleep.

★　★　★

Theo took a seat at the conference table and smiled at Tyson on his right, then Lola on his left. Palm Club staff meetings were always painful, but today's promised to be agonizing, because they were going to discuss the Lucy Cunningham project and Lola DiPaolo was already sneering at him.

Their boss, Ramona Cortez, regaled them with end-of-year sales figures and assigned trainers for several new clients, then gestured toward Theo. 'Get us up to speed on how your fifteen minutes of fame is going.'

He felt the heat of Lola's mascara-laden evil eye just before she said, 'Fifteen minutes that's gonna drag on for a whole frickin' year.'

Theo laughed along with every other trainer in the room, including his best friend, Tyson Williams, a bald and baby-faced former University of Florida running back who showed a bit of wear and tear that morning. Theo wondered which of Tyson's favorite clubs had kept him from his beauty sleep.

'We're doing great so far. We're in here every weekday morning at five, so give her a little encouragement if you see her. She's going to need all the support she can get.'

'And what are you gonna need at the end of this year? An updated résumé?'

Theo grinned at the remark from one of the trainers across the table and waited till the laughter subsided. 'Miss Cunningham and I will get the job done,' he said.

'Too bad the cameras weren't here the day she upchucked her M&M's,' Lola said with a laugh.

'No such thing as too many documentaries on how to perform the modified Heimlich maneuver,' Tyson added.

'It was Milk Duds,' Theo said.

Ramona jumped in. 'We're already getting an amazing amount of press with this project. It's possible some of you will be approached by the media for comment in the coming months, so please clear it with me first before you're interviewed.' She smiled at Theo. 'This campaign is costing a bundle up front, but we're going to reap the benefits for years to come.'

Lola frowned and shook her head. 'Have you ever had a client drop a hundred pounds in a year? I mean, get real, Theo!'

'No, I haven't.' It was the truth. He'd never tried something this ambitious, with this kind of timetable or public exposure. Of course, he'd cared for obese patients as a med student and helped some clients make dramatic changes in their lives, but lately it had been one nearly-perfect-on-the-outside Palm Club client after the next.

Frankly, it was getting old.

'Remember my client who lost sixty pounds?' Lola charged on with her story, oblivious to the fact that no one remembered any such client. 'Well, I heard she left her husband for the China Wok delivery boy.'

Theo wasn't sure what point Lola was attempting to make, as usual.

Tyson turned to Theo. 'Looks like she's sticking with it. You doing six days?'

Lucy was sticking with it, and though her first weigh-in was still a few days away, he could see the change in her. Her aerobic capacity was up. Her upper-body strength had already improved. She'd obviously lost weight. She was handling the nutrition plan well and had been sticking with daily journaling, short-term goal setting, and counseling. He'd done a boatload of research on cardio training and muscle toning for women, along with the newest motivation strategies. He'd picked the brains of a couple of his friends now in sports medicine. He'd even taped a few episodes of *Dr Phil*.

'We're doing five days on, one light day, and one rest day. She has access to me round the clock.'

'Oooh. Every girl's dream,' Lola cooed.

Tyson stared at Theo, his head cocked to the side, his dark eyes quite wide. '*One hundred* pounds, though, man. I still say better you than me.'

Ramona closed the meeting, sending the trainers out into the gym, but stopped Theo at the door.

'Got a minute?'

He leaned on the table edge and crossed his arms over his chest. 'Absolutely.'

Ramona smiled at him. 'You know, you're the best trainer I have and the only one I could have trusted with this. I wanted to tell you I appreciate how hard you're working.'

He nodded. 'Sure.'

'Look, Theo. I realize you've got your sights set higher than the Palm Club. I knew that when I hired you three years ago.' Ramona's warm brown eyes crinkled with her smile. 'You're going to handle Lucy and all the media attention beautifully. And I know that when it's over and you've got your money, you'll leave here and finish med school. How close am I to being right?'

Theo let go with a laugh. Ramona was so easy to work for that he sometimes found himself thinking of her as more a friend than a boss. But at her core, she was a shrewd businesswoman. When she held out that one-hundred-thousand-dollar bonus as bait, she knew he'd bite, and she even knew why.

'If they let me back in, yes.'

'They'll let you in.'

Theo shifted his weight from foot to foot. 'I love what I do here, Ramona.'

'And your clients love that you do it.' She let loose with a wide grin and patted his shoulder. 'When the agency suggested the idea, I knew it had to be you. All I ask is that you let Lucy Cunningham down easy when she falls in love with you.'

Theo was used to this kind of teasing. He had an undeserved rep for being a player, and nobody but Tyson knew that he rarely dated. Between raising Buddy, working two jobs, Special Olympics coaching, and studying his ass off for the reentry exam, there wasn't time for women, especially another one who'd break his heart. He hoped someday that might change, but that day seemed a ways off.

'And a year is a very long time for a lonely

40

woman to be in close proximity to Theo-dorable.'

He shrugged and decided to play along. 'I can't help it that I'm devastatingly handsome and perfect in every way.'

Ramona chuckled, headed for the door, then turned back toward him. 'To your clients, that's exactly what you are.' Theo tried to cut her off, but she held up her hand. 'Do you know you've got a waiting list of females a mile long? Have you noticed that out of your forty active clients there is only one man, and he's in love with you, too?'

'I've noticed.'

'Lucy is our meal ticket. The world will watch her go from frumpy to fabulous in your care and we'll be the hottest fitness franchise in the state — hotter even than Goldstein's Gym, and you know how long I've wanted to bury that sleazy bastard.'

'I know.'

'Your job is to keep Lucy Cunningham motivated and on track. Get as close to her as you need, but keep it professional. I know you can walk that line.'

Theo frowned at his boss, incredulous. 'She is not exactly my type, Ramona.'

She shook her head and laughed. 'But you're *hers*, Theo. You're every woman's type.'

Theo closed his eyes and sighed. 'I can handle Lucy Cunningham.'

Ramona had already shut the door behind her.

★ ★ ★

'You can open your eyes now.'

Lucy did. And the number on the scale seemed too good to be true. She looked up into the TV studio camera and gasped, 'I lost *twenty-two pounds?*'

She blinked into the lights while the *WakeUp Miami* audience applauded. Theo offered her his hand, helped her down from the scale, and escorted her back to the row of upholstered chairs on the set. Lucy felt the cameras trail behind her and heard an occasional whistle or hoot from the crowd.

'Congratulations, Lucy,' cooed cohost John Weaver, who clapped right along with the audience.

She felt a little self-conscious sitting there in her snug pink sweatpants and a T-shirt, all eyes and smiles focused on her. At least it was a new T-shirt. A pretty lime green color the makeup people said looked nice against her complexion.

'Do you feel any different, Lucy? Tell us — how in the world does that *feel*?' Carolina

Buendia's question caused the applause to taper off, and Lucy swallowed uncomfortably. She glanced at Theo, who gave her a wink.

Lucy tapped the small microphone clipped to her shirt, hunched her shoulder to bring her mouth close, and said, 'I feel smaller.'

★   ★   ★

Theo finished measuring Lucy for the second time that morning, then led her from the Palm Club's trainer room out into the gym.

'Well?'

'The measurements I got at the TV studio were accurate.' Theo shook his head in disbelief.

'But this is good, right?'

'Too good. I don't want you losing this fast.'

She stopped walking. 'What are you, *nuts*?'

They arrived at the treadmill. Theo punched in a ten-minute warm-up program and Lucy hopped on.

'I expected you to lose a lot up front. That's normal. But you lost eight inches and twenty-two pounds, and that's too much in one month. I need to keep you in the two-pound-a-week range.'

Lucy perked up at that. 'So I get to eat more?'

'You wish.' Theo playfully tugged on the towel around her neck, then made some notes on his clipboard. 'I'll weigh and measure you once a week for a while to keep a better eye on things, see if I need to make adjustments. But that will be for my eyes only. I don't want you to get too attached to numbers.'

He looked up, caught her eye, and smiled. 'The bottom line is you're doing great, Lucy. I'm proud of you. So how was your New Year's?'

Lucy tried to let everything he'd just said sink in. *She was a success.* She was *too* successful! Maybe she didn't have to tell him about the pecan pie after all. Obviously, it hadn't hurt her. Maybe this whole weight loss thing would be a snap. Suddenly, for the life of her, she couldn't figure out why she hadn't tried this sooner!

'My New Year's was marvy. Partied all night with the beautiful people.'

Theo gave her a crooked smile that made her stomach do a strange flip-flop. 'Yeah, I spent it with my family, too. Less aggrava-tion.'

'We obviously don't have the same family.'

Theo let his smile linger for a moment while he reached for her wrist and took her pulse. Lucy had become accustomed to Theo touching her, but it still sent a charge through

44

her nervous system every time, and she knew he'd never get an accurate pulse rate that way. She was tempted to tell him to subtract at least 10 from the figure.

When he was done, he patted her forearm affectionately and went back to his clipboard. 'How did you do with your nutrition plan the last few days?'

'Good. My journal's in my gym bag.'

She watched Theo bend down, push aside her water bottle, and root through her clean underwear before he pulled out the journal. She could have died. But really, was there anything left to hide from the man? He knew her weight to the digital ounce, her percentage of body fat — which was less than 98 percent, thank God — along with her body mass index, resting heart rate, base metabolic rate, and cholesterol level. He knew what foods she craved and exactly when she craved them. Besides, it wasn't like her white granny panties would trip his wire.

Lucy sighed, watching him flip through her journal. He would soon know about the pecan pie, too, because she'd finally admitted to it in writing. *Oh hell.*

Theo made a noncommittal 'hmmm' sound and glanced up at her, his little gold earring glittering in the overhead lights of the cardio studio. He held her gaze for a second, his smile soft and thoughtful. 'That's one whopper of a slip, Cunningham.'

'Look. I'm fully aware that pecan pie isn't on my nutrition plan.'

He said nothing but returned the journal to her bag, then leaned against the treadmill, long and relaxed, and looked at her.

'I know I'm supposed to stay away from refined sugar and white flour.'

He nodded.

Theo's nonchalance pissed her off. Why didn't he just come out and yell at her? 'And the last time I looked, a thousand calories worth of corn syrup and pie crust fit both those categories rather nicely.'

'Probably does.'

'Aren't you going to say something?'

'Any whipped cream?'

'No.'

'I don't like whipped cream on mine, either.'

A sudden change in treadmill speed nearly made Lucy trip. She had to push herself to keep up the pace. Her lungs began to pump.

'That's it?' she cried, breathing hard. 'That's all you have to say about the pie?'

Theo shrugged. 'The world didn't end, right?'

'Of course not.' She tried to scowl at him, but her facial muscles wouldn't comply. She felt too warm and relaxed this morning, her body loosening and swaying to the steady beat of her feet on the wide rubber belt. She could feel the blood moving through her veins. She was starting to sweat in earnest. She felt proud and happy and, she realized with a jolt of awareness, a whopping twenty-two pounds lighter.

'We're in this for the long haul. You made a mistake, but you didn't let it derail you. That's the important thing.'

She gave him a grateful smile.

'But if you do it again, I'll have to kick your ass. And that's the end of our little pie discussion.' Theo continued scribbling on his clipboard, one ankle casually crossed over the other.

Lucy sighed. She supposed he couldn't help it, but Theo Redmond throbbed with the good-looking guy vibe, that chromosomal-level confidence that made every female within a mile perk up, suck in her gut, and smile in an effort to catch his eye.

Except for herself, of course. It was understood that women like Lucy were automatically disqualified from playing those games with men like Theo. She'd once been stupid enough to believe she could be the exception to the rule, and look where it landed her. Never again.

47

She studied Theo, all that lean muscle and golden skin, and realized it was a blessing, really. There could never be any kind of sexual connection between them, and that left her free to be herself with him, the red-faced, sweaty mess she was.

Lucy was huffing now, starting to drip. She looked down at the digital readout on the treadmill console and frowned. 'Hey!' she gasped. 'I thought . . . we were . . . sticking to three-point-two miles an hour . . . maximum incline . . . of three!'

'Think again.' Theo didn't raise his eyes from the clipboard.

'But — '

He looked up, his grin spreading ear to ear. 'Don't want you to get bored, Cunningham.'

She shot him a glare.

'Keep talking to me. This is just a warm-up, and if you can't talk, then it's too much.'

'I can talk.' The sun was just starting to peek over the water. It made her smile. This entire experience made her smile — she was awake to see the sun come up. She was moving, sweating, breathing, meeting a challenge. She felt alive.

She turned and saw Theo scrutinizing her. 'Thank you, Theo,' she said, knowing she was beaming at him.

'For what? The pie thing? Don't thank me — just don't do it again.'

She laughed. 'Not that, exactly.'

Theo shook his head almost imperceptibly. 'Then what?'

'For being so cool about everything. For being good at what you do. I'm lucky to have you as my trainer.'

Slowly, Theo's grin began to fade, and Lucy watched him struggle to keep it in place. He shrugged off the compliment. 'It's just my job.'

Right. Lucy turned back to the windows and laughed out loud at herself for being flattered by his attention. Theo was looking at a huge payoff if he could get her to lose all the weight, and at this point it looked like she'd make it way before the year was through. That charm was professional courtesy. That smile was capitalism at work. She bet those cornflower blue eyes shone like that for all his paying clients. Of course it was his job. *She* was just a job. Nothing more.

Lucy told herself to remember that.

3

February

Journal Entry Feb 6

Breakfast: *½ whole wheat bagel; 1 tbsp natural peanut butter; ½ grapefruit; decaf with splash of skim milk*

Lunch: *2 cups romaine and raw vegetables; 4 oz turkey breast; 1 oz light cheddar; 1 tbsp olive oil; red wine vinegar; ½ c brown rice*

Dinner: *1 small baked sweet potato; 3 oz broiled chicken breast; 1 c steamed pea pods and mushrooms*

Snack: *1 c plain yogurt; 1 apple; cinnamon*

Affirmation for Today:
I'm sure that somewhere in the world there is a boss more psycho than mine. I just haven't met him yet.

★　★　★

Stephan Sherrod burst into the conference room without warning. 'Greetings, employees!' He settled into an armchair, his long legs stretched in front of him. 'I take it we're flexing our creative pecs and abs in here this morning?'

Stephan chortled at his own pun and waited for someone — anyone on his staff — to join in appreciation of his wit. Lucy didn't volunteer, but her assistant, Veronica King, managed a vague giggle.

'We're reviewing the Palm Club account,' Lucy said, handing Stephan the month's media summary.

'Marvelous. Don't let me stop you.'

Now *that* was truly funny. Everyone in this conference room knew that Stephan Sherrod could single-handedly suck the lifeblood out of anything — and did so as a matter of course. Meetings. Client outings. Parties. And, since his partner, Sarah Thoms, died eight months ago, Stephan had been doing it to his own company. Sherrod & Thoms had been steadily losing loyal clients, and it was a battle to find new ones. The company lost its heart and soul when it lost Sarah.

Lucy looked around the conference room and noted that Stephan had managed to ruin her team meeting as well. Moments ago, they'd been reviewing everything from graphic design to Web site development for the Palm Club account and the room had been filled with creative energy, good humor, friendly competition, and teasing. Now, there was nothing but discomfort.

Barry Neikirk stared at the ceiling. Maria Banderas clicked away at her laptop in silence. Veronica nervously snapped her gum and doodled on her agenda.

Lucy had taken the position with Sherrod & Thoms last year because of Sarah Thoms. Sarah had been in her mid-fifties, outgoing and witty, devoted to her clients, and full of life. Her creativity and drive had made this little company a big presence in the Miami-Dade market. It didn't take Lucy long to figure out that Sarah was the heart and soul of the operation and Stephan was the face man, the schmoozer. It had worked.

But Sarah died during elective surgery about eight months after Lucy moved to Miami. She looked around the conference table now and knew that everyone there — herself included — had stayed with Stephan because the job market was tight, not because they enjoyed working for him.

And in ten months, if she met her weight loss goal, she'd be walking out of this place with a hundred thousand in her pocket and a business plan for her own agency. The thought put a smile on her face.

'So Barry,' Lucy decided to salvage the meeting. 'What do you think about capitalizing on the idea that the gym can work around anyone's schedule?'

'It's the only way to go, frankly,' he said. 'The fact that the Palm Club has personal trainers available from five a.m. to ten p.m. seven days a week really sets them apart. They're leaving their competition in the dust.' Barry referred to his laptop screen. 'Goldstein's Gym only offers personal training from six to six, five days a week.'

Maria agreed. 'The Palm Club's ability to work around a client's schedule is really the only way to justify a price point much higher than anywhere else in town, including Goldstein's.'

'Exactly,' Barry said. 'You can't exactly put a price tag on the South Beach celebrity mojo thing they've got going.'

As everyone nodded their agreement, Lucy glanced Stephan's way. At some point in the last few moments, his expression had shifted from affable vacancy to pasty fear.

'Are you all right, Stephan?'

'Fine. Fine.' He cleared his throat and straightened in the leather chair.

'Well, I loved the slogan 'Fitness at the Speed of Life,'' Veronica chimed in.

Maria pointed across the table. 'That was your idea, wasn't it, Lucy?'

Lucy still had one eye on her boss. 'Yes, it was.'

'I think you hit a bull's-eye with that,' Barry said.

Stephan stood up.

'Thanks.' She watched her boss shuffle toward the conference room door, his shoulders slumped. 'I fiddled around with a few other things, including something a bit more blunt, but that's the one I like, too.'

Maria smiled. 'I'm all for blunt. What was it?'

Lucy studied Stephan's back. 'Oh, just something like, 'Wanna bet the fat chick can do it?'

Suddenly Stephan spun around, a glint in his eye. 'My God, Lucy! You look like someone stuck a pin in you and you've begun to deflate!'

Veronica snapped her gum a little too loudly.

'I'd heard you'd lost a few pounds, but I hadn't really noticed until now.'

If it weren't for past experience, Lucy would have assumed she'd misheard Stephan. But as she was now well aware, her boss had no manners.

'Uh. That's the whole point,' she replied.

Stephan laughed. 'Well, we need to take you out to celebrate. Whad'ya say? Lunch for everyone tomorrow at Bugatti? My treat. Anything you want. They have the best pesto ravioli in town.'

And with that pronouncement, he was gone.

★   ★   ★

Lola DiPaolo looked like she was hitting the tanning bed a bit too hard these days. At this rate she'd have skin like a wrinkled paper bag in another few years, Theo decided. But then, Lola wasn't known for her long-term approach to anything.

'Theodore.' She looked up from her bodybuilding magazine and smiled.

'Lola. How's life?'

'Fun as always. How's yours?'

'Busy.' Theo walked over to the wall of mailboxes in the staff lounge, where each trainer had a cubbyhole for mail and phone messages.

He sorted through a stack of messages and found the usual — clients who needed to reschedule, clients who wanted information on the military basic training course, clients who said they needed to stop their workouts because they were going to be out of the country or were moving.

He hated that. More than anything in the world, Theo hated seeing months of hard work fizzle away as people returned to bad habits, just because they felt familiar and took less effort. He hated it when people gave up on themselves.

He felt Lola behind him. This was bad news.

'Hey, Theo.' Her breath came hot down on his neck. He felt the front of her things nearly touch the back of his. 'You know, I was wondering — '

'The answer will always be no. Back off, Lola.' He continued to sort through messages and ignored her, then noted that the hours in the tanning bed must have damaged Lola's hearing, because her hands went to his hips and the rest of her pressed nice and snug against the back of his body, from calf to shoulder. He felt the outline of all her parts — the parts molded by endless hours of hard work as well as those that were God-given.

'I said *no*.' Theo grabbed her roaming hands and extricated himself from his coworker and near . . . What word could he use to describe what had almost happened with Lola? She hadn't been a date. She hadn't even been a friend. She'd been a perfect body, at a time when he hurt so much that he thought a few hours with a perfect body would dull the pain.

Thank God he'd recovered his senses in time to zip up and go home. Unfortunately, Lola didn't feel the same sense of relief — she'd taken his rebuff as a challenge.

'Well, Theo. As usual, it's your loss.' A nasty hiss hung off the end of the last word as Lola returned to the recliner and her magazine.

Theo headed for the door.

'So how's it going with the hopeless heifer?'

He stopped. His ears burned. His stomach twisted with anger. He turned to her. 'What are you talking about, Lola?'

She shook out her straight blond hair. 'You know. The fat marketing chick. Lucy Cunningham. You two seem to be getting very cozy.' She shot him a snide smile.

'She's a terrific woman and she's working hard.' Theo had every intention of leaving the room, but he couldn't believe what Lola said next.

'If you're sleeping with her, that's against policy. Not to mention disgusting.'

Theo whipped around and stared at her. He was so livid, his mind went blank. 'What did you just say to me?'

'You heard me.' She thumbed through the ads for protein bars and starch blockers.

It took a moment, but Theo's head cleared.

'You're a real class act, Lola.'

She giggled and kept her attention on the magazine.

'Listen up. From now on, keep your nasty comments — and your hands — to yourself. Not interested and never will be.'

Lola looked up at him, her eyes narrow and mean. 'You sure were once.'

And it was the lowest fifteen minutes of his life.

'We'd look great together, Theo.'

'No, we would not. Let it go, Lola.' He slammed the door on his way out, only to run right into Tyson.

'What's up, Theo? You look mad as a rattlesnake.'

Theo pushed past, shaking his head. 'Nothing.'

Tyson caught up with him. 'Hey! Whoa, Redmond. Is this about the Lucy Cunningham woman? I thought she was doing great.'

Theo stopped and looked at his friend. 'She is.'

'And you?' Tyson yawned, rubbing his eyes. 'How're you doin'?'

Theo grinned, amused by Tyson's efforts to stay awake. 'I'm keepin' it together.'

'Just remember, man, you're a personal trainer, not a miracle worker.'

Theo laughed. 'No, I'm a trainer *and*

miracle worker. Don't have any choice at this point. And you need to get more sleep.' He continued walking, spotting his nine o'clock appointment waiting for him on the leather couch, the cute, trim, red-headed Cecile.

'How's the little bro?'

Theo smiled at Tyson. He was always so cool about Buddy and had been a great help with coaching these last few years. 'He's good. He wants you to come over Sunday to watch the game. We're having some of the athletes over. You up for it?'

'Always.' A big grin burst across Tyson's face. 'Those boys know how to party.'

Coming from Tyson, that was a real compliment.

★　★　★

When Gia Altamonte called Lucy at work an hour before and invited her to lunch, Lucy had been shocked. She was way beyond shock now, staring at the supermodel sitting across the VIP table from her at Larios on the Beach, snarfing down a plate of rice and beans and roasted Cuban pork.

'I think I forgot to eat yesterday,' Gia said, her mouth so full it temporarily muted her unmistakable speech.

'Yeah. Happens to me all the time,' Lucy said.

Gia laughed. 'I've been meaning to check on you, you know, after the life squad, but I've been in Belize for the swimsuit shoot and then I had to go to Los Angeles and then frickin' *Greenland*. You ever been to Greenland? It's nice. So you doing better now, or what?'

Lucy loved Gia's voice. It made her smile. It was high enough to be painful to the ear, grating yet endearing, especially in person, when it could be seen emerging from those sultry, heavily insured lips.

Perhaps it was cruel that God gave Gia Altamonte that voice to go with that mouth, because an acting career would forever be out of her reach. Then again, maybe that voice was proof that God did have a sense of humor, or that he wanted to give the rest of the normal schlubs on earth some shred of superiority.

'I'm doing great. Haven't choked since.'

'You like Cuban food, Lucy?'

'Love it.' Lucy had ordered a side salad with oil and vinegar, a side order of black beans, and a grilled mahimahi fillet — not bad for an impromptu lunch out and nothing she'd have to be ashamed to write down in her journal.

'Good, 'cause I'm gonna have my mama make you something. She's a big fan of yours.'

Lucy started. 'I have a fan?'

'Of course you do!' Gia said, laughing. 'My mama and me make two!'

Lucy couldn't help but be amused at the otherworldly nature of this situation. She had been invited to 'do' lunch with a *Sports Illustrated* swimsuit model in the VIP room of a chic restaurant on Miami Beach. Lucy didn't even know models *ate* lunch. And she'd certainly never been inside a VIP room of anything before, except maybe for the back office at the Order of the Eagles Aerie 982 in Pittsburgh, when her dad once brought her along when he had to pick up a roll of raffle tickets.

'How's Theo treating you?' Gia asked after she'd ordered coffee for both of them.

'He's busting my hump, but it's going well.'

'Mmmm. He's a cutie, no?'

Lucy shrugged, hoping she hadn't started sweating at just the mention of his name. 'How long have you two been dating?'

Gia tilted back her exquisite chin and howled. 'Oh no! No, no, no! He's just my trainer, *chica*! Besides, I don't think the man dates much. He used to have a steady, but they broke it off a while back.'

Lucy was stunned. 'Theo doesn't date?'

'Not that I know of.'

'That can't be right. Everywhere he goes, women remind him what day they're supposed to go out with him.'

Gia giggled. 'Those are his clients, Lucy. He's bee-yoo-tiful, isn't he? But he's a very serious and private kind of guy, and he's got all these big plans for himself. He's always saying he doesn't have time for women in his life right now.'

Lucy sat perfectly still. She didn't know how many shocks her system could take in one day.

'You wanna do a little shopping, girlie?'

Lucy looked at her watch, intrigued at the idea of shopping with Gia but aware that she had a two o'clock with a potential client she'd been chasing for months.

She asked for a rain check.

★　★　★

Stephan was almost relieved to finally get the call from Murray Goldstein, because the waiting had been making him a crazy man.

Stephan held the phone away from his ear as the old gangster ranted about how the Palm Club was going to ruin him and how Stephan had betrayed a sacred trust when he

62

accepted their business. It was all insane shit from a nutso (but rich and powerful) geezer, and all Stephan could do was mutter 'yes' and 'I realize that' and let him rage.

Stephan supposed he was responsible for this mess. If old Murray Goldstein decided to tie a cinder block around his neck and throw him in the causeway tomorrow, he had no one to blame but himself.

It started that day a few months back when Lucy Cunningham went out and snagged the Palm Club account on her own. Since he hadn't been very hands-on around the office, it was a total shocker when she showed up with a deal so full of zeros his head spun. He wanted the money. So shoot him. But he had to find a way to get it without pissing off old Murray, who happened to own a dozen Florida fitness centers in direct competition with the Palm Club.

He owed Murray Goldstein. Five years ago, the old guy put few thousand in small bills in an envelope, and put the envelope into the hands of the district court judge presiding over Stephan's divorce case. In Murray Goldstein's world, that meant he owned Stephan. Always would.

'That girl's got to stay fat!' Murray yelled into the phone.

Stephan winced, trying to remain in

control of the situation. 'That's been my plan all along.'

'Your plan? What plan? You couldn't plan your way out of a toilet stall!'

Stephan didn't appreciate that comment. It was a good plan, one that could work if Lucy failed to lose the weight.

'She's never going to do it, Murray. Get real — how many people do you know who actually lose a hundred pounds?'

The earpiece remained blissfully silent.

'I'm setting her up; don't you get it? I've wanted to fire her for months. She's another Sarah — a woman too aggressive for her own good.' That part was true. Lately Lucy was prancing around the halls of Sherrod & Thoms like her name was engraved on the stationery.

'In fact,' he continued. 'I've been trying to get rid of her lard ass since Sarah died, but she threatened to sue me for discrimination against fatties!' That part was a lie, but it sounded good.

'No shit?'

Stephan smiled, admiring the ease with which he could think on his feet. No wonder all of Miami respected him for his creative genius.

'Absolutely, Murray. I can accomplish two things at once — get a bad hire out of my hair and pay you back for your magnanimous generosity during my time of trial. No pun intended.' Stephan laughed at his little joke.

'But if she stays a blimp, won't that make you look bad?'

'It'll make *Lucy* look bad. Then I'll fire her. And it'll make Goldstein's look good because the Palm Club couldn't follow through on its claim.'

'That's it? That's your whole plan?'

'Isn't it fabulous?' Stephan crossed his fingers, hoping to God this would keep the old crook off his back.

After a moment of quiet, Murray said, 'That plan is so fucking stupid it just might work. But Lucy Cunningham has got to stay fat.'

'Blimp City all the way,' Stephan replied.

* * *

It was only five thirty in the evening, but Theo had been going nonstop since 4:00 a.m., and it felt like he was right back in the middle of his general surgery rotation in med school — headache, muscle fatigue, overwhelmed brain, and heavy eyelids. He took another swig of coffee and propped his feet up on his back porch railing, checking his watch. Buddy would be home from track practice in a half hour, leaving him just enough time to finish one last question on the histology practice exam.

But his vision started to dull and his shoulders cramped and he couldn't stop thinking about Lucy.

She was doing great; that wasn't the problem. They'd had another weigh-in that morning on *WakeUp Miami* and she'd lost six pounds and a few more inches. It was her smiling that bothered him. Her big, gray, sweet doe eyes. He wondered if Ramona had been wise to warn him that Lucy would make too much of the trainer — client intimacy. The truth was, he didn't want to worry about Lucy's heart except in the context of her cardiovascular well-being.

Theo stretched his neck and rolled his shoulders, glad for the feel of late-afternoon winter sun on his face. With a deep breath he returned his focus to the practice question, pondering the cartilage matrix found in the cells of connective tissue.

That's what it was about — *connection*. He really liked Lucy Cunningham, and he wanted to enjoy this year without worrying she'd get too connected to him. All he wanted was to help her, get his money, and get on with his life. Was there anything wrong with that?

Theo tossed the practice test to the outdoor table and wandered into the yard. The grass felt crisp and cool between his bare toes. There was something else about Lucy that bothered him lately — something he couldn't quite pinpoint. And it was driving him crazy.

He stopped, staring down at his mother's prized rhododendrons. They needed some serious attention. Theo raised his gaze and looked around him. He blinked. It seemed everything here needed attention — the grass, the fence, the exterior stucco of the house his parents had left him three years ago.

Theo rubbed his chin with his hand, then raked his fingers through his hair. He began to pace the yard, realizing that the grass, the fence, and the house were the least of his worries.

His first priority was and would always be his little brother, who needed a hell of a lot more than just attention. He needed love and guidance and reassurance and security. Then there were Theo's jobs — the full-time one, the part-time one at the nightclub, and the coaching one. And his aunt and uncle. And somewhere in there were his dreams. His dreams deserved his attention, too.

He thought about Lucy Cunningham's painfully cute smile, the little frown of concentration she got when he introduced something new to her workout, and suddenly wished he could just get in his car and drive away. He collapsed in the grass instead, laughing, then stretched out on his back and stared at the clouds. He liked Lucy Cunningham. He wanted her to be happy. *So that's what it was!*

Theo laughed some more, seeing with clarity that he'd put Lucy on that long list of things he couldn't afford to screw up!

Theo heard the gate latch click and looked up to see Buddy standing over him, peering down through his thick glasses. 'Chinese again tonight?'

Theo found enough energy to nod.

Buddy offered his hand and helped pull Theo to his feet. They walked together toward the house. 'Is the pretty fat girl from TV wearing you out already?'

Theo threw an arm over Buddy's shoulder and laughed. The tests might show his sixteen-year-old brother had the mental acuity of a third grader, but he sure didn't miss much.

★   ★   ★

Office of Doris Lehman, MSW, PhD
'I must tell you, the change in you is already

quite apparent. How does it feel?'

Lucy stroked her upper arms and ran her hands down the tops of her thighs. 'Bizarre. For a long time I felt like a head walking around in the world, numb from the jaw down, not exactly sure how I moved from point A to point B. Does that make any sense?'

'Yes, it does.'

'Well, I feel my legs now. Sometimes I look down at myself on the elliptical trainer and I go, *Check it out! Those are my legs!* Same with my arms and my back and shoulders — it's like I'm waking up from a long sleep.'

Doris jotted that down. 'And how does that feel emotionally?'

'I alternate between euphoria and panic.'

'I see.'

'Panic when people talk about my body like I'm deaf. Euphoria when I see that my clothes hang on me, even after I had them taken in twice.'

'And how are things with Theo?'

Lucy scrunched up her mouth and looked over at the kimono-clad nymphs for courage.

'Fine. Good. Excellent.'

'Have you . . . ?'

'No, I haven't told him I have a crush on him. It's too embarrassing. What if I accidentally blurt out the Lorna Doone fantasy? How could I ever rebound from *that*?'

Doris blinked.

'You know, it doesn't even have to be Lorna Doones. It can be Oreos or Malomars for all I care, and they aren't even my favorites. The important part is he's naked and some type of cookie is involved.'

Doris blinked again.

'I'm just pulling your leg, Dr Lehman.' Lucy gave her an exaggerated grin. 'I sometimes worry that my issues aren't fancy enough for you, you know? I come in here week after week, just a Pittsburgh girl who took off her clothes in front of the wrong man ten years ago, wiped out a college football dynasty, and enticed a *60 Minutes* camera crew to camp out on her parents' lawn. I worry that I bore you.'

Doris smiled politely. 'What I wouldn't give for all my patients to be so boring.'

4

March

'Go away. Leave me alone. You make me mad.'

Theo sat down on the edge of the bed, his coffee balanced in one hand while the other stroked his brother's wispy blond hair. 'You gotta get up, Buddy. I need to take you to Aunt Viv's so she can drive you to school later.'

'Go away.' Buddy grabbed the edge of the comforter and yanked it up over his head, hitting Theo's arm, spilling his coffee, and sending Norton the devil cat leaping for safety. Theo checked his watch. This was insanity. Trying to get Buddy out of the house by 4:15 every weekday was getting harder as time went on, not easier.

Not for the first time, Theo wondered if a hundred grand was worth this hassle.

'We gotta rock-'n'-roll, Buddy. I have a client waiting for me.'

From under the comforter came a muffled, 'Another girl who loves you?'

'Get up, Buddy.'

'Do you still miss Jenna? I do. Why did she stop liking you? Because you're not a doctor anymore?'

Theo was quite used to Buddy's filterless questions but was still half-asleep and more vulnerable than he would have been at a later hour. He took a sip of coffee, gulping down the sadness that could still pierce him when he thought of Jenna. 'Yeah, I still miss her sometimes. Now get up.'

'Buzz off.'

'I don't appreciate your attitude.'

'Go away.'

Theo checked his watch. He was growing desperate. 'Look, Brian. If I get back in med school I'll really need your cooperation, so let's practice now. I have to meet my client. Get up.'

'The funny fat lady from TV?'

'Yeah. Her. Now get up.'

'No!'

'We can have cheesesteaks for supper.'

'I'm up.' And with that, Buddy burst forth from under his covers and nearly knocked Theo to the floor as he made his way across the bedroom, fully dressed, all the way down to his Reeboks.

Theo shook his head and laughed. He'd been got again, by a teenager alleged to have an IQ half his own.

He used the corner of the comforter to mop coffee off his work shorts, taking a moment to look around Buddy's room, listening to the usual morning humming coming from the bathroom down the hall.

The bedroom looked like your average teenager's room. Computer on the desk. An MP3 player and headphones tossed casually on the floor by the dresser. Clothes spilling out of the hamper. Sports posters all over the wall — with Lance Armstrong, Marian Jones, and Michael Phelps predominating.

But the trophy and medal collection surrounding Theo wasn't average at all. Pinned to a strip of corkboard encircling the room were hundreds of ribbons and medals. Dozens of trophies sat on a low shelf above the desk, engraved with the name 'Brian Redmond.' Though Theo couldn't read the small print on each from where he sat, he knew well enough what they were for. In swimming, the hundred-meter butterfly and the hundred-meter freestyle. In track, the long jump, hundred-and-ten-meter hurdles, high jump, marathon, half marathon, and pentathlon.

They were from school meets, local and state competitions, invitationals, and last year's international games. They reflected eight years of athletic achievement by a boy who surprised his parents by arriving sixteen years after Theo, with Down's syndrome.

Theo's eyes traveled to the neat little cross-stitch slogan that hung on the wall over Buddy's bed, matted under glass and nicely framed. Their mother gave it to Buddy a few months before she died. It was the Special Olympics athlete's oath, in a graceful cursive script:

> *Let me win.*
> *But if I cannot win,*
> *Let me be brave in the attempt.*

Theo knew those words by heart. And he knew they applied to him and the rest of the world as much as they did to Buddy and his fellow Special Olympians.

A horrible noise jarred Theo from his quiet thoughts.

'*I like the way you moo-oove!*'

As usual, Buddy's singing was very loud, very off-key, and had no identifiable time signature. And like he did nearly every morning, Buddy sang while brushing his teeth and flossing.

'*I like the way-ay . . .*'

Theo slipped into the bathroom doorway to watch Buddy groove his way through his oral hygiene. 'Anything cool going on at school today?'

'Never is.' Buddy spit and rinsed. 'So probably not today, either.'

'Track after school?'

'Yep.'

'Got your gear packed?'

'Yeah.'

Theo watched Buddy swivel his hips in front of the bathroom mirror, and couldn't help but smile at how happy he seemed. After the accident three years ago, Buddy had simply shut down. He stopped competing. He wouldn't hang out with friends. He became so angry at the world and so lost that it broke Theo's heart.

He did everything he could to make it easier for Buddy. Theo dropped out of med school halfway through his M-3 year, right in the middle of a general surgery rotation, which didn't go over well with the attending physician, not to mention Jenna. Then Theo moved back home to Miami Springs and took over his dad's coaching post with the Special Olympics of Miami-Dade.

Theo had no choice. His aunt and uncle were too old to keep up with Buddy, and Theo couldn't pull him out of his school and away from his friends and definitely couldn't move him out of the house. Buddy didn't do well with even the smallest changes in his routine, like grape instead of the usual strawberry jam on his peanut butter sandwich. Moving would have killed him.

Looking at him now, combing his hair and humming, Theo was proud that Buddy was doing so well. Theo was proud that with Aunt Viv and Uncle Martin's help he'd managed to keep his brother's world intact for these last three years.

Even at the cost of Theo's own.

'I have to work the door at Flawless Friday and Saturday nights, so you'll be staying with Aunt Viv and Uncle Martin. But we can train Saturday afternoon.'

'Sounds like a plan.'

'Get your backpack and let's roll, stud.'

Buddy laughed, and Theo enjoyed watching him tilt his head back and squint his already-squinty eyes behind his thick glasses, smiling so big that his gums showed all along the ridges of his small top teeth.

When Buddy stopped laughing, he playfully shook his finger at Theo. 'You're the stud in this house,' he said, strolling into the hallway and toward the foyer.

'Nope.' Theo grabbed his car keys off the hall table and opened the door for his brother. 'You're the only stud around here, dude, and we both know it.'

★　★　★

'How much have you lost now, Lucy?'

Veronica hadn't asked that question in about six days, which might have been a record for Lucy's assistant. 'Not sure. The month's not over yet.'

Maria Banderas munched on her taco salad and waved her fork around. 'I don't know how you do it! I'd be weighing myself every ten minutes if I were losing weight as fast as you are. You're a better person than I am!'

Lucy gave Maria a polite smile. 'If you were losing weight this fast they'd have you in the ICU, hooked up to an IV. Everything's relative.'

'It's good to see you're eating actual food.'

Veronica made that preposterous comment just as Lucy popped a cherry tomato into her mouth. She chewed desperately so she could respond. 'Of course I'm eating food! What else would I be eating?'

Her assistant looked sheepish. 'Well, Stephan said you had to be cheating to be doing so well — like a liquid fast or vitamin shots or something.'

Lucy shook her head in disgust. 'At least if he's paying attention to my weight that means he's paying attention to one detail of one account, which is a miracle.'

'No kidding.' Maria's eyes got wide.

'Thank God you're still here, because we'd be dead in the water if we counted on Stephan. It's like he's sleepwalking! Remember the asphalt company proposal I asked him to approve last week? He hasn't even picked it up.'

Lucy frowned. 'That's a potential big-money account. I'll talk to him.'

'You might want to talk to him about the phone bill while you're at it,' Veronica said. 'He didn't pay it last month — flipped out that it was too expensive and we could get a better deal and told me to do the research.'

Lucy put her fork down and stared at Veronica.

'So I gave him a couple options, right? But he still hasn't decided and he won't pay the overdue bill and we just got a cutoff notice. How's an advertising company supposed to do business without phones?'

Lucy closed her eyes, took a deep breath, and repeated the words to herself: *Eight more months.*

★ ★ ★

'Don't you *ever* do that to me again, Cunningham.'

Theo greeted her at the Palm Club door as usual, but he wasn't wearing his standard

Happy Trainer face. His lips were pursed tight. His marine blue eyes were stern and had none of the unnatural sparkle she'd grown accustomed to. And Lucy knew it was her fault.

'I'm really sorry, Theo. I left you a voice mail to apologize yesterday. I thought I hit the snooze but somehow fell back asleep.'

'Don't do it again.'

'OK. OK. I'm sorry.'

Theo punched in a fifteen-minute warm-up on the recumbent cycle and extended his hand for her to have a seat. He started scribbling on his clipboard.

'I hate getting out of bed at four in the morning as much as you do, Lucy, if not more.'

'I understand. But for the record, I hate it a lot.' She started pedaling.

'You're the one who picked this ridiculous time.'

'It's the only time I had. I have to be at work at eight!'

'Where's your food journal?'

'In my bag.'

'I don't see it.'

Lucy watched in horror as Theo tossed aside her new zebra-striped panties. In the last couple weeks, her underwear had begun to fall around her knees, so in a moment of

79

recklessness in the Filene's lingerie department, she'd decided to oomph up the style
while she bought three sizes down.

Now Theo knew she wore zebra-striped
panties.

Lucy comforted herself by stealing a peek
at Theo while he bent over her bag, noting
the perfect man butt in those navy blue
shorts, those golden legs etched into bands of
long, strong muscle. She decided to use small
talk to smooth things over with him.

'I suppose getting up at four puts a real
damper on your busy social schedule.' She
pedaled along at a comfortable pace, knowing
Gia had to be wrong when she claimed Theo
didn't date much. Look at him! He was Prom
King material! 'In my case, it doesn't matter
if I go to bed before your average fifth grader.'

Theo stood up with her food journal in his
hand and an annoyed expression in his eyes.
'Uh-huh.' Then he leaned toward her and
with lightning speed adjusted the program-
ming on the cycle. Lucy immediately felt her
leg muscles burn with the effort.

'Hey!'

'Those things you're feeling now are called
hills, Cunningham. They go up, and then they
go down. The hard parts won't last long, so
just do it and look happy.'

Lucy tried not to laugh. Theo's foul temper

made her want to giggle. 'You're in an ugly mood.'

'You didn't write down a goal for today. Where's your damn goal?'

She continued to huff and pedal. 'Right now, Master and Commander, my goal is to get through this appointment without running you over with this bike.'

'Stationary bike, empty threat.' Theo snapped the journal shut and put his hands on his hips. 'Look, I'm sorry if I'm grumpy, but you just have no idea how hard it is to get Buddy out the door in the morning.'

Lucy had never heard him mention his dog before. 'What kind is he?'

'Who?'

'Buddy.'

Theo seemed even more annoyed, if that were possible. Her attempt at chitchat was obviously a flop. She tried again. 'Your dog, Theo. What kind of dog is Buddy? That's all I'm asking.'

She watched Theo go from annoyance to full-out laughter in a flash. 'Buddy is my brother. It's a nickname for Brian. And there is no dog. We have a goddamn feckless, evil cat.'

'You have a *cat?*' That just wasn't right. Men like Theo didn't have cats. Unless they were gay. Could it be? The no dating? The earring? The perfect hair?

'He's my brother's cat. He's possessed by Satan and his name is Norton.'

'You really have a *brother*?' Mercifully, Lucy had reached the top of a hill and was headed down. Her legs tingled with relief and her lungs stopped seizing.

'Sure do.'

'I'm sorry, but I just have to ask. Are you gay? You're single and attractive and you wear an earring and have a cat. This is Miami Beach, right?'

Theo closed his eyes and slowly shook his head, a look of near pain on his face. Eventually, he opened his eyes. 'I like women, Cunningham. Always have. Always will.'

'I knew that. The cat thing threw me, I guess.'

'By any chance, are you done interrogating me? If so, I'm going to check my mail. I'll be back in a few and we'll stretch out.'

'Fine.'

He turned to go, then looked over his shoulder, offering her a mischievous grin. 'So is there a zebra-striped bra to match?'

Lucy's mouth fell open. She watched Theo jog across the nearly empty cardio studio toward the offices, where he opened what Lucy knew was the door to the trainer lounge and disappeared.

It had taken more than two months, but she'd just discovered Theo had a temper. Theo had a cat! He used words like *goddamn*. He had a *brother*. And he liked zebra-striped underwear.

Then she wondered if his brother was as good-looking as Theo was and why in the world he had to worry about getting him ready in the morning. Was he ten years old or something? If so, where were the kid's parents?

Suddenly the bike switched gears on her again, and she was pedaling for all she was worth. Lucy made a mental note not to miss any more workouts, because clearly, payback was a bitch.

★   ★   ★

They'd been inside Nordstrom's all of five minutes when she heard the shocked whisper behind them: '*My God! It's Gia Altamonte and the fat woman from* WakeUp Miami*!*'

Gia whipped her head around so fast her Versace sunglasses went flying off her head and clattered to the parquet flooring of the designer shoe department.

'Is that you talkin' to my friend like that?' Gia placed her fists on her hot pants-clad hips. 'Yes, I'm speaking to you, Grandma.'

Lucy cringed at Gia's fingernail-on-chalkboard verbal assault on a woman in her sixties wearing a pale peach linen skirt set and a horrified expression. Gia looked the woman up and down and added, 'Who you think you are, lady? If you worked twice as hard as she does, she'd still look twice as good!'

The woman slinked away into the atrium, her shoulders slumped in defeat.

'I'll tell you, people can be so frickin' *rude*.' Gia bent in half and scooped her sunglasses from the floor and set them back on her pert little nose. 'You OK or what?' She placed a hand on Lucy's elbow and nudged her out into the aisle and toward the designer sportswear collections.

'I'm fine. You're probably accustomed to people recognizing you. I'm not.'

'You get used to it, but you can't let them say nasty stuff to you like that.' Gia ran her fingertips over a filmy blouse with a plunging neckline and a price tag with way too many numerals on it. 'One day, I swear to God, a total stranger came up to me at the corner of Seventh and Fifty-fourth in New York and tells me I had visible panty lines in my *Vogue* layout. Can you flippin' believe that garbage?'

Gia shook out her dark tresses and flashed her mahogany eyes over the gold rims of her sunglasses. Lucy smiled at her friend. She

84

simply loved the way Gia had just said 'gar-bahjz' in that high-pitched squeak of hers. Lucy had been hanging out with this woman for the last few weeks and couldn't remember a time when she'd had so much fun.

'So what did you say to him?'

Gia smiled, pushing up those world-famous lips into a sweet curl of naughtiness. 'I told him, 'Baby, I don't wear no panties,' and then I cross the street and he's still back there, and I think maybe he was having a coronary or something.'

Lucy laughed, then leaned up to whisper in Gia's ear, 'You really don't wear underwear?'

'Of course I do. Mama would kill me if I went out into the world without my privates covered. You?'

Lucy gasped. 'Me? Of course I wear them! I just bought a bunch of new stuff the other day.'

Gia grabbed her elbow. 'God. Let's get more. No such thing as too much lingerie.'

*　*　*

If she were brutally honest with herself, Lucy would have to admit she was going to all this trouble for Theo. She wanted to impress him. Make him proud of her. She wanted to show

85

the world what they'd done.

She smoothed down the jersey fabric and ran her hands over her hips again. Not so bad. She'd lost enough girth that control-top panty hose actually did some controlling. And the size 16 was snug but not obscenely so. She supposed it fit perfectly.

Gia had been right about the dress. The open shawl-collar coatdress exposed the smooth skin of Lucy's throat and upper chest and accentuated her curves. It made her look sleek and feminine. The dark gray-blue matched her eyes and provided a contrast to her pale skin that would look good on camera. The dress was worth every dime she paid for it, even if she only wore it once. Soon it would be too big. And soon it would be too hot in Miami for a dress like this, anyway.

But today was important. She deserved to look pretty today, right now, didn't she? She didn't have to wait until she was wearing a size 8 to dress like the beautiful professional babe she was, right?

Lucy smiled at her newfound boldness, brushing aside her shoulder-length hair to put in the small gold twist earrings. She slipped on her watch, seeing she'd have to have the band tightened soon.

She caught her reflection in the mirror just

as she turned to go, and winked at herself. Gia had been right about the lingerie — even if nobody saw it, it didn't mean it wasn't having its desired effect.

Because Lucy knew that beneath this dress was the most extravagant bra and panty set she'd ever owned — something so delicate and soft that it gave her goose bumps when she put it on. And just knowing what lay against her flesh made her stand a little taller. It gave her a blush Lancôme could never duplicate.

She needed to stop by the office on the way to the TV studio, and during the ten-minute drive she thought about Theo and how he would react to seeing her dressed up like this. Would he hug her? Would he kiss her cheek? What would his mouth feel like on hers? That clean, sweet smile turning serious as he backed her against the wall, crushed her breasts against his chest, took her mouth —

Whoa. There wasn't a cookie to be seen in that fantasy.

Lucy looked in the rearview mirror and was greeted by a guilty reflection. Was that really what all the preening was about today? Was she determined to have Theo see her in a different light?

She returned her attention to the road and

sighed. Surely that would only be setting herself up for rejection. And she was too smart for that.

Lucy ran smack into Stephan Sherrod in the hallway outside her office.

'Ah, Lucy! Just the gal I wanted to see.'

'Stephan. You're here early.' She looked at her watch to see it was not quite six thirty. 'Will you be at the team meeting this afternoon?'

'Well, no. I have a late lunch, but I'm sure Maria and Barry can handle anything that comes up.'

For a split second Lucy let the insult sting her. Then she nodded, smiling at the thought of the freedom all that money would bring, how in about eight months she'd walk out the door of this place without so much as a good-bye, many of Stephan's clients begging her to take them with her. 'Of course, Stephan,' she said to him.

Ooooh, she couldn't wait! First, she'd snag a few of the agency's smaller but more fun clients. The yoga center. The private marina down in the Gables. The artsy clothing boutique in Boca Raton. After working with these people for over a year, she knew they sorely missed Sarah Thoms but were happy to put their businesses in Lucy's hands. They didn't trust Stephan — they made that perfectly clear. She'd use that to her advantage.

And after those clients jumped, there was no telling who would follow. She hoped it would be the teachers' credit union and the quick-lube chain.

'Lucy?' Stephan's voice interrupted her plotting. 'I know you're on your way to the studio, but do you have a minute? There's something I wanted to run by you. I need to give you a quick heads-up.'

She didn't like the sound of that. Lucy knew that when Stephan said he wanted to run something by her, he was telling her to drop whatever she was doing and do something else. And when he said he wanted to give her a heads-up, that meant he'd done something stupid and he wanted her to clean up the mess.

She looked up slowly from her desk, prepared for the worst — because she couldn't recall a time when Stephan had used both bad business metaphors in one sentence.

'I have *just* a minute. I can't be late. We're going on live at seven thirty.'

'Of course.' Stephan sat down in a chair and waited for her to do the same. He smiled at her.

'You've certainly spruced up the scenery

around here lately, Lucy.'

She looked around her office. 'I haven't redecorated.'

Stephan let out one of his tight smug little laughs. 'I'm talking about you. You're fast becoming a real asset to this company.'

Lucy's heart skipped a beat. This man's loutishness knew no limits.

'I'm just saying that it's a vast improvement — no pun intended. Get it? Vast?' He chortled again.

Lucy nodded, letting her eyes wander to the ostentatious Caran d'Ache fountain pen tucked into Stephan's dress shirt pocket, thinking how satisfying it would feel to jam the eighteen-karat gold nib into his left eyeball, thereby causing his head to deflate.

The bastard. There she was, the person who'd landed the Palm Club account in the first place — the biggest in Sherrod & Thomas's history. Lucy was the creative director of a team that had conceived a fun, fresh campaign that was going to forever change their agency's reputation. She'd even sacrificed her body and pride for this account. And she was supposed to be walking out the door right that minute to make this man even richer than he was by getting on a scale in front of a live studio audience and tens of thousands of viewers — and he just informed her she hadn't been an asset until she'd become *thinner*?

She stood up. She glared down at him. 'Unless this is about business, it will have to wait.'

'Don't be so sensitive. Loosen up. Sit down. I've got good news.'

'I really only have five minutes, tops.' Lucy's blood boiled. She'd taken this job for one reason — Sarah Thoms. In Sarah, Lucy had seen a kindred spirit, a real mentor, someone who'd managed to remain a decent person while she'd made her way in the business world. This position had appealed to Lucy because it would allow her to keep a hand in a variety of projects. The pay was excellent, too. But from the beginning, the one downside of this job had been Stephan. Lucy had figured Sarah would serve as a buffer between them. And she had, until she went in for routine cosmetic surgery and died. Now there was no Sarah — just one weird-ass boss, who sat in front of Lucy, his face lit up with malevolent delight.

'I've nominated the Palm Club campaign for this year's Eddies.'

'You *what*?'

'I just sent in the preliminary application.'

The Eddie Award was like the Academy Award of the advertising industry, and every year the professional association gave out honors for excellence in advertising, marketing, and public relations. Lucy had never been nominated for anything in her life. She'd never even gone to the awards ceremony.

This was incredible news, but the look on Stephan's face cautioned her not to get carried away with her excitement.

'What's the catch?'

'Well, the application process is quite detailed. You'll have to start coming in a little early to work on it. It's due in two months.'

'I can't come in early, Stephan. That's when I work with Theo.'

'Ah, right. Well, maybe you can skip a day here and there. It probably won't matter much. I've managed to stay in shape with a three-day-a-week regimen, myself.'

As Stephan tapped his belly contentedly, Lucy found herself speechless. Stephan was encouraging her to slack off. Why in the world would he do that? The reputation of his company was riding on this enterprise.

'You aren't trying to lose a hundred pounds, Stephan.' Something else was off about this. 'Besides,' she pointed out, 'the Eddies are for ad campaigns with quantifiable results. This campaign won't be done for another nine months. To send it in now would make me look like I don't know what I'm doing.'

Stephan shifted in the chair and chuckled again. 'Well, let's give it a shot anyway. You can just talk about how much you've lost so far. So where are we now — fifteen pounds?'

Lucy shook her head in incredulity. 'I'll be weighed on the show this morning, but it will be over thirty-five pounds, I'm sure.'

'*Shit!*' He jumped up from his seat and stood over her, his mouth hanging open. 'You've managed to lose thirty-five pounds? Are you absolutely sure? Let me see you! Stand up! Turn around!'

Stephan had always been an odd bird, and Lucy had never judged him too harshly for his decidedly strange behaviour since Sarah's death. The two of them had started this agency twenty years ago, and losing her had been hard on Stephan. But today's display had Lucy worrying about his mental stability.

'I am not your 4-H entry, Stephan.' Lucy stood up from her chair and hoisted her laptop onto her shoulder. As she made her way toward the door, she heard him say something under his breath that she swore sounded like, '*You have to fail, you bitch.*'

When she spun around, he looked quite innocent, a pleasant smile on his face.

'What did you just say?'

'I said, 'You've really found your niche.''
Stephan motioned for her to pass ahead of
him. 'I'm proud of your initiative.'

'Uh-huh,' she said, taking a step forward.
Under her breath she added, 'You ain't seen
nothing yet.'

★   ★   ★

Lucy knew Dan was visiting her parents, but
she had no idea Mary Fran was there, so the
sight of her peeling potatoes at the kitchen
sink threw her.

'Frannie?'

'Hey, girl!' Mary Fran made one step
toward the back door and stopped. The
potato peeler fell to the floor and she gasped.

'Oh, sorry. Mary Fran, this is my friend
Gia. I brought her over for her first-ever Saint
Patrick's Day party.'

Frannie's eyes continued growing in
circumference. She stood as still as a statue
and said nothing. Lucy had never known her
sister to be so impolite.

Gia didn't seem bothered by the stare and
moved quickly to introduce herself. 'Nice to
meet you.' She stuck out her hand. 'I'm Gia
Altamonte.'

'No shit,' Frannie said, then smacked
herself on the cheek. 'I'm sorry. It's just . . . I

mean . . . I didn't expect Lucy to walk in the back door with — '

'*Sweet baby Jesus and Mother of God!*' Dan nearly fell over his tongue when he stepped into the kitchen, and Lucy feared he would need surgery to reattach his jaw. Holden was squirming in Dan's arms to be put down.

Lucy gestured toward Gia. 'Dan, this is my friend from the gym, Gia Altamonte. Gia, this is my charming and sophisticated brother, Daniel Cunningham.'

Dan shuffled forward, bending as he eased Holden's feet to the floor, his hand outstretched and his cheeks redder than the day their dad caught him using his Norelco to shave the heads of Lucy's Barbies.

Dan stood in front of Gia in a hunched position, as if in deference to the queen.

'You can stand up, Dan,' Gia said, smiling down at him beneficently.

'I'm sorry,' he said, shaking his head as if to clear his vision. 'I just keep seeing these two words: *Swimsuit Issue.* Am I dead? Is this heaven?'

Gia laughed and patted his head, and in her rather irritating nasal voice she said, 'So, we gonna drink green beer today or what, Danny boy?'

Lucy was pleased at how easily Gia slipped

into the rhythm of the Cunninghams. She entertained everyone with the description of a recent photo shoot in Los Angeles, all while bouncing Holden in her lap. She explained that she had eight siblings and eleven nieces and nephews and was quite used to kids.

'Do you want children of your own?' Dan asked over dessert. Though he'd only had one beer, Dan had sported a look of drunken reverence through the entire meal. At least he'd stopped gawking, and for that Lucy was grateful. She had to admit it was cute the way Dan said their guest's name — '*Gee-ahh.*'

'Sure. Someday I'd like a few kids of my own.'

A satisfied smile crept across Dan's face. 'Wanna have mine?'

'Oh Lordy,' Mary Fran mumbled.

'Daniel!' Lucy's mother refilled Gia's teacup and looked apologetic. 'Would you like more sugar, sweetheart?'

'Thank you.' Gia wrenched her head to the side to avoid Holden's attempt to rip out one of her hoop earrings, then smiled at Dan. 'I'm not sure what would happen if a redheaded Irish dude and a Cuban girl had kids. They could turn out cute, I guess, with a little luck.'

Dan turned his twinkling eyes and a wide grin upon Lucy and shook his head in wonder. 'You look marvelous, Luce. Have I told you that?'

'No, actually. You haven't.'

'You do. Fabulous. And when was the last time I told you that you were the best sister a guy could have?'

Lucy let her eyes flick toward Mary Fran, then back to her brother. 'That would be never.'

'Ah. My oversight.'

Lucy had to laugh. If she wasn't mistaken, Gia really liked Dan, sitting over there in his chair just being who he was — an average-looking pediatrics intern in a pair of Levi's and a nondescript cotton sweater. She had to admit Dan was funny and smart and would probably make a decent catch for somebody at some point. She just hadn't thought it would be anytime soon or that he'd catch the attention of somebody as glamorous as Gia Altamonte.

It was almost as far-fetched as someone like her snagging someone like Theo.

★   ★   ★

Theo didn't even recognize her at first. He walked into the green room at the TV station and took a seat near the doughnut table. He let his gaze move casually around the room to the three TV monitors bolted to the wall and to the small knot of people chatting nearby.

That's when he saw an attractive woman seated on the edge of a table, talking on a cell phone, one leg bent, her hair falling in glossy waves of at least three different colors. Then she clicked the phone shut and looked up, tossing her hair back.

'Lucy.' Her name came out like a gasp. Theo sat very still, realizing with confusion that his pulse was tripping.

Well, of course it was. He was just surprised. That was all. He was looking at the cumulative effect of a good balance of freestyle, cardio, and core strengthening along with lean protein, complex carbs, and fruits and vegetables.

He was merely reacting to all the changes in her numbers made visible. Her body fat mass was down. Her lean muscle mass was up. She'd lost a bunch of pounds and a bunch of inches from her upper arms, chest, hips, waist, thighs, and calves.

He'd done a great job with her. He had a right to a little increase in his pulse.

The soundman walked toward Theo and nodded. 'She's looking *awesome*,' he said, stopping in front of Theo.

'Thanks.' As soon as Theo said it, he realized the guy's compliment wasn't really meant for him but for Lucy. Theo heard his own nervous laugh.

He continued to study Lucy as she chatted with one of the morning show's assistant producers. Lucy smiled confidently, at the young woman nodding and listening as the producer waved her hands and laughed. Theo stared at the soft curve of Lucy's cheek and felt a jolt of surprise when she tucked a thick segment of hair behind her ear.

Lucy had pretty hands. Long fingers. He'd seen them a hundred times — why hadn't he ever really *seen* them? And what was with her hair today? It almost looked like it had red in it, and he could have sworn it had been just plain brown. Why couldn't he take his eyes off her face? Why was he feeling like this while looking at Lucy?

Theo wiped his palms on his pants and looked around the room uncomfortably. He'd never seen Lucy dressed up. That had to be it. She'd worn sweatpants the first two times they'd done the show. And he knew he'd never seen her with her hair down or with makeup on, at least never anything on her lips, which looked shiny and soft today.

He had to get out of there.

'Hey, Theo!' Lucy waved to him, her beautiful eyes looking right into his. Theo felt his heart thud in his chest as she stood up from the edge of the table and smiled.

She wanted him to look. She stood tall, with her shoulders back, showing herself to him. She looked at him like she knew something he didn't, and frankly, it left him a little unhinged. It was like Lucy was daring him to accept the changes in her. Theo took the dare and let his eyes devour her from head to toe and back again. Lucy Cunningham was curvy and female and flat-out beautiful. *Oh hell . . .*

Right then, Ramona walked into the green room along with Lola and Tyson. In today's installment of *WakeUp Miami*, the trainers were scheduled to work with four members of the studio audience. The theme of today's show was designing a personalized motivation strategy.

Lola sat down next to Theo and he caught a whiff of her perfume. Theo glanced her way and quickly tried to figure out what he'd ever thought was attractive about her. Lola's quads were so hard you could bounce a quarter off them. Her arms were nothing but corded muscle. Her collarbones stuck out in the vee of her shirt. He recalled how the tanned skin pulled tight over every one of Lola's ribs, the corrugated surface of her abs, and the sharp bones at the barely there swell of her hips.

Then he looked at Lucy. She was soft and round and glowing. She was funny and sweet. She was complicated. She was brave. She was feminine. And she was smiling at him like they were sharing a very private joke.

And he wondered, *Who's the one with doe eyes today?*

Tyson plunked down on the chair next to him. 'Dayum. She's looking *fine*.'

Theo turned to see Tyson leaning forward, his elbows balanced on his knees as he stared at Lucy. Theo didn't like the laserlike focus of his friend's expression. Not one bit. He glared at him.

Tyson looked Theo's way and laughed. 'What? What I do?'

Just then, the assistant producer left the room and Lucy turned to pick up her laptop from the floor. Tyson let out a big rush of air. 'She's getting a real nice booty on her, Redmond. Squats? Lunges?'

Theo's brain started to burn hot. He couldn't see straight. 'Her booty is none of your business.'

'Hey, it's just part of my continuing education refresher course. Gotta keep my booty-ologist certification up-to-date, you know.'

'Go refresh yourself with someone else's booty,' Theo said.

Tyson laughed. 'Don't tell me you hadn't noticed what you've been working with! C'mon, Theo — open your eyes. She's a nice-looking woman, and in about another ten pounds I plan to ask her out, so don't you even think about slackin' off now.'

Before Theo could recover enough from the shock of anger to respond, Tyson gave him a playful punch and strolled across the room to chat with Lucy. Theo watched his friend elicit a shy smile from her and was shocked again — this time by the stab of jealousy. He was *jealous*?

The realization sobered him up but quick.

This was not a part of his plan. Since Jenna left him six months ago, he'd decided to shut down his heart and focus on his own dreams. Of course his heart still did the job for Buddy and Uncle Martin and Aunt Viv, but not for women. That was the plan — there was no time or energy to waste on a woman. All Theo's life, all he'd ever wanted to do was be a doctor, and it was finally within reach again. He could not afford the distraction.

Besides, Lucy was not just any woman — she was his *job*, for God's sake, not to mention his ticket back to med school.

Theo watched Tyson put his big hands on Lucy and guide her into the hallway. It took everything he had not to run after them.

5

April

Theo heard the familiar sound of Jenna's Acura pulling up to the curb. He brushed the sandy soil from his knees and stood up, turning away from the rhododendrons in time to see Jenna pop out of her shiny sedan. She strolled up the driveway, her long, smooth legs carrying her with the same sensual strength she'd always possessed.

'Theo.' She stopped in front of him and crooked her head. Her straight light hair fell against a shoulder and her smile was sweet and a little sad. Then she broke eye contact with him and studied the yard. 'The place looks great. Do you have a minute?'

Theo tossed down the pruning shears he'd been holding in a death grip and nodded, trying not to stare at the way her skirt hugged her slim hips or the soft skin at the opening of her blouse. It had been a few weeks since he'd last talked to her and seven months since he'd kissed her, and he wasn't sure if the steady in-and-out of his breathing meant he'd finally gotten over her or if he was in a daze. 'To what do I owe this honor?' he asked.

'How've you been, Theo?'

Jenna's face was aglow with her bedside manner persona. He'd seen it often enough when they were med students, and he didn't like that it was directed his way this morning — it implied bad news was on its way.

'Fine, but we're going to have to talk out here. Buddy's home and I don't want to confuse him.'

Jenna's eyes lit up. 'How *is* he? God, I miss him. Would you tell him I miss him?'

Theo nodded, watching as Norton strolled through the pine bark mulch and approached Jenna's ankle as if he planned to rub against it. At the last instant he stopped, arched his spine, and hissed like the demon-possessed thing he was.

'Norton! You've gotten so fat!' Jenna reached down to stroke his large orange head and he slashed at her with a declawed paw. 'Well, I see you're still quite the sociopath.'

'You did call him fat.'

Jenna laughed.

'I'll tell Buddy you said hi.' Of course, there was no way in hell Theo would mention her name to his brother. It would only result in weeks of nonstop questions about when she was coming back. 'So what's up, Jenna?'

'I've been watching you on TV. You're famous now!' Jenna watched Norton skitter away. 'I can't tell you how I feel for that client of yours! I don't know how she could have let herself go like that. She seems fairly intelligent. But you're doing great with her. I even saw your billboard at a bus stop near the med center. I guess you've been able to quit the bouncer job at the club?'

Theo sighed, trying to tally up all the vaguely condescending things she'd managed in one breath. 'Did you come here to get my autograph or something?'

She laughed, and her pale gold eyes filled with affection. For a brief moment, Theo thought maybe she still loved him. Maybe she'd come here on a Saturday morning to beg him for another chance. He straightened his back at the thought.

'Actually, I've come to ask for your blessing.'

That definitely did not sound like begging.

'I wanted to tell you before you heard it through the grapevine.'

Theo's eyes flicked to the ring finger of her left hand, and there it was — *bam!* — the door-slamming end to whatever he'd built in five years with Jenna. At that moment, it felt like a whole lot of nothing.

'He asked me last weekend and I said yes.'

'I'm happy for you.'

'Are you?' Jenna's whisper was shaky. 'It's important to me that you're OK with this, Theo.'

OK with this?

He had to get a few additional feet between himself and all the sweet-smelling, cool beauty that was Jenna. He turned away and rubbed a dirty hand through his hair and tried to find his balance.

That dick got her to commit.

'He's a lot older than you.' Theo turned to squint at her there in the sun, all pretty and unruffled and everything he'd ever wanted — smart, determined, steady, logical, built, gorgeous.

Jenna smiled. 'Yes. He's fifty-one.'

'Has lover boy had a recent stress test? Have you checked his lipids?'

'Come on, Theo — '

He couldn't decide what to do with his hands. He had no pockets in the old pair of running shorts he'd worn to work in the yard that morning, so his hands just hung there, feeling rubbery and useless when all he really wanted to do was punch a big-ass hole in the stucco side of the house.

'Are you going to join his surgery practice when you're done with your fellowship?'

'We've talked about it.'

'The call schedule is going to be hell on your marriage.'

'Theo — '

'When's the wedding?'

'We're not sure yet.' Jenna allowed a little giggle to escape. 'We've talked about maybe eloping.'

'Oh boy! Won't that get him in trouble with his *wife*?'

'His divorce is almost final.'

'Good, because I think the state of Florida frowns on bigamy.'

'*Stop* it.'

'Look, I'm sorry. Congratulations.' Theo found himself taking the two steps required to reach Jenna and wrap her up in his arms. He hugged her, feeling her solid suppleness, the so-familiar shape that perfectly sealed the hole she'd left in him seven months ago. He patted her arm and pulled away.

'Thank you.' Jenna blinked and wiped a little tear from her cheek, and the flare from the megadiamond nearly scorched Theo's corneas. 'I'm so glad you're taking this well.'

Theo shrugged and bent down to retrieve the pruning shears. 'Yeah, Jenna. I take everything well. Just bring it on, babe. That's my motto.'

Jenna's hand landed on his shoulder. 'I've been thinking about this a lot, Theo, and I don't think there's a logical way to explain it. I don't think love is logical.'

Theo chortled and kept snipping.

'Seriously. I was trying to decide if I owe you an apology.'

He didn't look at her when he asked, 'So do you?'

'No.' She removed her hand. 'I think we love who we love and there's not a damn thing that can be done about it.'

Theo hung his head and stared at the mulch under his old running shoes. 'That sounds rather fatalistic for a woman who's had to fight for everything she's ever wanted in life.'

'I just knew what I wanted, and I wanted him.'

'Yep. You knew what you wanted, all right.'

Though Theo faced the house, he could feel the heat of Jenna's anger. He peeked around to see her glaring at him.

'We've been over this, Theo.'

He turned to face her full-on. 'You know, I don't think we ever really cut through the bullshit and told each other the truth — and the truth is you wanted more than a personal trainer with a retarded little brother. You wanted more than a guy who still works the door at Flawless on weekends because he can't say no to the money.'

Jenna gasped. 'That is *so* unfair.'

'No, what is unfair, Jenna, is that my brother's entire life was altered because of one tiny error in cell division. What's unfair is that my parents died in the prime of their lives because of a freak accident in a brand-new boat. Those things are unfair. What happened with us was your premeditated decision.'

'We'd grown apart and you know it.'

'Nope.' Theo shook his head. 'You grew away from me. I've always been just who I am.'

Jenna put a hand on one hip and narrowed her eyes at him. 'Bitterness doesn't look good on you. It almost makes you look ugly.'

He let go with a raucous laugh. 'There you go! Yet another reason to marry your attending physician — not only does he have more prestige and money than me, but he's better-looking, to boot!'

With a forced bedside-manner smile, Jenna told Theo to take care. Then she turned, walked back to her car, and drove away.

Buddy opened the front door a few moments later.

'Who are you arguing with out here?' He scanned the street in front of their house.

'Norton. You know how he is.'

'Yeah.' Buddy laughed. 'Need some help raking?'

Theo looked at the mess under the live oak and had a better idea. 'Whad'ya say we get medieval on the kickboxing dummies at the gym instead? I could use a good fight right about now.'

Buddy peered around the yard until he located the cat, then frowned at Theo. 'I don't even want to know what Norton said to you.'

★ ★ ★

Journal Entry April 16

Breakfast: *¾ c oatmeal; 1 Granny Smith apple; 1 c skim milk; decaf*

Lunch: *3 oz chicken breast; 1 cup stir-fried veggies; ½ c brown rice*

Snack: *1 c plain yogurt; ½ banana; sprinkle of low-fat granola*

Dinner: *3 oz sirloin; 1 small baked potato; 1 tbsp light whipped butter; 1 c sautéed spinach*

Affirmation for Today:
Just because Theo wants me to meet him at a running track doesn't mean I'll have to do actual running. Right?

* ★ ★ ★*

Lucy arrived at the Miami Springs High School parking lot shortly before five, peering in the dark until she could locate the open chain-link gate Theo had described. She grabbed her gym bag, locked her car door, and trudged down the walkway to the track.

She could make out the white lines that glowed under her feet, but not much else. She looked up to see the shadowy outline of Theo's form, standing next to what appeared to be a large ball.

It was so quiet she could hear her footfalls on the spongy surface as she walked.

'Good morning, Luce.' As soon as Theo spoke, she detected a slight change in his voice. It was like some of the zest was gone from it, and she suddenly wished she could see his face, just to make sure he was all right.

'Come here often?' she asked, setting her bag down in the dewy grass.

Theo laughed and patted her on the shoulder. 'I do, as a matter of fact. Maybe it'll become a hangout for us. Did it take you long to get here?'

Theo wanted to hang out with her? That was news. 'Uh, it's about the same as my place to Miami Beach. Not a problem at all.'

'Good.' Theo shuffled his feet, shoved his hands in his pockets, and looked off into the dark morning.

There was something wrong with him. She could sense it. And she was just about to ask him what it was when he said, 'I want to tell you something, Lucy.'

She straightened at how serious he sounded, and all her senses went on alert. The darkness made the few feet between them shrink to nothing. She heard Theo's even breathing and could smell the soap and shampoo on him and the now-familiar scent of his skin.

Suddenly he moved toward her and his face was so close she could feel his heat. Then his lips brushed over her cheek, soft and sweet. They stayed there about three seconds, but it felt like forever.

'I am extremely proud of you.'

Lucy felt his breath on her neck just before he pulled away. She squeezed her eyes tight and tried to breathe normally, wondering if that kiss had branded her cheek with a sizzling imprint of his lips. 'Thanks, Theo,' she managed.

'And you looked wonderful at the studio last week.' He flashed his teeth at her in the dark. 'Everybody was talking about you.'

Lucy thought her heart would melt. He

just said she looked *wonderful*! She was thrilled!

'Now it's time to kick your ass, Cunningham.'

Lucy laughed. She loved the way Theo talked dirty to her.

He took her by the hand, slipping his fingers between hers, and they walked along the track at a nice clip. He squeezed her hand and smiled again before he let go.

As they walked, Theo explained they were entering a new phase of her training, one that would put more emphasis on the quality of her cardio, not just the quantity. He explained interval training to her, that it would consist of alternating running and walking at varying speeds, including sprints. Lucy figured now would be the time to mention that she didn't do sprints.

'Ever hear the blues song that goes, 'I'm built for comfort, not for speed'?' Lucy asked. 'That's my theme song.'

The sun had begun to tiptoe its way over the horizon, and she could just make out the amused look on Theo's face.

'That's bull, Luce. You ran just fine that day at the News Café. You ran right out onto the sidewalk.'

She laughed. 'OK, but I was running away from you and your *tank*. It was a self-preservation thing.'

Theo laughed, too, and Lucy realized that she'd developed a real fondness for the sound of that laugh. She'd grown accustomed to its cadence over the last few months, along with all the other little noises Theo made, like the sigh when she exasperated him, the little devilish chortle when he added five pounds to the standing tricep pull-down, the way he gave her his seal of approval — *you rock, Cunningham* — after she'd made it through something difficult.

'I'm not too proud to chase after women,' Theo said, then lunged toward her with a dramatic roar.

Lucy yelped, turned, and took off down the track.

She couldn't remember the last time she'd felt her body surrender to the rhythm of running. She listened to her breath move in and out and the steady tap of her feet on the track. She knew she wasn't going all that fast, but it didn't matter. What mattered was that her body instinctively remembered how to do this, that her body could still do what it was designed to do.

'I'm right behind you, Lucy.' Theo's voice dripped with pretend menace.

Lucy smiled, reveling in how her lungs were expanding, thinking that the response she'd had to Theo's peck on her cheek was proof her body remembered other joys as well. Maybe sensual pleasure was something a woman's body could never forget, no matter how hard the woman tried to pretend it wasn't important.

Maybe being in close proximity to Theo Redmond, day after day, was all the reminder a body needed.

As her lungs pumped and her head cleared, she wondered if all the effort she'd put into blotting out the pain had deadened her ability to feel pleasure, too. What a shame. What a loss.

And then she asked herself: how much had she really allowed Brad Zirkle and the Pitt State football team to steal from her that day?

Lucy's eyes began to sting.

'You'd better keep going, little girl.' Theo was trying for a downright creepy delivery, but to Lucy he sounded like a cross between Mr Rogers and Arnold Schwarzenegger. He leaned in close to hiss in her ear, 'You're in the woods. It's dark. The big bad wolf's right behind you, and you look good enough to eat.'

The stands had been packed that day her freshman year. If the team managed to beat Purdue they got their shot at the Taco Bowl. And, thanks to Brad Zirkle's record-breaking rushing performance, they did it. Lucy cheered as the students stormed the field in celebration. It was all chaos and excitement. And then Lucy watched team members unfurl something . . . a bedsheet? . . . and the first words appeared: *Thank You, Lucky Lucy Cunningham . . .*

Lucy stumbled on the track, and she felt Theo's hand steady her. She pushed herself to keep running. She needed to run through the memory, push her body through the hurt.

She'd felt joy when she first saw those words, because for a second she really thought Brad was thanking her. He'd just had the game of his college career, the game that made up for his season-long slump. She'd been dating him for three weeks. They'd slept together. The big sign unfurling on the field had to be his way of thanking her for his change in luck, for all the world to see.

And then the rest of the sheet snapped open. The team went wild with hoots, the TV cameras swarmed, and everyone within earshot began to mumble, 'Who's Lucy Cunningham? And what's a *slump buster?*'

On some level, Lucy knew it was bad. Real bad. But it wasn't until she was leaving the stadium nearly fifteen minutes later that she learned precisely what she was.

Two frat boys were trying to explain the

concept to a girl Lucy recognized from Brit lit class. She overheard them say, 'If a jock is in a slump, his teammates dare him to find a fat or ugly girl and have sex with her. If the act is witnessed and he can survive it, his luck will change.'

For an instant, Lucy had been unable to move and got jostled around in the exiting crowd. But then she ran — she ran as fast as she could in a blind panic of shame, falling in the parking lot, scraping her palms bloody. Someone tried to help her up, but she pushed them away and scrambled to her feet, running all the way back to her dorm.

The Miami Springs High School track blurred under Lucy's feet, and her lungs began to burn like they had that day so long ago. Her heart pounded so hard it hurt, just like it had that day. Her legs felt like Jell-O, just like that run from the stadium ten years ago.

She heard herself make the strangest sound, and it struck her as interesting that she could sob and run at the same time.

'Lucy!'

She stopped in the middle of the track. She stood, panting, her legs braced wide apart, her hands on her knees and her head hanging as she gulped down the air. Theo bent down to peer into her face.

'Are you all right?'

The instant Theo's hand caressed her back, her scream pierced the silence. Lucy spun around, unable to stop the screech of words already leaving her lips: *'Don't touch me!'*

The sun had risen enough that she could clearly see the bewilderment in Theo's face. His mouth hung open and he stepped back, shocked.

Their eyes locked for a long moment.

'What in the world is going on, Lucy?'

Theo hadn't felt the anger pulse off Lucy's body like this since that day at the News Café. And not only was the anger back; it was back with a vengeance, and it was raw and nasty and, for some reason, aimed directly at him.

Lucy pushed out her chin in an attempt to stop its quivering. 'Don't ever touch me again without my permission. Got it?'

Where did this come from? He'd only been playing with her, and he wondered if somehow their little Robin Hood game had flipped a switch in Lucy's brain. He'd never seen her so pissed. He'd never seen *any* woman this pissed.

Or this hurt.

He made his voice as gentle as he could. 'I touch you all the time, Luce. I just wanted — '

'I know you touch me! Do you think I haven't *noticed*?'

Theo took another step back and felt torn between appreciation for Lucy's warrior princess body stance and the devastation in her eyes. Something — someone — had really hurt Lucy Cunningham. It had been obvious to him from the beginning. And there she stood before him now, a ticking time bomb in a pair of pink sweatpants, and he didn't know how to defuse her.

'You've got to talk to me, Luce.'

'Just don't touch me anymore, Theo.'

She turned away and began to cut across the oval infield of grass, arms swinging high as she took big strides toward her gym bag.

Theo arrived at her side — a polite distance away — and said nothing. After they walked for a few moments, he risked a sidelong glance, only to find her face contorted and streaked with tears.

'What in the hell is this about? Tell me!'

She shook her head and held up a hand. 'I'm sorry. That was completely ridiculous.'

He sighed. 'Look. We all have our hot buttons, and it seems I just hit one of yours. So tell me what's going on.'

There was no humor in Lucy's eyes or curve to her lips, which now formed a grimace. She turned away without comment.

He decided not to push. Like everything else about Lucy, he would have to discover it one little piece at a time.

'How about we just move on to the exercise ball?' Theo tried to sound cheerful. 'You're warmed up, and I've got a few new tricks up my sleeve I'd like to show you.'

She came to a halt, then stomped her feet in the grass in indignation. 'You want to keep going after I've had a complete mental breakdown?' She waved her arms in the air. 'All I want to do is go home and eat a large pepperoni with extra cheese and a box of Fiddle Faddle! I don't want to do any stupid tricks on your fucking big red exercise ball!'

'Lucy — ' Theo somehow kept himself from brushing away the strand of hair swaying across her forehead. Then he restrained himself from taking her in his arms, holding her, and telling her everything would be all right. This woman baffled him. She made him laugh. She stirred up feelings in him that he had no business having. He didn't know how to handle this. He didn't know how to handle her.

So he said, 'Junk food isn't the way you deal with bad days anymore, remember?'

'Oh, fuck off!' Lucy leaned down, gripped the exercise ball in her arms, and threw it at him.

Theo caught the ball and stared at her. She was glistening and her hair was a mess and her breasts heaved from exertion and her lips were red and her eyes wild — and he suddenly needed to kiss her mouth hard, rip off her pink sweatpants, and throw her down on the dewy grass before the *WakeUp Miami* camera crew got there.

Theo felt himself go numb.

Lucy blew the hair out of her face. 'What is *wrong* with you?' she spit out. 'Why are you looking at me like that?'

Theo threw the ball down. 'I happen to be flipping out a bit myself today.'

Lucy let out a loud snort of a laugh. 'Oh, really? And what could possibly be bothering *you*? Did they discontinue your favorite brand of hair gel or something?'

Theo stared at her, letting her comment sink in. 'You don't think very much of me, do you?'

She sighed. 'You didn't deserve that.'

'Damn right, Cunningham.'

'Do you want to talk about it?' She bit her lip. 'Is everything OK with your brother? Your cat?'

Theo shook his head slowly, wondering once again if a hundred grand was worth the loss of his sanity. She insulted him. He lusted after her. There was something very wrong with that picture. 'My brother and cat are excellent. My hair is excellent, too.'

'Yeah. OK.' Lucy moved a little closer to him, trying to gauge his expression. 'I'm sorry, Theo. I can get real ugly with self-pity sometimes. But I'm a good listener. Let me make it up to you.'

She reached for his hand, and the soft touch of her fingers sent a bolt of awareness through him. This was nuts. It was almost like Lucy's outburst had opened something in him that he was now unable to close. Theo suddenly ached with desire for that fiery, passionate, angry woman he'd just seen revealed in all her glory.

He looked down at their joined hands. 'You said no touching.'

Her gray eyes searched his face. 'I take it back.'

'Oh yeah?'

'Yeah. Now tell me — why are you having a bad day?'

Theo opened his fingers and entwined them with Lucy's. 'My ex stopped by to tell me she's engaged,' Theo said. 'She's marrying the middle-aged dude she dumped me for seven months ago. It took me off guard, I guess.'

Lucy took a step back. *Someone actually dumped Theo Redmond?* 'What a complete idiot!'

Theo shrugged. 'He's a jerk, but an extremely smart one, as it turns out.'

'No, I meant your ex-girlfriend! She's obviously not the brightest crayon in the box if she left you for someone else.'

Theo shot her a smile so full of mischief that it stunned Lucy. She was suddenly burning up, and she knew it wasn't because she'd just run a mile for the first time in a decade. It was because Theo's smile acted like gasoline thrown on that secret little flame inside her, the one he'd ignited the day she met him.

He grabbed her other hand in his.

She had to be imagining this. Theo was holding both her hands in his, and it had nothing to do with adjusting her grip on a fitness machine. All she could think was, *Don't blow it, Cunningham!*

'I thought Gia Altamonte was your girlfriend at first. Did I ever tell you that?' *Oh great — bring up the most gorgeous woman on the planet while he's holding your hands.*

'Gia?' Theo's eyebrows shot high on his forehead. 'She's not exactly my type.'

'Of course. Homely creature that she is.'

Theo laughed a little and noticed how the exercise ball had come to a stop near Lucy's feet. He gave it a tap with his toe until it was directly behind her.

'Gia is a live wire, Lucy. She has the attention span of a gerbil. She's great, but I prefer my women a little more predictable. Besides, I don't date clients.'

'Why not?' He gave her a gentle nudge and Lucy found herself lowering her bottom onto the huge ball, Theo still holding her hands.

'Palm Club policy.'

'Of course.' Lucy bounced a few times, getting the feel of the weight of her body balanced on the curved surface, anchored by her widely spread feet. When she let go of Theo's hands, the ball felt like a life raft on choppy seas.

'Now it's your turn. Tell me what just happened back there.'

Lucy tried to get up from her perch but should have rearranged her legs first, because once her butt cleared the ball, her center of gravity pulled her backward. 'Uh-oh . . . '

Theo grabbed her, and in an instant she was standing in his arms, his nose up against hers and his lips not two microns away from her own. She feared her beating heart would punch a hole through her damp T-shirt.

Theo whispered, 'A kiss is not dating. Just so we're clear on that.' His lips brushed hers even as he spoke.

'Of course.' Her lips grazed his.

'I don't want to violate company policy.'

'Then just violate *me*.'

Theo pressed his mouth full against hers while he gripped her hard by the upper arms. Lucy closed her eyes and swayed. OK, perhaps she vaguely remembered kissing as a concept, but she'd never felt a kiss like this in her whole life.

His mouth seemed to know exactly what it wanted, and took it. Theo's kiss had a unique rhythm. Its own language. Theo's kiss was like visiting an exotic foreign land that she'd only seen in travel brochures. It felt so strange. So perfect. And she thought to herself, *So this is a kiss*.

Lucy let herself sink into it, the heat and the connection and the soft, sweet questions Theo seemed to ask her. And at that instant, her answer to everything was, *Hell yes*.

Theo found it difficult to kiss and smile at the same time, but he found he had no choice with Lucy. He *knew* it would be like this. He knew she'd be soft and delicious and responsive and he'd get one taste of her and not be able to stop himself — so why had he started? Now all that mattered was that he feel every inch of her body, kiss her until they both couldn't breathe, until he knew her down to her very last secret.

His hands roamed around her back, down her sides, and they were just about to grab onto the full globes under those pink sweatpants when the camera crew pulled into the parking lot.

★ ★ ★

'I kissed her.'

Tyson crammed a handful of popcorn in his mouth and dragged his gaze from the basketball game to Theo. 'Kissed who?' he mumbled.

Before Theo could answer, Tyson's focus wandered back to the TV screen. The room erupted in hoots and jeers, and Buddy and his Special Olympic teammates gave one another high fives and pranced around the family room. The noise was deafening.

'Lucy.' Theo said it in a near whisper.

Tyson jumped to his feet, dumping the bowl of popcorn on the floor.

'Hey! We were eating that!' somebody complained.

'We got to have a talk, boy.' Tyson grabbed Theo's forearm and herded him through the dining room just as Buddy tossed the empty bowl their way and asked for a refill.

'So when did *that* happen?' Tyson leaned up against the kitchen counter, crossing his arms across his big chest. He found a stray kernel of popcorn on the front of his polo shirt and popped it in his mouth. 'And does this mean I can't ask her out?'

Theo laughed. He'd always appreciated how Tyson cut to the chase. That's probably why the athletes enjoyed his help as an assistant coach — he gave it to them straight. 'It is what it is,' had become the unofficial slogan of the Special Olympics of Miami-Dade track-and-field team, thanks to Tyson's all-purpose application of the saying.

'Yesterday at the high school track. I'm not sure what happened.'

Tyson laughed loudly. 'What do you mean, you're not sure what happened? Your lips don't go running around smacking into women without your knowledge, do they? Where's the popcorn?'

'Second cabinet to the right. Set the microwave on three minutes or it'll fry.'

'Gotcha.'

'I will come after you if you hit on her.'

Tyson tapped the buttons on the microwave and chewed on the inside of his cheek, clearly trying not to laugh again.

'Lucy is more than one of your flavors-of-the-week.'

Tyson shook his head. 'Ramona doesn't want us dating anyone on our own roster.'

'I'm not dating her.'

'But you're kissing her.'

'I kissed her *once*. And it would be a lot simpler for both of us if it doesn't happen again.'

Tyson spun around. 'So your plan is to kiss the woman one time, walk away, and then forbid anyone else to date her?'

'I knew you'd catch on.'

'Dayum, bro. That's just not right.' Tyson grabbed the big plastic popcorn bowl out of Theo's hands. 'It's plain selfish, in fact.'

Theo sank down onto a kitchen chair. 'Yeah? Well, I think there's something going on with Lucy that she won't talk about — maybe some unresolved issues about men. I feel like I should . . . I don't know . . . look out for her.'

Tyson frowned. 'You mean she's got sex hang-ups?' He smiled. 'I have experience working through those things. I even got references.'

Theo laughed softly. 'Exactly what I was afraid of.'

'You know, it's not your job to fix everything about her, Theo — just help her get in shape.' The microwave dinged and Tyson got up from the table. 'You don't have to go around carrying everyone's burden like it's your own.'

'I know.'

'Well, sometimes you don't act like you

know. You've got to learn to del-e-*gate*.' An explosion of cheers came from the living room. 'I'll be right back.'

Theo listened as the popcorn was met with great enthusiasm in the other room. As Tyson chatted with the kids about basketball, Theo realized his friend had a valid point. Theo's only responsibility toward Lucy was getting her to lose the weight — what she did or didn't do with her issues after the fact was her own affair.

Of course he and Lucy should keep it strictly business. He shuddered at the thought that come December, she'd be completely in love with him, right as he went back to medical school. She'd expect to keep seeing him every day, which would be a scheduling nightmare. Maybe she'd even want a commitment, which would be impossible — not when he was about to immerse himself in the pursuit of his dream. Medical school and residency was hell on even the strongest established relationships. He'd only end up disappointing her. He'd only end up not being enough for her.

Theo rested his chin in his palm and slumped. The immediate problem was that kiss. Oh God, he'd never felt anything so good in his life. She was so hot and sexual, and if the camera van hadn't pulled up in the parking lot there was no telling what would have happened! Since when did a single kiss make him lose it completely like that? What was his problem?

He needed to think. He needed to stop remembering how it felt and start developing a plan for damage control. If he simply pretended the kiss had never happened, it would come off as rejection, which would mess with Lucy's head, chip away at her confidence, and possibly set her back. Which made it his problem, too.

He should never have kissed her . . .

'Now what was I saying?' Tyson returned to the kitchen chair.

Theo stared at his friend for a moment. Then smiled. 'I believe you were saying that you'd take Lucy out every once in a while, give her a lot of attention, make her feel special and make sure she has a great time but not do anything to make her uncomfortable.'

Tyson's eye twitched. 'I don't remember saying any of that shit.'

'Ah, but you were going to.'

'I was?'

'Yeah.' Theo laughed. 'I will come after you if you don't hit on her within the next week.'

Tyson shook his head. 'Correct me if I'm

wrong, but I believe you have just *del-e-gated* my ass.'

★   ★   ★

Office of Doris Lehman, MSW, PhD

'Have there been more kisses?'

'No.' Lucy couldn't sit still that morning. She paced in front of the love seat, her hands fidgeting, her teeth digging into her bottom lip. She stared at the kimono girls for advice, but their small red mouths remained closed.

The little bitches.

'Have you talked about the kiss?'

'He apologized right after, when the camera crew arrived. Then last week he said I was wonderful and special but that we needed to stay focused on our goal. He hasn't said another word about it since.'

'Do you want to kiss him again?'

'I've thought about it, and I've come to see that Theo kissed me because he didn't know what else to do. You know how men hate it when women flip out — they feel kind of helpless.'

'You didn't answer my question.'

Lucy stared at her therapist. 'Sure. I'd kiss him again if need be.'

'Hmm. As I recall, you once referred to Theo as . . . ' Doris flipped through the chart

131

balanced on her knee. 'Hot.' She looked up at Lucy. 'Was the kiss hot, too?'

Lucy's mouth fell open in astonishment. 'You want his phone number or something?'

'I have his number and he has mine. What do you find most attractive about him?'

Lucy cocked her head and stared at Doris, wondering about her therapist's personal life, about Mr Doris. She hoped to God Doris wasn't getting her ya-yas out by asking these questions.

'If you must know, Theo Redmond is downright biscuit-worthy,' Lucy said.

Doris hitched up her left eyebrow. 'Care to elaborate on that?'

'Sure.' Lucy grinned. 'Have you ever met a man who looked so damn delicious that you wanted to sop him up with a hot buttermilk biscuit and inhale him in one gulp?'

'Why, yes, I have,' Doris said.

That was a shocker. 'Really? What happened?'

'I married him.'

★ ★ ★

The angle of incline on this particular machine had always annoyed Lucy. She didn't like the way her legs fell open a little too lewdly and how her boobs seemed to stick out like boulders, and she really didn't like the way Theo always put his fingers just under her upper arms.

If there was one place on her body she didn't want him fondling, it was the underside of her upper arms. Or her stomach. Or her thighs. Or the pads of flesh on her hips. Or her waist, because it was still so soft.

'You rock, Cunningham. Exhale on the extension.'

'Stop doing it for me!' She would have batted his hands away, but she was busy pushing the stupid bar up over her head. Theo kept his fingers on the vulnerable bare flesh of the underside of her arm.

'I'm not doing it for you, Lucy. You're doing every bit of the work.'

She exhaled on the extension, feeling her shoulders and arms shake with the weight on this last of fifteen repetitions, her abdominals contracting to provide the stability for the movement. 'Then why are your hands all over me? Take your hands away and let me do it.'

With great relief she returned the bar to its berth and sat up. Theo guided one of her arms up over her head and bent it at the elbow so that her fingertips touched between her shoulder blades.

'Breathe into the stretch and chill out, Luce. I'm not doing anything for you. I'm just here if you need me. That's my job.'

She harrumphed.

'That was an excellent workout. You're a machine, Luce, a lean, mean fitness machine.'

She stood and grabbed her gym towel and water bottle from the floor and glared at Theo while she chugged. Then she wiped the sweat from her face.

'That might be overkill,' she said into the terry cloth.

'The man has a valid point, Lucy.'

It was Tyson. She peeked around the towel to see him standing at Theo's side, and it was the first time Lucy had noticed that Tyson was at least two inches taller than Theo.

She immediately felt self-conscious. The sweat stains under her pits were so big they had blended with the sweat ring around her neck, which ran all the way around to her back and down into the seat of her yoga pants. She was basically one large, wet rag. Her hair was pulled up in a clip that had long ago lost its fashionable position and was now balanced on her shoulder.

She took another swig of water for fortitude, then fixed her hair clip as best she could. 'Hey, Tyson. How've you been?'

'Fine, except I don't get to see you much around here. Our schedules don't seem to mesh.'

He was one handsome man. Deep-set dark eyes with decadent eyelashes and a nicely trimmed mustache over one beautiful set of lips. Big and hard and bald and black. And he'd just smiled at her, and Lucy wasn't sure she'd be able to stand up much longer.

'Well, it's nice to see you, Tyson. And I'll catch you tomorrow, Theo. Thanks for the workout.'

She turned to head to the locker room and Tyson was at her side. 'Mind if I walk with you?'

She shrugged and tried to appear nonchalant. She could feel Theo's eyes on her. He was staring at her, sending heat her way, from his increasingly distant position behind her. She felt it. She felt him. She was so tempted to look back . . .

'I was wondering if you'd like to go out with me some evening. I've been meaning to ask you for quite a while.'

Lucy stopped and grabbed the towel from around her neck and wiped her face again. She glanced up to Tyson and saw him waiting patiently for her answer, a hint of a smile on his lips.

'Look, I've got to ask you this one little thing.' Lucy took a quick sip of water. 'Are you *sure* you want to go out with me?'

Tyson's laugh was sexy. She liked the

sound of it. 'I'm very sure. So is that a yes?'

'No. I mean . . . I have one more question.' She took a steadying breath. 'Weren't you a Division I football player in college?'

'Uh. Yeah. University of Florida. You got something against bigger schools?'

She could tell by the way his eyes sparkled that he found her amusing. Nothing about this subject was amusing to Lucy. And she just knew that if she accepted his offer, Doris was going to have a field day with the deeper meaning of it all. 'I have nothing against the schools themselves, just the football programs.'

'Is that right?' Tyson put one of his huge hands on her soaking wet shoulder and encouraged her to continue her walk to the locker room. 'Well, how about you shower and change and we'll go have a cup of coffee across the street and you can tell me all about the activities you *do* like.'

'Parcheesi. I like Parcheesi. Nobody ever gets hurt playing Parcheesi.'

'You haven't played Parcheesi with me.'

Lucy giggled. Her worry was ridiculous. Tyson went to school down here, not in Pennsylvania where it was news. He didn't recognize her. That was paranoia. Plus, maybe going out with Tyson would accomplish two things at once — she could face her fear of jocks and end her dating drought all in one fell swoop.

She looked up at him and realized the most important reason for her to say yes was that Tyson seemed genuine, had a fine sense of humor, and was an incredibly attractive man. It might also help her to get over her completely irrational and dead-end crush on Theo.

'I'd love to have a cup of coffee and talk about Parcheesi. Twenty minutes?'

'Absolutely.' Tyson smiled big at her. 'I'll see you in the lobby.'

Lucy dared to turn around before she entered the locker room, and there Theo stood, right where she'd left him, an expression on his face she swore looked just like jealousy. He gave her a wistful smile, tapped the clipboard against his thigh, and walked away.

You snooze, you lose, Redmond.

★　★　★

Tyson turned out to be the kind of man who liked to laugh and dance and be in the company of women. He seemed to know quite a lot about the female species, and Lucy figured it was knowledge that came from years of intense hands-on study of the subject matter.

In fact, Tyson had his hands on her during much of their first date. A hand on her elbow. A hand wrapped around hers when they walked. A hand on her knee to illustrate a point.

She enjoyed it. She enjoyed his laugh and the easy way he had with everyone they encountered. When they strolled together toward Bicentennial Park for the reggae festival, she relaxed into his strong arm and leaned up against him.

At one point, she turned her head to look up at Tyson, only to find him smiling down at her with that bright, devilish grin of his.

'What's on your mind, Tyson?' She smiled back at him.

'Just thinking that you're the sweetest woman I've met in a long time, Lucy. Are they all like you in Pittsburgh? 'Cause if so, I may be relocating.'

She laughed. 'There's only one of me.'

Tyson moved his hand to her waist, pulling her tight against him. 'You're damn cute, Lucy. So tell me, how many other men are you seeing these days? I mean besides Theo of course.'

Lucy stopped and wrenched away from Tyson's embrace. 'I'm not seeing Theo!' She realized she sounded huffy.

'Whoa, girl. Relax.' He pulled her close

again and resumed walking. 'That was a little joke, you know? Because everybody knows you see Theo every damn day. Unless — '

Lucy shook her head. 'Don't go there.'

'You got a thing for our man Theo?'

Lucy brought her arm up around Tyson's waist and squeezed. It was a bit of a shock. Tyson's body was more than buff, it was carved out of granite, and she felt his muscles ripple under her fingers. 'Dear God,' she whispered.

'You like that?'

'It's impressive. What's your percentage of body fat?'

'You gonna tell me yours if I tell you mine?'

Lucy tilted her head back and laughed. 'Like you and the rest of Miami don't know it already.'

Tyson stopped this time, pulled her close to the revolving door of an office building, and held her steady in front of him. 'Listen, Lucy, I like you a lot.' The feel of one of his big fingers stroking the side of her cheek was very nice. Very nice indeed. She felt her eyes close. 'But all you have to do is say the word and I'll back off. Theo's my friend. I respect him and like him and I'd never want to get in the middle of something you two are working on.'

'The only thing we're working on is my body,' Lucy said.

'Sounds like nice work if you can get it.'

Lucy smiled up at him, stood on her tiptoes, and brought her lips to his. She wanted to thank him for being so considerate and figured a nice kiss was a way to do it.

Their lips touched. His were warm and cushiony. They welcomed her, moved on her, felt so nice and smooth. And Lucy stood there on her tiptoes, waiting . . .

And waiting . . .

She waited patiently for the *zing!* she'd felt when she'd kissed Theo. She counted to herself, *One, two, three* . . . but there was no *zing.* Where the hell was the stupid *zing?*

'You feel good, girl.'

Tyson's lips went back to hers and his arms went around her and she was off the ground. He was lifting her up off the sidewalk! She started kicking.

'My God, put me down! You're going to snap your vertebrae!'

All he did was laugh and try to get his lips back on hers.

'Tyson! *Put me down!*'

He did, and she stood there out of breath and bewildered, his hands still gripping her around the waist. She watched a little smile play on his lips.

'Baby, I've been known to bench press three hundred. I could lift you with one hand.'

Lucy did the math, and knew he was sort of close to being right.

Tyson laughed hard and grabbed her hand in his. 'C'mon. Let's go hear some music.'

The outdoor music festival was loud and joyous and he kept her close in the throng. Lucy felt safe and relaxed with Tyson and enjoyed the feel of his arms around her as he swayed to the beat.

Many people came up to her to congratulate her. One woman gave her a bear hug and began to cry, explaining that Lucy's success had inspired her to lose ten pounds and quit a dead-end job. Tyson took all the attention with grace, yet Lucy noted how he stayed right by her side.

'Are you my bodyguard?' she asked him at one point that night.

'Like I said, sweet Lucy, nice work if you can get it.'

★ ★ ★

'Delivery for you, Lucy.'

Veronica tilted the dolly on its back wheels and used her sandaled foot to steer it though the door of Lucy's office.

Lucy looked up from her food journal, where she'd just had to fess up to eating an entire multigrain bagel for breakfast instead of just the half she'd intended, and stared at the dolly. Three nondescript shipping cartons were stacked on top of one another.

'I'm not expecting anything.'

Veronica shrugged and tossed an invoice on Lucy's desk. 'The UPS guy just brought them up. They're all addressed to you. From the Palm Club. They're not all that heavy. Want me to open them?'

Lucy frowned. 'No. It's OK. I'll unload them in just a second.'

She wondered what Theo could be sending her — new workout clothes? A lifetime supply of food journals? Several exercise balls? A self-help book for women who never get kissed a second time?

'And there's a bunch more fan mail this morning,' Veronica said. 'I think it's so cool you've got a fan club. I've never known anyone who had a fan club.'

'Yeah. Fifteen members at last count. I'm gonna be bigger than Britney Spears soon.'

'But still, it's a club. I don't have a fan club.'

'You're young yet.' Lucy walked over to the dolly and grabbed one of the cartons. 'At this rate, every man, woman, and child in America will be required by law to do

142

something humiliating on television before they die, so your time will come.'

Lucy hoisted the package on the top of her desk, then used a letter opener to slice through the packing tape. She pulled open the flaps and her eyes landed on the familiar small yellow boxes with brown printing. Dozens of little yellow boxes, the sight of which caused her heart to race and her mouth to water.

Impossible.

'Why in the world would the club send you three cases of Milk Duds?' Veronica peered over Lucy's shoulder and sniffed. 'That's really mean.'

Lucy reached for the invoice with trembling fingers and studied the sender information — sure enough, it listed the Palm Club's Miami beach address and number. And it listed Theo by name.

She grabbed her phone. Then put it back down.

Could somebody have put his name on that invoice as a joke? Who would want to hurt her like that? Who would like to see her fail? Who on earth could be so malicious?

Veronica stared at her, openmouthed and bug-eyed. 'Ohmigod!' she said. 'I thought you were going to rip Theo to shreds. That was close.'

'Yes, it was.'

Veronica eased a hand into one of the packages and held aloft a few boxes of candy. 'Because I was just thinking maybe somebody used Theo's name as a kind of sick joke. I mean, it makes no sense that he'd send you these.'

If Veronica had just reached a logical conclusion before Lucy, the end was near. 'I think that's exactly what happened,' Lucy said.

'I wonder who would do that to you?' Veronica shook the boxes like marimbas and sashayed toward the door. 'You don't mind if I eat these, do you?'

★ ★ ★

'It's time to WakeUp, Miami!'

Lucy spread her arms wide and smiled as the vaguely salsa-like theme music kicked in. The applause was punctured by sharp whistles and a chant of 'Go, Lucy; go, Lucy,' as the cameras left her and focused on hosts John Weaver and Carolina Buendia.

'Good morning, everyone, and thank you, Lucy, for waking us up today!' Carolina said. 'We've got a great show for you this morning, including what's fast becoming everybody's favorite monthly segment here on WakeUp

144

Miami — Lucy Cunningham's check-in on her journey from chubby to chic!'

From his spot just off camera, Theo cringed, and caught Lucy's eye. She shrugged it off and gave him a little smile.

She was wearing a pair of sleek black yoga pants today and a form-fitting scoop-neck shirt in a pale blue. He wondered if Gia was taking her shopping, because he hadn't seen the hideous leggings or the pink sweatpants in ages. He watched her walk across the stage and wave to the audience, which seemed to get more pumped with each of their appearances. A middle-aged couple in the third row held a poster that said; *Lose, Lucy, Lose!*

John Weaver spoke to the camera. 'Stay tuned. We'll be back with Lucy and personal trainer Theo Redmond and all of Miami will see just how close Lucy's getting to her goal of losing a whopping *one hundred pounds* in a year!'

They cut to a commercial and Theo studied Lucy as she walked across the set toward him, moving with a level of confidence he'd not seen before, almost with a little sway of her hips. Maybe it was the flared legs of the yoga pants.

Maybe it was all the dates with Tyson.

Theo laughed at himself. Despite his

logical approach to the kissing fiasco, he now faced another fiasco — Tyson was dating Lucy, and loving it. He'd taken her to a concert, a movie, a couple dinners, lunches. Theo no longer asked. He'd also managed to stop himself from asking how much petting — heavy or otherwise — was going on. He didn't want to know.

Because the woman walking toward him had melted in *his* arms once, surrendered to *his* mouth, showing Theo that beneath Lucy Cunningham's surface lurked a babe who felt like paradise and tasted like lust. And what had he done after that discovery? He gave her to another man.

He should be taken out and shot.

'My public adores me,' she whispered, standing beside him at the edge of the set. 'I think my fan club membership just sky-rocketed to sixteen.'

She smelled especially soft and sweet today and he took a deep breath of her. 'Are you wearing a new perfume?'

She smiled up at him, and Theo examined her lips for any telltale sign of paradise. He was alarmed to see the scenery hadn't changed, and decided he'd have to simply avoid looking at her mouth.

'I am. Thank you for noticing. It's called 'Paradise Awaits.'' Lucy tipped her head to the side and her smile mellowed. 'Gia's modeling for their new ad and gave me a freebie. You like?'

Theo had to laugh. Sometimes the ways of the universe could be as subtle as a sledgehammer. Sometimes it hurt like hell, but other times it was just a gentle reminder to pay attention. And at the moment, he certainly was rising to attention — everywhere. It started with a heat in his face and moved down into his chest, where his heart stirred to life, and kept on moving southward. Everything about him was perking up right there in front of John Weaver and Carolina Buendia and an audience full of people watching their every move.

'I like,' he said.

She nodded. 'Hey. Two Cuban sandwiches and a bag of Fritos were delivered to my office yesterday at lunchtime.'

Theo frowned at her. 'You ordered that for lunch?'

Lucy made a *tsking* sound followed by a sigh of exasperation. 'No, Theo. This is not another pecan pie confession. What I'm telling you is that someone called in that order to be delivered to me at work — the Milk Dud scenario again — with your name on the receipt.'

'Wow. That's so strange.' Theo was doing

his best to sound casual, but the truth was, this had 'creepy' written all over it. It was true that Lucy's notoriety was increasing, and it could be that she had attracted the attention of an admirer with a twisted sense of humor. Theo hoped that was the only thing twisted about him. 'Do you think we should call the police?'

Lucy laughed so loud that the stage director slashed her finger across her throat and glared at her an instant before she counted down to action.

Lucy leaned her shoulder against Theo and whispered, 'I'm not sure the unauthorized delivery of swine is a felony.'

Theo put his lips to her ear and enjoyed the scent of paradise before he said, 'Damn well should be.'

Lucy lost only three pounds that month. Theo's heart just about cracked in two as he watched her step down from the scale in front of the live audience, trying her best to put on a brave face as the crowd groaned in disappointment.

He felt her tremble from head to toe as he measured her in front of the cameras. She had lost five more inches, three from her hips alone.

Theo took the opportunity to explain to John and Carolina that this was a perfect example of why people working toward improved health and fitness should not be too focused on the numbers. Lucy had obviously lost many pounds of fat and gained lean muscle, which weighs more. Her loss of inches was proof that her body was finding its own pace of transformation.

'I wouldn't be surprised if next month is a big number loss for Lucy. Sometimes it works like that.'

Carolina leaned forward in her chair, her great legs crossed at the knees, and she patted Lucy's forearm. 'Do you feel like you've failed this month?'

Ah, hell. This was the kind of crap that they'd managed to avoid so far and the last thing he wanted Lucy to have to deal with. But Lucy — sweet, funny Lucy — looked right into the camera and said, 'The only thing I'm losing is weight.'

Theo tried not to smile as Carolina fidgeted with her cue cards and blinked in discomfort before they started taking questions from the audience. The woman with the *Lose, Lucy, Lose!* poster stood up and asked if she could give Lucy a hug.

'Sure,' Lucy said, standing up and waiting for the woman to reach her.

'My name is Sonja Gallegos and I've lost eleven pounds following the Lucy and Theo health and fitness plan,' the woman announced.

That was interesting news — considering Theo didn't know there was such a thing.

'When are you going to have your Web site up and running?' Sonja asked. 'And when's the book coming out?'

Lucy laughed good-naturedly and gave Sonja a squeeze. 'We'll keep everyone posted. Promise.'

Theo ended up giving Lucy a ride to her office after the show because she told him her car was in the shop.

'So how'd you get here this morning?' he asked.

'Taxi.'

Theo sighed, pulling into the crazy morning rush hour traffic of downtown Miami. 'I could have picked you up at your place, Luce. It wouldn't have been a problem.'

'But what about your brother? And you live all the way up in Miami Springs. I didn't want to cause any more problems than I already do.'

'It would have been OK. You can ask me for things like that anytime. That's what friends do.'

He watched her turn her face toward the passenger-side window. She'd lost a total of forty-three pounds now, and it was fascinating how the bone structure of her face had come out of hiding. When he looked at her he no longer saw a round-faced woman. He saw Lucy. And Lucy happened to have been blessed with a nice heart-shaped face, high cheekbones, big, perfectly spaced eyes, and beautiful skin.

But if he had to pick one thing he loved most about the way she was designed, it would have to be her neck. It was graceful and long, and the way she had her head turned away at the moment made him want to kiss her right behind her cute ear.

'Are we really friends?' Lucy swiveled so fast she caught him gawking at her. A shadow passed through her eyes and she frowned.

'Of course we're friends.'

'Just checking.'

'Why did you have to ask me that?'

She didn't say anything for a moment, then smiled. 'We're the kind of friends who've kissed once by mistake.'

Theo swallowed hard, pulling onto First Avenue and getting flipped off in the process. He knew her office was near Twelfth Street and he needed to switch lanes, which was going to be near impossible at this hour of the morning. He also knew he needed to respond to that last comment but had no earthly idea what to say to her.

That kiss had been hot and confusing and tipped his world on its axis. It had been unforgettable. And Lucy had just referred to it as a mistake. Maybe that was the easiest way to put the issue to rest.

'We all make mistakes, Lucy. We're human.'

'You can drop me off right here.' She reached for the door handle and grabbed her clothes hanger from the backseat.

'But your office is six blocks away!'

'I'll walk.' She waited, her hand on the handle. 'Unlock the car, please.'

'We need to talk about this.'

Her eyes flashed at him and she gritted her teeth. 'Unlock the car. Now.'

'You're dating Tyson.'

'The door, Theo.'

'Fine.' He hit the button and the sharp little click echoed through the Honda interior like a gunshot. 'I'll see you tomorrow at — '

Slam!

She was already gone.

★ ★ ★

Lucy changed her clothes in the ladies' room of Sherrod & Thoms and tried to find the perfect balance between deep-relaxation breathing and hyperventilation. But the way her sinuses hummed and her vision ebbed and flowed, she feared she'd already crossed that line.

She fumbled with the back button on her skirt and looked at herself in the mirror. 'What the hell?' Granted it was difficult to keep her wardrobe organized with the constant size changes, but she could have sworn this particular skirt was a size 16. But it sagged at the waist and made the bottom half of her body look like it was draped in a sack.

She yanked at the waist and twisted the fabric around so she could read the tag. Yep. A 16. This was very weird.

'Good morning, Lucy!' Veronica balanced her Starbucks cup on the edge of the sink and began to touch up her lipstick. 'Having a problem with your zipper?'

'No. I'm having a problem with my trainer.' Lucy shoved the waistband into her panty hose and pulled her cotton twinset down over her hips and admired the effect in the ladies' room mirror. 'I look like I have a tumor.'

'So what's wrong with Theo? What did he do? I watched you two this morning on *WakeUp Miami* and he sure seemed nice to you. It looked like he was taking care of you.'

Lucy blinked hard at her own reflection, then looked at Veronica. 'What in the world are you talking about?'

'I said . . . ' Veronica rubbed her lips together and popped the lipstick tube back in her bag. 'It was obvious he really cares for you. Just the way he looked at you when you talked. The way he smiled at you. It was real sweet. Gentle. If I didn't know better, I'd say he had the hots for you, but I know you've been going out with that other trainer babe.'

'Oh, for God's sake, Veronica!' Lucy scooped up the empty hanger and her workout clothes from the floor and shoved them in her gym bag.

'Hey, you asked and I answered. You're my boss. I don't lie to you. That's what I saw.'

Lucy stood a moment at the restroom door and tried to remember if she'd seen any of what Veronica described. Maybe. But then, Theo was usually sweet. Always gentle. Like a friend would be.

The dangerously high lust level she'd felt in his kiss must have been a figment of her imagination, a result of her naïveté.

'Thank you, Veronica. I didn't mean to snap at you.'

'No problem. So what did Theo do? Why are you so pissed at him?'

She held the door open for her assistant. 'Nothing. It's all in my head.'

Lucy made her way down the still-quiet halls of Sherrod & Thoms. She liked getting in at eight because that left her an hour of peace before everyone else showed up and the fax machine started going crazy and the phones rang incessantly and Stephan popped his head in to make as many pointless suggestions and godawful strange comments as one man could produce in a day's work.

She parted company with Veronica and rounded the corner past Stephan's office, which used to be Sarah's. Lucy remembered interviewing with Sarah, how much she loved the older woman's sense of humor and her worldliness. How they'd hit if off immediately. With her gone, the one hundred thousand couldn't come soon enough.

'*I said I'll make it work, so enough with the bullshit threats about the IRS or anything else. You got it?*'

Lucy stopped dead as she heard Stephan slam down his phone and scream, 'Nasty old unscrupulous fuck!' The words echoed through the quiet hallway.

She took a steadying breath and opted to walk by his door casually, greeting Stephan with a smile and a wave. He saw her, and his face fell. He ran after her.

'Lucy. Hold up.'

She turned in time to see him adjusting the collar of his dress shirt, looking for all the world like he was nearly stroking out from stress, and they hadn't even opened for business yet.

'Everything OK, Stephan?'

'Sure. Sure. Great.' He put his hand at the small of Lucy's back and directed her toward her office. She absolutely *hated* him touching her like that. 'How's the Eddie Award entry coming? And what the hell's wrong with your skirt?'

Lucy sighed. She threw her gym bag behind her desk and motioned for Stephan to have a seat. 'My skirt is too big and I'm done with the Eddie entry. It's an incomplete mess. I'm embarrassed to put my name on it. But it's done. Veronica's making a copy.'

'I'm sure it's fine.'

'It's seven pages and fourteen graphic attachments of bullshit and you know it.'

Stephan didn't blink. 'I think it's important for the agency's visibility that we at least try this year.'

'I disagree. The Palm Club campaign would be perfect for next year's entry, but not now. But I did it, just as you asked. Anything else?'

Stephan shuffled his feet on the carpet and looked around restlessly. His eyes landed on hers and he grinned. 'Tough break on the weight gain this month.'

Lucy would have to call the look on her

boss's face outright glee. 'I lost three pounds, Stephan. That's not a gain.'

'Well, Lucy, it hardly matters. What matters is the fact that at this rate it doesn't look like you're going to make it, and I won't lie to you — I'm quite concerned.'

Lucy sat back in her chair and crossed her legs. She'd just started doing that again, and it made her feel a little smug that she could once again get her thighs to lie on top of each other like a normal person. 'Is this your way of empowering me?'

Stephan snickered and steepled his fingers in front of his face. 'You're plenty empowered. I don't want to put additional pressure on you, but it's clear I need to remind you that the firm's reputation is in your hands.'

'I see.'

'You and the pretty-boy trainer can be as bubbly as fuck on TV, but if you don't keep dropping the pounds we're going to start dropping clients. If you don't keep losing weight, you could ruin us. You and everyone else around here could be out of a job.'

Once again, Lucy couldn't quite figure out the man who was supposed to be the captain of this business enterprise. She wondered if maybe Sarah's death had sent him over the edge.

'Did you see the show this morning,

Stephan? Did you see the woman who wanted to know when our Web site would be up?'

'The poster was quite a classy touch.' He shook his head.

'I think she's hit on something. I think Theo and I should have our own site — not just the progress reports on the Palm Club site. We can have chat rooms and online support groups for those trying to get fit. We can link to the Palm Club, of course, and have guest trainers do weekly question-and-answer columns. I can make a blog of my daily workouts and food journal. What do you think?'

Stephan's eyes had glazed over and he appeared ready to fall forward onto Lucy's desk.

'Stephan? Hello?'

'I'll think about it.' He pushed himself up into a stand, still not making eye contact with Lucy. 'Don't do anything until I've had a chance to mull it over.'

'Mull what over?' Lucy stood up to study her boss. There was something more funky than usual about Stephan this morning. Was he not getting enough sleep at night? Had the man started using drugs? What was that ugly phone conversation about? 'I think this is a no-brainer. We could generate so much excitement — '

Stephan simply turned and left without comment, like a ghost, or a man who'd just realized he'd stepped into the wrong room and was lost.

Men. Lucy didn't think she'd ever understand them.

Her phone rang. She picked it up and heard the unmistakable sound of Mary Fran in tears.

'My God! Frannie, what's wrong? Is it the kids?'

'No. No. They're fine.' More sobs.

Lucy figured she might as well give in to the fact that today was going to be a doozy. Before most people could get their butts settled in their desk chairs, she had been publicly weighed and measured only to disappoint thousands; had learned without a doubt that Theo thought of her only as a friend; was dressed like a bag lady; had engaged in a nonsensical conversation with her borderline-insane boss; and had just been informed that her big sister was running away from home and moving in with her.

'You're *what?*'

'I'll be there tonight.'

'Fran, you can't. What about the kids?'

'I told Keith I was leaving him and he'd have full responsibility for the children for as

159

long as I decided to stay gone. We'll see how long he survives.'

'Are you serious?'

'Well, no. Maybe I just need a wild girls' weekend.'

'But Frannie — '

'Don't try to stop me.'

'But — '

'I have to go. One of the twins just puked. My flight gets in at Miami International at ten.'

Lucy pulled the phone away from her ear and stared at it. Mary Fran had hung up.

6

May

Some nights, Theo didn't think he did enough to earn five hundred dollars manning the door at Flawless. Other nights, it seemed they couldn't pay him enough for this gig. Tonight was one of those nights.

The early crowd was already sloshed and rockin'. Theo looked at his watch to see that it was eleven — he had five more hours of this before he could go home and collapse. He'd sleep in until about ten, then hit the books. His test was in three months and it weighed heavily on his mind.

Theo knew it was rare for someone to reenter medical school once he'd dropped out, especially after what would be a four-year hiatus. Sometimes he thought he was nuts for even trying. The brain absorbs information at an astounding rate in med school, and once you leave that environment, it's like a stopper is removed and the draining begins. Much of what he'd learned had already hemorrhaged, and he was attempting to shove it all back in, trying to reacquaint his

161

mind with the pounding demands of medical school.

It was the hardest thing he'd ever done.

The score on his readmission test would determine how much of his life he'd wasted. There was a distinct possibility he'd have to start all over again, from the beginning of his M-1 year. It would be demoralizing, and he wasn't sure if it would be worth it. But if his scores were high enough, he could start at any point prior to where he left off and maybe even pick up right at the middle of the M-3 year. That would be ideal, but he wasn't counting on it.

'Hey, Theo, baby.' He looked up to see one of the club's regular honeys sashay inside. For women like her, there was no cover. All she had to do was look gorgeous and occasionally dance on the bar, a huge mahogany structure built for just that purpose. No one sat at the bar at Flawless. Few people sat at all. It was just a writhing sea of techno dance music, sunbaked bodies barely covered in shamefully expensive clothing, and naked hunger.

It's what South Beach was all about.

'Good to see you. Enjoy yourself tonight.'

'I'd enjoy myself more if I had you.'

Theo tried to smile. He'd seen this woman operate more nights than he could remember.

Safe sex with her would require the use of a full-body condom. 'Sorry, but I gotta work.'

When she pouted and shook out her hair, the glitter she'd spritzed on herself from eyelids to toenails twinkled in the lights. 'Maybe some other night.'

The patrons poured in. Theo had to turn away a female foursome with the lamest fake IDs he'd seen in some time. 'Come back in a few years, girls,' he'd said to them.

Theo put up the rope at about eleven forty-five. From now till about two thirty he'd be cajoled and tipped and begged by those who knew it was uncool to show up before midnight but weren't cool enough to make it through the rope after then.

He despised this game but smiled and joked to pass the time. He looked at his watch. It was just after midnight.

He recognized the voice long before he saw Gia. There wasn't another person on the planet with that cackling laugh and that grating, fast, Spanish-laced speech.

She kissed his cheek. 'Hola, Theo.'

He kissed her back. 'You missed your appointment Wednesday.'

'You mad at me, or what? I forgot to tell you I had to fly to New York.'

Something in Theo's brain snapped. He could swear he just got a whiff of Paradise

163

Awaits and he sniffed at Gia, but it wasn't her.

Then Gia stepped out of his face and his eyes landed on the most amazing sight. It was Lucy — two Lucys, really: the one he knew and a shrimpy version, standing next to two other women he'd never met.

'You gonna make us stand out here all night or what, Theo?'

He hardly heard Gia. He blinked. Lucy was wearing a sparkling silver top with tiny straps and a black skirt that fell well above her knees. He hadn't seen this much of her skin since he dipped her in the hydrostatic tank. But she hadn't looked like this back then. Back then she'd been a big, out-of-shape woman. Tonight, she stood before him a voluptuous, curvy, solid, glowing, slightly larger-than-average woman.

So he was shallow. He admitted it. All he knew was the Lucy standing in front of him, her eyes wide and her shiny hair falling free, was *hot*.

'I'm Lucy's sister, Mary Fran. I've heard all about you, Theo.'

A soft little hand was shoved into his palm and broke his fixation on the real Lucy. The small Lucy began to shake his hand with gusto. 'So is this when I tip you?' she asked, holding out a five.

Theo laughed, pushing the money back into her hand. It was amusing seeing someone who looked like Lucy but was so different. He raised his eyes to see the real thing smiling at him.

'And this is Veronica King and Maria Banderas,' Lucy introduced her coworkers to Theo.

'Please, come right on in, ladies.'

Lucy passed by last, and Theo inhaled — paradise indeed. 'You look beautiful,' he whispered in her ear.

Lucy spun her head around, and a section of her hair slapped him across the chin. He loved it. Though he knew it would be the stupidest thing he could do, he wanted to reach out and grab that hair and crush his mouth against hers — just one more time.

'Thanks, Theo.'

Her eyes were beguiling. She stood on her tiptoes and pressed her lips to his cheek. On the surface, it was exactly the same kind of perfunctory, social kiss that Gia had given him just a moment ago. But it didn't feel the same, and when Lucy's warm lips touched his face he automatically turned toward the kiss, and the very corners of their mouths touched.

It was electric.

Lucy pulled back and looked away, running

to catch up with the other women, already swarmed with admirers. Theo worried about Lucy in there. He worried she'd get hit on. He worried she'd not know how to protect herself.

Then he pictured her warrior princess stance on the Miami Springs High School track last month and knew she'd be OK.

Besides, there was no way he'd let Lucy out this door without knowing what time she left and whom she left with. He'd make sure of it.

Theo took a break about one thirty and decided to search for her. It didn't take long — he found her dancing with a Latin lover type, her head thrown back as she laughed. Theo stood stock-still, staring at her hips. She was moving in a way that had nothing to do with building core strength and everything to do with seduction. He swallowed hard, just as Lucy turned to see him staring.

The song ended, and he watched Lucy shake her head several times, turning down whatever offer her dance partner had extended. Theo sighed in relief as Lucy sat down at a small cocktail table just to the side of the bar, alone.

'What are you drinking?'

She grinned at him. 'Diet Coke,' she shouted over the music. 'Is this a journal check?'

He laughed. 'Nope. I was going to get you another one. Be right back.'

Theo helped himself to two sodas and returned to the table, hopping up on the stool right next to Lucy. He knew that conversation would be tough with the music, but just sitting by her side was better than nothing.

He let his eyes scan the club and saw Gia holding court on a red velvet sofa on the raised dais toward the back. This club didn't have a VIP room, but the platform cluttered with sofas, chairs, and Persian rugs served the purpose.

His eyes fell on the miniature Lucy named Mary Fran, who was shaking her thing on the bar with Veronica and Maria. He raised an eyebrow in surprise.

'My sister is having a marital crisis!' Lucy shouted in his ear. 'I think she just needs to blow off some steam!'

He looked down on Lucy's glistening face and smiled. Without thinking, he brought his hand to her cheek and touched her smooth skin. Her eyes flew wide. Theo wanted to smack himself. Not only did he have to stop *thinking* about touching and kissing her — he also needed to stop *doing* it.

'Wanna dance?'

'I don't think so.' She shook her head and took a sip from her straw.

'Why not?'

Lucy shrugged. 'Too self-conscious, I guess.' She leaned closer to him, and thoughts of paradise clouded his mind. 'I'm a little worried about what other people are thinking.'

Theo laughed. 'You didn't seem too concerned about that with Ricky Romance back there.'

Lucy laughed, too. 'He wouldn't take no for an answer.'

'Let's dance.'

'No.'

'Sorry. Not acceptable.' Theo grabbed her hand and pulled her out onto the dance floor, all the while his brain was crying, *Stupid, stupid, stupid!* He told himself to shut up and snuggled her tighter, feeling every inch of her feminine softness against every hard place on his body, including the parts that seemed to be getting harder by the second.

It wasn't exactly a slow dance number, but Theo didn't give a damn. This was what he craved.

'Are you trying to camouflage me with your entire body, Theo?'

He laughed. 'I'm only here to help.'

'This is not helping anything. Let me go.' Lucy tried to shove away from him.

'Hey, relax, Luce. I'm going to say

something to you and it may sound harsh, but you need to hear it.'

He let her pull away enough that she could look up into his face. She was frowning. 'What? I can't even hear you!'

Theo took her hand and led her past the bar, through the kitchen, and out the back door of the club. Lucy gasped as they entered the serene little courtyard that led to the club owners' apartment.

Theo motioned for her to have a seat on a cushioned lounge chair next to a potted fern. He sat in the one across from her.

'You have a habit of obsessing about what people think when they look at you.'

'Not accurate.' Lucy adjusted herself so she was poised on the chair edge, as if preparing for a quick escape. 'That *used* to be one of my habits — obsessing over the fact that people were staring at me, then being pissed off about it and eating too much, then getting more obsessed and pissed off because I ate too much and people were staring at me. Fun, huh?'

She tried to get up, but Theo grasped her hand. 'You're a different person now.'

Lucy's face softened. She nodded her head. 'I'm trying.'

'Look, Luce. What I'm getting at is there's a lot more to life than how much you weigh and what size you wear.'

Her mouth opened. She blinked at him.

'You need to get your mind off that crap for a while. It really isn't all about what you look like.'

'Thanks for the pep talk.' She stood up, and Theo stood with her.

'All I'm saying is there's a bigger picture. Maybe you need to expand your horizons a little.'

She cocked her head to the side and smiled at him. 'Since when did you become a philosopher, Theo?'

'I think about three years ago. So what are you doing two weekends from now?'

'Nothing.'

'Then I'd like to show you someplace where nobody gives a rat's ass about your percentage of body fat. Where nobody will judge you by your appearance. A place where you can stop judging yourself for maybe the first time in your life.'

The music stopped inside the club for an instant, and it got quiet out in the courtyard, so quiet they could hear the ocean.

'I don't know any places like that, Theo,' she whispered.

'I do.'

Lucy shrugged. 'All right. So what's a girl wear to a place like that?'

'Sensible shoes and sunscreen,' he said, smiling.

★ ★ ★

'I'm Buddy, Theo's brother. I have mental retardation and I'm a track star.'

Lucy had barely made one pass around the University of Southern Florida stadium before she found the brothers Redmond, or they found her. She'd really had no idea what to expect — Theo had told her only that Buddy was sixteen and had Down's syndrome and that Lucy should come to Tampa for the weekend to watch him compete in the Florida State Games.

And now Buddy stood very close to her, his face on fire with delight, his smile very wide and a little wet, and he was staring at her through thick glasses, waiting for her response.

'Cool. I'm Lucy,' is what she said, and they shook hands.

Theo hung back, relaxed and hunky as always, in a red polo shirt with the words *Special Olympics Miami-Dade Coach* stitched on the left upper chest. Theo was a Special Olympics coach? Why hadn't he mentioned that?

'I know who you are, Lucy.' Buddy gave

her a slow nod. 'You're the pretty fat lady Theo goes on TV with. Your butt looks a lot better now than it used to.' He kept going. 'I weigh one hundred twenty-six pounds and I don't eat junk, except on nights Theo's too tired to cook, so I can win in competitions. My mom wouldn't let me get fat like a lot of Down's syndrome people.'

Lucy had no idea how to respond to all that.

Just then, a pack of four teenagers strolled by, all in different-colored T-shirts, all obviously Special Olympics athletes, and they pulled Buddy into their group with excited hugs and loud greetings.

Theo hollered after him, 'Meet me at the main registration tent at four! Do *not* be late — we're having dinner with Aunt Viv and Uncle Martin before the opening ceremony!'

'You got it, stud!' Buddy waved at Theo, winked at Lucy, and was swept off into a sea of people walking toward a banner that read: *Olympic Village.*

Theo turned to her and grinned. 'He can be a little direct sometimes.'

'And you said nobody here would care about the size of my butt!'

He laughed, putting his arm around her shoulder and giving her a friendly squeeze.

'So how was your drive? Did you enjoy Alligator Alley?'

There was little to enjoy on the highway from Miami to Tampa via Naples — unless you reveled in endless desolate swampland and no mobile phone coverage. 'It was relaxing. I listened to some good tunes and got here in no time.'

'Great. Do you think you would be comfortable staying with us this weekend? It would be much better than a hotel.'

Lucy frowned at him. 'Us who? You and Buddy? I don't think that's — '

'My aunt and uncle's best friends have a winter home here but are already back in Boston. They gave us the place for the week.'

Whoa. Lucy had planned on the Red Roof Inn, not living under the same roof with Theo and his family.

'There's more than enough room for all of us. And Viv and Martin would love to meet you.'

She shook her head. 'I could never impose like that.'

Theo laughed. 'Don't be silly. I'd love your company, and that house is so big we could lose each other in it. Plus, it's staffed, as in there's a maid, a cook, a gardener, and a pool man. Come enjoy it with us.'

She felt her eyes go wide.

'Please say yes, Luce.'

Theo was looking down into her face with such adorable tenderness that Lucy nearly lost her breath. She couldn't be angry at him, she supposed — he obviously had no idea what he did to her with those sea blue eyes, how he confused her with his affection, excited her with his touch, left her feeling lost when she wasn't in his company.

The man squeezing her shoulder so tightly was her friend. Her trainer. Her business partner. Yes, she'd been ga-ga over Theo since the moment they met. But he was not her lover, and despite the sparks she felt in his presence, he seemed to be happy just being friends.

The faster she could come to grips with that, the saner she'd be. And the more she could just enjoy her next date with Tyson.

'Sure, Theo. I accept.'

Theo had led her to a big blue-and-white-striped tent where dozens of volunteers handed out badges.

'Theo!' An older lady in a hat decorated with an array of fishing lures smiled warmly at him. 'What can I do you for, handsome?'

'Hi, Mimi.' Theo kissed her cheek. 'This is my friend Lucy Cunningham, and we need to pick up her pass for the weekend.'

'Welcome, Lucy!' Mimi opened her arms

174

and leaned over the utility table, pressing Lucy to her big bosom. 'Any friend of Theo's is a friend of mine.'

Mimi rooted through a box of manila envelopes. 'Ah. Here we go.' She opened the flap and pulled out a long white neck strap looped through a laminated card that read: *All Access Pass.*

'Is this your first time at the State Games?'

Lucy poked her head through the strap and flipped the ID badge faceup. 'Actually . . . uh . . . ' Lucy forgot what she was saying because Theo had just reached over and extracted her ponytail from the strap, then stroked the back of her neck. 'It's my first Special Olympics anything.'

Mimi's mouth opened in surprise. 'Oh, wow!' She smiled at Theo conspiratorially, then squeezed Lucy's hand in both hers. 'It's going to blow your mind, sweetheart.'

They went to a Mexican place on Fowler Avenue for dinner, where Lucy ordered the grilled sirloin, pinto beans, and a salad and was thoroughly charmed by Theo's family.

Vivian and Martin Redmond were much older than Lucy anticipated, in their early eighties if she had to guess, and she soon learned they were Theo's great-aunt and great-uncle. Vivian was gracious and kind and Martin was a firecracker and had them all laughing. Lucy saw immediately that Theo's stunning blue eyes were a trait among males in the Redmond clan and Martin must have been a real looker in his day. Lucy glanced from Theo to his uncle and back again and was hit by this wistful thought — that it would be nice to know Theo when he was an eighty-year-old charmer, telling jokes to his grandchildren while they ate dinner at some Mexican joint.

Irrational longings like that did nothing to lower her expectations, Lucy realized. She had to stop being such a sentimental goofball.

'Lucy, we've been so impressed by your progress on the *WakeUp Miami* show.'

As nice as it was, Vivian's comment brought Lucy right back to reality. It made her realize she'd gone several hours without thinking of herself as Lucy Cunningham, media makeover guinea pig. She'd gone most of the day without worrying how her legs looked in her shorts, whether her upper arms were too fleshy for this conservative tank top, or whether she was sweating like a sow in the sun.

She glanced at Theo across the round table and he smiled at her.

'Thank you, Vivian,' Lucy said.

'So tell us about your family, Lucy. Do you have any brothers and sisters?'

And apparently, that was it — there would be no haranguing her about calorie intake or how many abdominal crunches she did each day or the total inches lost off her upper-thigh circumference. They'd already moved on to another subject. Lucy sighed in relief.

'My mom and dad retired to Fort Lauderdale a couple years ago, and I left Pittsburgh and moved to Florida to be near them. I have an older sister who's married with three little kids — she lives in Atlanta — and a younger brother who's in his medical residency back in Pittsburgh.'

The table got very quiet, and Lucy looked over to see that Theo's fork had paused in midair. He put it down and cleared his throat.

'Interesting,' he said. 'I didn't know your brother was in medicine.'

'Mmm-hmm. Pediatrics. He's in the internship year of a three-year residency. We don't see him often because I guess the internship year is the worst.'

'I've heard that.'

'Theo was going to be a doctor,' Buddy announced matter-of-factly. 'But then Mom and Dad died and he had to come home to be with me and then his girlfriend said she couldn't love him if he wasn't going to be a doctor. Norton didn't like her, anyway.'

Buddy reached up and stroked Theo's hair,

as if to comfort his big brother. Then Buddy started to cry.

Lucy's body buzzed in embarrassment. She felt like she was intruding on a private family matter.

Vivian caressed Buddy's shoulder and Martin shrugged sadly and Theo looked at her from across the table and grinned.

That was the last straw for Lucy. Theo was so completely *not* what she'd first assumed him to be. He was single-handedly raising his brother. He had the patience to coach special athletes. He was brilliant enough to get into med school. He'd had his own share of loss and pain. And he was able to hang on to his fine sense of humor in the process.

She felt ashamed at how she'd once assumed Theo was just a pretty face and a perfect body. She'd done the one thing she'd always despised most — she'd judged someone by his appearance.

And right then, Lucy knew that no matter how hard she tried to deny it, it would be a blizzardy day at Disney World before she'd ever find a man she wanted more than Theodore Redmond.

★   ★   ★

The pageantry of the opening ceremonies surprised Lucy. She was expecting something schmaltzy and low-budget, not something so powerful. Seventeen hundred athletes ranging in age from eight to eighty stood in clusters under bright field lights and a cobalt blue evening sky, their T-shirts forming a rainbow around the stadium track.

Loud, inspiring rock music blared from the sound system as a cavalcade of law enforcement vehicles roared onto the grass, their lights and sirens sending the crowd into a frenzy. Then the torch was carried into the stadium by a small group of police officers who'd completed the last ten miles of a statewide torch run.

After a rousing welcome speech from the emcee, a young woman assigned the job of reciting the Special Olympics oath rose from her chair onstage. Little by little, she neared the microphone, her left leg dragging, her physical imperfections clear for all to see. She stood tall in front of the huge crowd and said the words slowly and deliberately, in a voice thick with difficulty: 'Let me win,' she said. 'But if I cannot win, let me be brave in the attempt.'

Lucy sat in the bleachers between Martin and Vivian, humbled to tears. She wondered how many hours of practice had gone into that short walk to the podium and those simple lines of speech. She wondered how much courage it had taken for that woman to do what she'd just done.

Suddenly it was clear why Theo wanted Lucy to be here. He wanted to teach her a compelling lesson in a gentle way. He wanted her to learn to put her own struggles in perspective. Theo, who was out there somewhere in the sea of red shirts, was a very smart man.

Lucy tried to surreptitiously wipe the tears from her cheeks.

'Don't worry, sweetheart, I cry every year.' Vivian handed her a tissue. 'It can be overwhelming to see how much potential there is in all of us.'

Lucy appreciated Vivian's words and her quiet smile and told her so. Together they watched as officers handed the torch to a few Special Olympics athletes, who took off around the track to light the Special Olympic Flame of Hope, the fire shooting high into the dark sky.

The emcee announced, 'Let the Games begin!'

★ ★ ★

Competition began early the next day and ended late into the afternoon. Theo's aunt and uncle lasted only a few hours before the sun and the heat sent them back to the house. They did stay long enough to see Buddy win the one-hundred-meter and the long jump and then receive medals for the events.

Twice that morning, Lucy, Vivian, and Martin left their seats in the stands for the shady picnic area, where the award platforms were arranged behind potted plants. Twice Buddy stood atop the highest of three blocks while a volunteer hit the play button on the boom box and the Olympic theme blared. Twice Buddy smiled, pumped his fist in the air, and the instant the music ended shouted, 'Who loves me now?'

The second time he did this, Lucy turned to Theo to ask him what Buddy was doing, but Theo had already started to explain. He said it was Buddy's good-luck ritual, one he'd used since he was eight, when he won his first Special Olympics event.

'It was the two-hundred-meter breast-stroke, and right before it started my mom went to the side of the pool and hugged him and said, 'Everybody loves you, Buddy.' So when he touched the wall first, he ripped off his goggles and pumped his fist in the air and yelled, 'Who loves me now?' Everyone laughed, and he's been winning ever since.'

By four that afternoon, Buddy had six gold medals hanging from his neck and Lucy felt like she'd run a marathon herself. The heat and all the pure emotion was exhausting, but she couldn't take her eyes off the competitions. There seemed to be a lot of hugging going on, which fascinated her. Hugs seemed to be as important as the medals. After a singles tennis match, the victor dropped to her knees and kissed the court before she was crushed with hugs from her coach, parents, friends, and even her competition. When a tall, strong high jumper hit the bar with his shoulder and cried in disappointment, he was hugged by his rivals.

At about five, Theo drove them back to the house, where they planned to eat and get showered and changed for the evening's festivities — the closing ceremony and victory dance. The dance was all Buddy talked about on the drive from the stadium. Apparently, the dance was the best thing about the Summer Games.

'Are you going to dance tonight, Lucy?' Buddy had turned his excited sun-brown face around toward her in the backseat of Theo's car, where she sat enjoying the airconditioning.

'I'm not a big dancer, Buddy.'

'Oh, don't be such a party pooper!' He

turned around in his seat, clearly disappointed.

Theo caught her eye in the rearview mirror and smiled. 'Tonight just might change all that, Luce,' he said.

Dinner was ready when they arrived, and Martin and Vivian waited for them in the cavernous dining room, sipping cocktails and looking cool and rested. Lucy was starving. It was all she could do not to attack the meal of grilled halibut and vegetables, cold corn relish, and salad. She wanted to shove it in with her bare hands until she was so stuffed she couldn't move. Instead, she forced herself to eat a sensible portion slowly, with utensils and everything, and enjoyed the company.

After dinner, Lucy had just enough time to get a shower and change before they had to leave again. She'd only brought one nice outfit — a new sundress in a size L — no 'Xs' anywhere on the tag. It was a simple sheath in muted oranges and pinks, with a zipper in the back and a scoop neck. It hit just above her knees. She put on a pair of fisherman sandals and dabbed on some lip gloss and gave herself a spritz of Paradise Awaits. She kept her hair loose around her shoulders so it could dry naturally.

Lucy was writing in her food journal when

Buddy began calling her name from down the long hallway.

'Lucy! Let's go! I can't be late!'

She met Buddy in the foyer, immediately noticing how dapper he looked in his white cotton button-down and chinos, his short hair glistening with gel, his face scrubbed clean. When Lucy asked Buddy why he wasn't wearing his gold medals, he looked at her like she was from Mars.

'It's uncool to wear your medals to the dance,' he said. 'It looks like you're bragging.'

Theo strolled into the foyer, jangling his car keys and patting his pants pocket for his wallet, and Lucy's heart just about fell to the white marble floor. He was wearing a pale blue loose-fitting rayon shirt with an open neck, white linen slacks, and sandals. He looked squeaky clean. He glowed from the sun. He smelled like heaven. A little patch of golden-brown hair appeared just below the hollow of his throat.

She had the strangest urge to lick him there.

Theo stopped, turned, and gave Lucy an odd little frown — almost as if he'd just heard her thoughts out loud. That would be a problem, since throat licking wasn't something friends did to each other as a rule; at least it wasn't something she'd done with any friend she'd ever had.

'Can we just *go* now?' Buddy stood by the front door with his hands on his hips. 'You are staring at each other like you do on TV and I just really feel like dancing.'

The closing ceremony was short and sweet, and as a few special awards were handed out Lucy's body stung with awareness. Theo sat next to her in the stands, the long solid length of his thigh pressed up against her from hip to knee. All Lucy could think about was the kiss they'd shared on another track in another town, the one that they'd agreed was a mistake, and how she could go about getting another one.

Lucy turned slightly and looked at Theo. He was staring at her with that odd little frown again. But he didn't look her in the eye. He scanned her face, stopping with particular concern on her lips. Then his nostrils flared.

Lucy needed to say something funny and say it now or she was going to throw her arms around Theo Redmond's neck and kiss her trainer in front of thousands of mentally retarded Floridians.

She was saved from this humiliation when the emcee announced that the Games had come to their official close and added, 'Would anyone care to dance?'

It was mayhem. Athletes stampeded out of the stands and swarmed the infield, jumping and running and shouting as the DJ began his program.

Lucy and Theo hung back in the stands for a while to get a good view of the action.

Many of the girls and women wore nice dresses, all along the spectrum from church clothes to chiffon prom dresses complete with matching corsages. The boys and men sported everything from the usual shorts and tees to slippery oversize suits and spats.

The crowd went into a frenzy when the disc jockey played 'The Chicken Dance,' followed by 'Wooly Bully,' then the Village People's 'YMCA,' and 'The Macarena.'

'That DJ has got to start pacing himself,' Lucy said to Theo. 'He's already played all the greatest songs known to man and it's not even eight thirty.'

'Dance with me, Luce.' Theo grabbed her hand and pulled her to her feet.

'But — ' Lucy stumbled forward, tugging on the hem of her sundress.

'No buts tonight.' Theo led her down the steps and across the track, greeting at least a dozen people he knew on the way, never stopping, finally pulling her onto the grass and into his arms.

'I'm not the world's best dancer, Theo.'

'And that's going to be a problem here?' He gestured broadly at the crowd around them and smiled down at Lucy.

She had to admit he had a point. There was some rather unconventional movement taking place on the grassy dance floor, and much of it didn't require a partner or even a beat. One woman was happily doing the 1960s-era Swim. There was a long and disjointed conga line snaking through the crowd, gleefully knocking apart small groups as it went. There was a Rockette-like kick line of women with decidedly un-Rockette-like physiques. And some waltzing. Plus a lot of jumping around and hollering.

Lucy didn't think she'd ever been around so many people who couldn't care less what others thought of them.

'Thanks for asking me here this weekend.'

Theo's face softened, and in the bright stadium lights his eyes twinkled down on her. 'Thanks for coming.'

The DJ chose that particular moment to play Elvis's 'Can't Help Falling in Love,' which made Lucy groan and turn her face away from Theo's.

'Does Elvis make you uncomfortable?'

'Just some of his lyrics.'

Theo's hand pressed into the small of Lucy's back and brought her even closer. She felt herself mold into him, rest her cheek on his hard but comfortable chest. Why did everything about Theo have to be just right? Why couldn't his chest feel too bony under her cheek, or too fleshy? Why couldn't she be disgusted by the scent of his skin? Why couldn't she be annoyed by the sound of his voice?

One of Theo's hands moved to her hair and Lucy started. She tried to pull away, but he kept her there, and that's when she felt his lips press down on the top of her head.

'Viv and Martin like you, Luce.'

'I like them.'

'You look lovely tonight.'

'God. Just stop, Theo.'

She pushed away enough to break his embrace, only to find her face right below his. He inclined his head enough to bring his lips too close to hers.

Her pulse kicked up to heart-attack speed. 'I think we need to stay away from running tracks. We make mistakes on running tracks.'

'Damn, Lucy.' Theo's breath was warm and sweet on her mouth, and all it would have taken was the slightest forward movement on her part and they would be kissing again. It's what she wanted. It's what she feared.

'Can I dance with you?'

They pulled apart to look down at the

source of the request. It was a man no more than five feet tall, at least sixty years old, wearing four bronze medals around his chubby neck and a very wide grin on his elfin face. He stared at Lucy with open adoration. He drooled just a little.

'Of course,' Lucy said, feeling Theo's hands fall away from her body. It was probably for the best. Of course it was. So she welcomed her new dance partner and put one hand on his shoulder as he put a hand on her waist and gazed up at her.

'You are so beautiful,' he said. 'I'm Fred. Are you married?'

★   ★   ★

They arrived back at the house about ten thirty. Viv and Martin were already asleep and Buddy went right to bed. It had been a very long day for him.

Lucy said good night to Theo and was about to venture down the long hallway toward her guest suite when he called her.

'Wanna go for a swim?'

Of course she did. Or did not. Of course she wanted to spend more time with Theo. No she didn't.

'I didn't bring a swimsuit. Sorry.' She gave him a nice smile. 'Good night.'

'You don't need one.'

Her brain seized momentarily. Then she said, 'Oh yes. Yes, I do. I need a suit so bad you wouldn't freakin' believe it.' Theo's laughter caused the heat of embarrassment to spread over her face. 'Good night, Theo.'

'We can turn off the pool lights, Luce. And with the twenty-foot privacy fence, only NSA spy satellites could see us.'

He was serious! Theo wanted to go skinny-dipping!

'No thank you.'

'OK, fine. I give up. There's a whole closet of swimsuits in the cabana. Let's find one for you.'

She laughed, admiring his strategy, then found herself following Theo through the foyer and the main hallway, through the family room, and out the double doors leading to the huge screened-in lanai around the pool. She walked with him past the pool's two elaborate fountains, trickling and bubbling in the background, along the side of the house to the cabana, where he flicked on the lights.

Inside was a large sitting room furnished in tasteful wicker and white wrought iron, and off to the side were two small changing areas. Theo opened a louvered closet near the entrance to the ladies' room.

'Here you go.' The door swung open to reveal a bathing suit selection that rivaled that of the average Kmart. 'What size do you wear?'

It was such a simple question. But her lips went numb.

Theo looked over his shoulder. 'Do you want a one-piece or a two-piece?'

Lucy laughed out loud. She hadn't worn a two-piece swimsuit since fourth grade. It had been a burnt orange color and she remembered it had an annoying habit of giving her a wedgie when she went off the high dive.

'One-piece,' she mumbled.

Theo pulled out a tankini on a hanger, the price tag still attached, and peered at the size on the side seam. 'It says twelve. Will that be too big?'

Too big?

Lucy snatched it out of his hand and disappeared into the changing room.

'So I'll meet you in the pool?' Theo asked. 'Do you want a drink?'

'I want a margarita!' she shouted. 'A big-ass frozen margarita with salt on the rim, and a plate of chicken nachos dripping with guacamole and sour cream!'

There were a few seconds of silence before Theo said, 'One light beer coming right up.'

Lucy saw her reflection in the mirror and

her eyes bugged out. Yes, the tankini fit. It fit nicely, in fact.

'A light beer would be perfect,' she answered. 'And I was just kidding about the nachos. I swear.'

★ ★ ★

Theo changed into his trunks, then padded over to the fully stocked kitchen across the lanai. This was a nice way to live, he had to admit, but he wondered what Viv and Martin's friends had sacrificed for this kind of wealth. Theo knew nothing about them, other than they were generous and had money and taste, but he figured people who had to work hard enough to be this rich had missed out on a few of life's simple joys. Like relaxation. Like spending time with their families. He wondered how often they even used their own pool.

Theo popped the tops of the beers and brought them to the pool's edge, then dived in. The water felt soothing, cascading over his hot skin, rippling coolness over the length of his body as he swam. He decided to do a few laps while Lucy got changed, hoping maybe he could clear his head a bit.

He had a problem. His problem was Lucy and his out-of-control desire for her. He was aware that holding her in his arms and nearly kissing her were the absolute wrong things to be doing, yet when she stood there in front of him tonight on the infield, her eyes so wide and pretty and all of her smelling so good, he succumbed to his lesser self. The only thing that mattered was getting her as close as he could.

They had more than six months left together. Lucy was the walking wounded, and she still wouldn't tell him why. What he needed to do was keep things simple with her. He had no right to tease her or lead her on. He had no right to act on his attraction to her when he had no intention of starting a relationship. There was a real possibility that he could hurt her. And he would rather die than hurt her.

Theo did a flip turn at the wall and out of one watery eye he saw her standing above him. He stopped, burst up from the shallow end, and pushed the water off his face.

He hadn't seen Lucy in a swimsuit since last November, and the sight was giving him the kind of perspective he couldn't get from numbers alone. A transformed woman stood in front of him. She was breathtaking.

She held her head high. Her elegant arms and hands hung to her sides, and he could see the very feminine curve of her hips, the indentation of her waist, the swell of her breasts. He saw a little bit of her belly peeking through the tankini, and it was round and full and female.

Seeing her like this almost made him wish they didn't have to keep pushing for her to lose more weight. She looked perfect to him just as she was.

She daintily dipped a toe into the water and Theo knew that if he were thinking straight he'd be focusing on her quad definition and not how he wanted to nibble on the velvet-soft inside of her thigh.

'Jump in.'

She did and barely missed his head.

He wiped the water from his eyes and laughed. 'I said jump in, not *on*!'

'Sorry.'

She didn't look sorry. Lucy smoothed her hair back and smiled at him, then giggled. She was a wet minx. A slippery vixen. Theo had to touch her or he'd splinter into a thousand pieces of frustration, but was there any way to make that touch appear accidental? The only thing he could think of would be to dunk her and chase her around in the pool like they were kids, but who was he fooling? That would be so transparent.

Then suddenly he was underwater, Lucy's hands forcing his head deeper below the surface. He laughed in surprise, feeling the bubbles shoot out of his nose up through the water. In a burst of playful revenge, he grabbed her around the knees and flipped her over his shoulder, hearing her scream just before she splashed down behind him.

Lucy swam hard to get away, but he was quick. Theo pulled her by the ankles and yanked her back to him, and as she flailed in a vain attempt to escape, he realized this was fun. He hadn't had this much fun with a woman in a long time. And it was anything but innocent.

She twisted in his grasp and came up for air, her ankles still in his hands. He opened his arms wide, spreading her legs, then pulled. She smacked right up against him and she squeezed her legs around his waist before he could even suggest it.

Then Lucy's arms were around his neck and she brought that beautiful mouth of hers close and pushed open her lips with the pink tip of her tongue. Theo blinked the water from his lashes, knowing this was going to be the kind of kiss neither could pretend was accidental.

He knew this kiss was going to be anything *but* a mistake or the biggest freakin' mistake he'd ever make in his life.

Theo moved his hands through the water

until they cupped Lucy's butt. She gasped. He squeezed, feeling muscle and flesh and woman, and Lucy let out the most appealing little whimper he'd ever heard. Right then, Theo's nose caught a hint of Paradise Awaits mixed with chlorine and that was all she wore. He didn't care about what happened after that kiss — he only cared about the kiss itself, that kiss and those legs around him and that luscious, full ass cupped in his hands.

Theo slammed his mouth on hers just as Lucy desperately sought him out, and they hit so hard it hurt. But they didn't stop. They soothed the momentary pain with each other's lips and tongues and Theo realized he was starving for this. He was starving for a woman — a woman he could connect with, a woman he could play with.

He was starving for a woman like Lucy.

Her hands were in his hair and she was grabbing him, pulling him even closer, squeezing him so tight between her thighs he feared for his ribs.

The sound of a slamming patio door was followed by the sudden glare of an overhead bank of lights. The two thrashed around in the water to separate, gasping for breath.

'What the hell . . . ?' Uncle Martin stood on the lanai in a pair of white boxer shorts so loose they made his legs look like toothpicks stuck in marshmallows.

He shook his head. 'Sorry, kids. I told Viv it was a 'making whoopee' scream, not a 'help-I've-fallen-and-I-can't-get-up' scream, but would she listen?'

Martin sighed, flipped off the light, and went back inside without further comment.

Theo got thoroughly splashed as Lucy swam toward the pool steps, kicking furiously. He admired her freestyle stroke and her speed, and then he just plain admired her when she climbed out and ran like a gazelle toward the guest wing. The girl could certainly make time on land or water when she was running away from him.

'Lucy, stop.'

She turned, clutching her arms over her chest, the water streaming off her body as she panted for breath.

'I want you bad, Luce.'

'No.' She shook her head.

'This is nuts. I'm not going to fight it anymore.' Theo began to exit the pool, knowing that just how much he wanted her would be evident when his hips cleared the waterline.

Lucy's eyes locked onto the front of his swim trunks. 'Oh, jeez,' she breathed. 'This is *so* not going to work.'

Theo looked down at himself. 'I have to disagree.'

'If we do this, it'll change everything, Theo! You still want to be just friends?'

'Hell, no.'

'Because I sure don't want to wake up with you in the morning and be told that we all make mista — '

Theo grabbed her, kissed her, and began to back her up toward the house. When they arrived at the sliding door to the guest suite, he deftly reached around, unlatched the handle, and shoved the door wide, all while managing to push down a swimsuit strap and nudge her inside.

'You're really good at this,' she said against his mouth.

'I'm severely out of practice.'

'You? I don't even remember what happens next.'

They both laughed while they kissed, Theo slamming the door shut behind him with a blind kick of his leg. 'You're in good hands, Lucy Cunningham.'

★　★　★

Lucy spent five minutes wandering around the room adjusting the lighting. She was still in her swimsuit. The idea of being naked in a man's presence after all this time had launched her into a panic.

'You're running away again.'

'No, really, I'm not.' She opted for one 60-watt bulb in the reading lamp in the corner of the huge bedroom, her orange sundress draped across to temper the glare. She stood back to admire the effect.

'I'm dying over here, Luce.'

Lucy turned to see Theo lounging naked on the kingsize platform bed, and it was obvious nothing on the man was dying or even wilting. He was breathtaking — long, lean, muscular physical perfection — with a soft fuzz of light brown hair all over his big chest. The trail of hair grew narrow as it grew darker, pointing like an arrow directly at . . .

Lucy bit her bottom lip to stop from moaning. She raised her eyes to his handsome face, not knowing if fear prevented her from closely scrutinizing what jutted from between his legs or if she was simply saving the best for last, like when she used to eat all the cup cake before any of the icing.

'Lucy, come over here.'

She sat on the edge of the bed.

Theo took both her hands in his. 'You're shaking. Why?'

'It's the icing on the cup cake.'

One of his eyebrows arched high. 'Yes, it

certainly is. But your suit is wet. Take it off.'

So easy for him to say. There he was, sprawled out confidently on top of the comforter, every inch of him on display. She supposed hanging around in locker rooms made men blasé about nudity. Having no discernible body flaws probably helped, too.

'This is hard for me, Theo.'

'It's been hard for you nearly all night, in case you haven't noticed.' Theo's smile was kind, but his eyes were hot. He brushed the side of her face with his fingertips, cupped her chin softly. 'Go on. Look at me. See how much I want you.'

She hesitated.

'Fine. Then *feel* how much I want you.'

Lucy closed her eyes tight and let him take her left hand and bring it toward his body. Her fingertips encountered something velvety smooth and warm. He then guided her hand around his girth, and he was big and rigid and behind her dark eyelids she was being treated to a Fourth of July fireworks show.

'Oh God. Theo.'

'This is how much I want you.'

Lucy moaned.

Theo left her hands where they were and reached out to slide down both straps of the tankini. Lucy kept her eyes shut when she felt her breasts being exposed to the air, ecstasy and anxiety fighting it out for top billing. Then he stroked her bare flesh and said, 'You are so beautiful, Lucy,' and ecstasy won.

Her eyes remained closed and her hands began to move along the length of him as his palms soothed, his fingers pinched. Then she felt his mouth, wet and warm lips that landed on her left nipple, where she was laved, nibbled, licked, and sucked until she was squirming and moaning and felt overwhelmed with the shocking amount of pleasure she felt.

'Oh, Theo — '

He removed his lips from her breast and kissed her, pulling her down on top of him.

Lucy's eyes flew open.

'This is all that matters, Lucy — you and me. And the only thing that's going to keep this from happening is if you don't want it.'

She let out an abrupt laugh and pushed away from his embrace. 'All right. OK. I'll be right back.'

'Where are you going?' Theo looked worried.

She jumped from the big bed and ran over to the dresser, rooting through her bag for the little cotton nightie she knew she'd packed. She found it, raised it in her fist in triumph, and said, 'Who loves me now?'

Theo collapsed back onto the pillows and

laughed. When she returned a moment later, he was still there, an arm flopped over his eyes, his body still beautiful and his cock still erect.

'I'm ready, Theo.'

He opened his eyes and smiled at the vision before him. Lucy had towel-fluffed her hair and put on the little nightgown, something low cut and short and as thin as gauze. He could see everything through it — the round female form punctuated by the dark triangle of her sex and the dark, hard peaks of her nipples. Lucy's eyes were wide. Her smile was shy. Her hair was thick and tousled, and the combination of vulnerability and va-va-voom sexuality had Theo wondering how he would ever find a way to protect her and debauch her at the same time.

When she got on the bed and began to crawl toward him on all fours, Theo forgot all about the protecting and went right for the debauching. He rose to his knees. When she reached him, he pulled her up and kissed her, his hands clutching her upper arms, his mouth desperate with months of pent-up hunger.

Theo put his arms around her and clutched her close. He could feel every bit of Lucy, from her knees to her lips, every curve, every swell and dip and soft place. He felt her breasts crushed against his chest, nipples like little rocks, and he felt the heat radiating from between her legs.

His lips and tongue caressed her mouth, opened her, dived into her, and though he loved the feel of her pressed tight up against him, he couldn't stay like this long. He needed to move. Theo reached up under the back of the nightgown and pushed it up and over the round globes of her ass. He caressed her back, slid his hands around her waist, rubbed her tummy and hips and breasts all with the hem of the flimsy nightie resting on his forearms. He'd much rather have her buck naked, but if this little piece of cloth made Lucy feel comfortable enough to be here with him, like this, then he'd live with it.

'Touch me, Theo,' she whispered. 'Oh God, please touch me.'

He put his fingers between her full, silky thighs and stroked her, coaxing her to spread her legs. She shifted, opening for him, and his fingers were instantly covered in slick heat.

'God, Lucy. You're so wet. Are you always this wet?'

She laughed. 'I don't remember.'

He laughed with her, pulled her until they fell to the comforter, where they rolled and laughed more, and Theo knew he'd never felt this much joy in a woman's presence, this much connection and happiness. It hadn't felt this way with Jenna, or with anyone.

They fit. He and Lucy fit like they were made for each other. That's all there was to it.

As if she'd heard his silent verdict, Lucy wrapped her legs around his waist and her arms around his neck in clear invitation. Theo gazed down into her face and saw his own certainty — and his own lust — reflected back to him in her shining eyes.

'I'm not running away anymore,' she whispered.

Theo pushed inside her, slowly, inch by inch, and the joy spread and grew and rushed at him with a force he'd never known was possible. Theo had found joy and pleasure and certainty in the paradise of Lucy.

* * *

Stephan stared at the television, watching Theo Redmond's right hand flick against the metal, making a *tap, tap* sound. His heart flopped in his chest like a dying fish. 'Dammit,' he hissed.

Chin in hands, Stephan watched the trainer flick his fingers again, *tap-tap-tap*. The camera zoomed in close to Lucy Cunningham's fat face. Stephan hated that face.

204

That fuckin' goody-two-shoes triumph-of-the-human-spirit chubber-nugget was really starting to fuckin' annoy him.

Redmond kept going. The suspense was killing Stephan. *Tap, tap . . . slide . . . tap, tap, tap.*

'Oh for God's sake, stop with the drama already!' He slammed back more coffee and rooted around in his desk drawer for his ibuprofen and a Snickers bar.

Finally, thank God, the scale's balance found its equilibrium at 170 pounds and Lucy's face lit up like a harvest moon.

Stephan was fucked.

'This month's loss was a whopping seventeen pounds!' Redmond announced, smiling into the camera like he was a spokesmodel for a laxative. 'That's phenomenal!'

Then Stephan had to endure the sight of the trainer lifting Lucy into the air like he'd just come home from the war, twirling her around on the set, her hair flying out around them. The nitwits in the audience were eating this shit up. The camera panned the rows of jumping and clapping housewives and that's when Stephan froze.

A whole goddamn section of the studio audience was wearing matching T-shirts that read: WE LOVE LUCY!

Stephan let out a howl of agony. This was just too much!

All Lucy Cunningham had to do was *not* lose weight! How hard could that be? The woman had been as big as a house the whole time she'd worked here! For over a year he'd watched her pop Milk Duds from morning to night.

Wasn't it true that every damn diet and exercise ad on the planet had to include the caveat *results not typical*? All he wanted was fuckin' typical! But Lucy Cunningham was actually doing it! She was doing the impossible, and causing a public relations sensation in the process!

His phone rang.

'The girl. She's skinny.'

'I wouldn't exactly go that far.'

'Hasn't she been getting my deliveries?'

'You can lead a horse to water, but you can't make it — '

'Horse? How about *horse's ass*? Because that is what I am going to look like if you keep doing such a bang-up job of making the Palm Club look bad.'

'Murray — '

'You said you'd take care of it!'

'It's still salvageable.'

As Murray Goldstein cussed him out, Stephan glanced at the TV screen and watched with revulsion while Theo calculated the size of Lucy's body parts with a tape measure.

Goldstein's voice became hushed. 'You disrespect me,' he said.

How was Stephan supposed to know that Lucy Cunningham would turn out to be his own personal big, fat walking Friday the thirteenth? A cow of bad karma grazing on the field of his life?

'I was there for you when you needed me, Sherrod, and this is how you treat me? Shame on you. You will pay the price for this disrespect, you lowlife piece of — '

Stephan hung up on Murray. With shaking hands he began to unwrap the Snickers bar. He shoved it in his mouth, all the while crying like a baby.

'Ohmigod! Mr Sherrod! Are you all right?' Veronica King stood in his doorway, staring at him.

Stephan stopped chewing and shoved the candy in his desk drawer. He swallowed. 'Allergies,' he said.

Veronica didn't seem convinced. She scowled at him. 'You look like death warmed over, Mr Sherrod.'

Stephan wiped his mouth and smacked his hand on his desk. 'Since when do you get in this early? And what are you looking at, you nosy little bitch? Close my door!'

If he didn't find a way to stop Lucy Cunningham, he'd look like death, all right, the cold, hard, bloated, dead-weight-at-the-bottom-of-the-ocean kind of death.

The kind Murray Goldstein was rumored to prefer.

7

June

Journal Entry June 4

Breakfast: ¾ c Kashi; 1 c skim milk; 1 c blueberries; decaf

Lunch: 3 oz grilled tuna; 1 c steamed zucchini; 1 whole wheat roll; 1 tbsp light butter

Dinner: 3 oz roasted lean pork; ½ large baked sweet potato; 2 c salad and raw veggies; 2 tbsp oil and vinegar

Snack: 1 c light yogurt; 1 apple

Affirmation for Today:
If I ever go out in public wearing spandex shorts, life as we know it will continue, and the time-space continuum will remain intact. Unless they happen to be a neon color. Then the fabric of the universe could be ripped asunder. Perhaps I should stick with basic black.

★　★　★

'Anybody home?'

Stephan entered Lucy's office with Veronica in tow, and the manic look on his face had Lucy instantly on alert. Veronica rolled her eyes as she sat down in one of the chairs near Lucy's desk and propped the notebook on a knee. Stephan sat next to her.

'What's up?' Lucy asked.

'Well, I figured since the party was coming up, we needed to discuss our plan of attack.'

Lucy squinted. 'Attack?'

'Well, yes. I think we need to introduce some fresh elements into the Palm Club campaign, maybe change direction here and there, and the party is just the place to do it.'

Lucy studied her boss, noting that Stephan's eyes were red-rimmed and his cheeks feverish. She slid her eyes over to Veronica, who made a fish face.

Lucy cleared her throat, trying not to laugh. 'Actually, Stephan, the halfway celebration party *is* the fresh element.' She spoke with all the patience she could muster. 'The NBC affiliate is on board for an evening news feature, and the *Herald* is sending a Style reporter. Our guest list is top-shelf. And I'm not sure the Mandarian Oriental Hotel is the ideal setting for any kind of sudden change in

210

direction or *attack*, since there's a lot of expensive, breakable stuff sitting around in there.'

Stephan's eyebrows met in a deep vee of anger. His mouth went rigid. 'I don't appreciate your snide sarcasm, Lucy. Regardless of your faux-celebrity status, you are still my employee, and I expect you to remember it.'

Lucy knew she was straddling a fine line here. She'd been dealing with Stephan's preposterous bullshit for far too long, but she was six months away from walking out of here, money in hand. It would be six months in hell if she didn't stand her ground.

'I apologize for my sarcasm, but my concern is that you don't respect my ability to handle this campaign. It seems that you're either completely disinterested in what I'm doing or trying to sabotage my efforts, and I never know which it's going to be day-to-day.'

'Don't be ridiculous, Lucy.'

She laughed. She didn't feel ridiculous. She felt sure of herself, competent, and strong. She stood up behind her desk.

'Have you seen the latest numbers, Stephan?'

'What numbers?'

'The media report. The publicity summary.

The ratings for our *WakeUp Miami* appearances. The sales figures from Ramona Cortez. Web site hits. Have you looked at any of it?'

'Of course I have.'

Lucy nodded. 'Then you know that I have everything under control.'

Stephan looked up at her from his chair, a puzzled expression on his face. 'Web site? You mean the Palm Club Web site?'

Veronica made another fish face, then snapped her gum.

'Yes, and our TheoandLucy.net site. It went live two months ago.'

'I never gave permission for that! Maria kept hounding me and I told her *no*!' Stephan shot up from the chair. 'Don't I have control of this agency anymore? Whose name is on the fucking door outside this place, tell me that? Does it say 'Sherrod & Cunningham'?' He sounded out of breath. 'Does it?'

Lucy could barely contain her disbelief. She watched Veronica slink out of her seat and move toward the door, her eyes wide. 'Actually, Stephan,' Lucy said calmly, 'the name Thoms is on that door, and Sarah would be ashamed at what you're doing to her company.'

Stephan snorted. 'No, she'd be ashamed of you, Lucy, prancing around this town like you were *the shit*, when you're nothing but an

212

overweight hick chick with a painfully obvious crush on her pretty-boy trainer. Do you know how ridiculous you look on TV with him? Do you have any idea what a joke you're making of yourself? People all over town are talking about you, how you'll never make it, how the Redmond gigolo is playing you like a harp, how he's using you for the money.'

Lucy went numb from her scalp to her big toes. She had to ignore Stephan. She could not allow him to get under her skin like this. Not now. Not when she was doing so well. Not when Theo had shown her it was more than just a lopsided crush — that it was real and true and the best thing that ever happened to her.

Not after she'd had sex with him. Five times!

He would never do that to her.

Stephan started for the door, then turned. 'I'm going to be out of town for a couple weeks. Do me a favor and try to show up at the party wearing something decent.'

His eyes traveled up and down Lucy's body and she felt like she was going to be sick. 'I hear you can get formal wear at Wal-Mart nowadays. You can get anything at Wal-Mart.'

Stephan left. Veronica fell back against the door-jamb with her mouth hanging open.

Lucy stood behind her desk breathing like she'd just run a few miles.

The two women stayed like that for a long, silent moment. Then Veronica returned to her seat and flopped down in it. Lucy fell into her own chair.

'OK,' Lucy said. 'He's officially fucking nuts.'

'You have no idea,' Veronica whispered. 'Wait till I tell you about — '

There was a knock on Lucy's open door. Maria and Barry stood in the hallway looking worried.

'Come on in and shut the door.' Lucy gestured for them to hurry in. Maria sat next to Veronica, and Barry leaned against the window frame, arms crossed over his chest.

'Strange things are afoot at the Circle K,' Barry said. 'I think he's completely lost it.'

Maria looked near tears. 'He's really starting to scare me. He just screamed at me about the Web site when I've been sending him memos about it for months! I don't think he's even remotely connected to reality these days.'

'He called me a bitch a couple weeks ago,' Veronica said, snapping her gum. 'I swear to God I heard him crying in his office, so I look in and he says, 'Go away, you nosy bitch,' or something. I couldn't believe it!'

Barry straighted and moved to Lucy's desk. 'I've been wooing the Lucky Chef gourmet grocery chain for eight months now, right? Well, I went in there to tell him they're interested in my meals-to-go idea and he said he didn't have time to discuss it.'

'Maybe Stephan's doing drugs,' Maria said. 'That would explain a few things.'

The thought had crossed Lucy's mind.

'I've never seen him like this, not even when Sarah died,' Veronica said.

Maria gripped the armrests so hard her knuckles went white. 'Oh my God! I just had the worst thought! You don't think Stephan *killed* her, do you?'

Everyone went still.

'She died from a reaction to anesthesia,' Lucy said quietly.

Barry patted Maria's shoulder. 'So unless Stephan was in the operating room during the tummy tuck, I sincerely doubt he had anything to do with Sarah's death.'

'Fine. But he's crazy. That's all I'm saying — making one totally loco decision after the next.'

'Especially since Lucy landed the Palm Club account,' Barry said.

Lucy fiddled with the cuff of her jacket, listening, thinking about the ill-timed Eddie application, the erratic behavior, the bizarre phone conversation about threats and the IRS, the crying, the lack of focus . . . If he were a woman, she'd be thinking menopause.

Barry smiled at her. 'Hey, Lucy. I only ask one thing — when you get rich and go out on your own, please don't forget to take us with you!'

That was her plan exactly.

★　★　★

'No, no, no, no, no! That looks like a grandma dress on you and I won't let you to go out in public lookin' like nobody's grandma! Especially not on your special night!'

Lucy was getting a headache. It had turned out that shopping for formal wear with Gia was hard work and involved a huge investment of human resources. There were no fewer than four saleswomen fawning over them at that very moment.

'Go back and try the light blue one on again.'

Lucy sighed in resignation and was about to return to the dressing room when a saleswoman arrived with another dress draped over her arm. It was a champagne color, with a sheer plunge neckline and cap sleeves constructed of a dainty nylon mesh. It

216

looked like it weighed about an ounce and would reveal every bump and roll on the surface of Lucy's body.

'I don't have a good feeling about that one.'

The saleswomen looked despondent. 'Would you at least try? I've seen it on other customers and it drapes nicely. It could be quite flattering on you.'

'Let me see that.' Gia held out her hand and examined the dress. 'Yeah, OK, I thought so. This is an Olorio. I wore this for his Paris spring show. It felt good on.' Gia smiled at the saleswoman, then looked at Lucy. 'So you'll try it for me, or what?'

'There's just one thing.' The saleswoman tilted her head and smiled at Lucy. 'It's a little over your budget.'

Lucy held up the dress and looked at the tag. Yes, it cost more than the GNP of some countries and was also a size 10, two good reasons it wouldn't be leaving here with *her*.

Gia waved her hand and made a little dismissive huff. 'Don't worry about the money. I'll call Isaac and tell him I need it. He'll work it out with the shopkeeper.'

Lucy held the dress and stared. Since she began this makeover gig seven months ago, she had found herself in a situation every now and then that seemed just downright dreamlike, as if it were happening to someone

217

else. This was one of them.

She was being catered to by a staff of saleswomen in a posh South Beach boutique, a *Vogue* cover girl acting as her personal fashion assistant, shopping for formal wear in a size 10 that she would wear to a black-tie dinner thrown in her honor.

'You forget how to move or something, girlie?'

Lucy shook her head and entered the dressing room. A few minutes later, she emerged from behind the ornate partition to find Gia sprawled on the sofa laughing into her cell phone. Gia looked up, continued talking for a second, then looked up again, her mouth wide.

'Holy moley, *chica!*' she shrieked, then went back to the phone. 'Danny, baby, I gotta go. Your sister needs me.' She snapped the phone shut and a torrent of Spanish words came tumbling out of her mouth, only a few of which Lucy understood. Gia stood up and nodded.

'You look like a million-freakin'-dollars.'

'With the proper foundation garments, this dress will flow perfectly.' The saleswoman swiped a hand down the side of Lucy's hip.

'A girdle?'

She laughed at Lucy. 'No, dear. Just a strapless body smoother. Many ladies wear them for form-fitting dresses like this, and you'll need it anyway so there is no bra visible.'

Gia crossed her arms over her chest and nodded. 'You look hot. No questions about it.'

Lucy almost couldn't look at herself. She began at her bare feet, moved up her legs to two inches above her knees, where the hemline hit, then up her thighs to the way she filled in the dress at the hips.

'Isaac? It's Gia. Are you in Cannes?'

While Lucy turned to look at her bottom in the mirror she half-listened to Gia on her cell phone. Theo seemed to appreciate that bottom. It was a good bottom. And it was now a size 10 bottom.

'I think we have a couple different body smoother styles in nude. I'll see what we can do.' The saleswoman was gone, and Lucy stood by herself, alone with her reflection, as Gia talked in the background.

Lucy couldn't wait for Theo to see her.

Gia came up and stood behind her. 'I think you are the most beautiful friend I have,' she said, leaning down and kissing Lucy's cheek. 'You look better in this dress than I did. I think I'm jealous.'

Lucy smiled.

'Isaac says just take it. It's his gift to you.

Now let's go see how else we can spend that money of yours.'

Lucy was stunned. 'The man who designed this dress is giving it to me for free?'

'That's what I said.'

'Wow.' Lucy swallowed hard. 'So what else do I need?'

'Shoes, my little mango. Shoes and stockings and a bag and some sparkly things.'

'I'm exhausted already.'

'Vamanos, girlie. We're going to do the loaves and fishes thing with your money. Just you watch.'

They stopped for a late lunch at a sidewalk café, Lucy steadying the array of shopping bags at her feet, still amazed that the day she'd just spent had been a day in her own life, the life of Lucy Cunningham.

At Gia's urging, she called Frannie to tell her about the dress. She screeched into the phone in approval, then chatted briefly with Gia.

Halfway through lunch, Gia frowned at Lucy and tapped her hand. 'You OK? All day you've been going back and forth between looking like you just won the Powerball and like you're gonna cry. What's going on with you? Is it hormones or what?'

Lucy shook her head slightly, knowing this was the kind of thing she usually saved for Dr

Lehman. It had been a while since she'd had a friend she could truly confide in.

'Then it's gotta be Theo-dorable. What he do to you now?'

Lucy laughed. What *had* he done to her? He'd made her delirious with pleasure and drunk with happiness. He'd given her a refresher course in her own sexuality. He'd shown her that he cared for her, adored her, wanted her.

'Oh no, girlie! Did you go to bed with him?'

Lucy's head snapped up. 'Why did you say 'oh no' like that? Like it was something he does all the time with his clients? Like I'm just another pitiful girl who's fallen under his spell?'

Gia's eyes went wide and she looked around the outdoor restaurant, as if she was unsure who Lucy was talking to. 'Where did that come from?'

'I don't know.' Lucy took a big gulp of her unsweetened iced tea, hoping it would extinguish the uncomfortable heat she felt rising in her.

'Spill it, Lucy.'

'I did sleep with him. In Tampa. Then four times since we've been back.'

'Dios mio!' Gia put a hand to the surface of her diminutive tank top. 'Was it good? Wait

— I don't want to know if it wasn't, 'cause it'll ruin my whole image of Theo, OK?'

Lucy smiled. 'It's been everything, Gia. It's tender and wild and good and everything I've ever dreamed of.'

'OK.' Gia scrunched up her mouth. 'So if it's so good, how come you're sitting over there looking so sad?'

Lucy shrugged. 'It's just that I'm not sure it's as important to him as it is me. He says it is, but I'm feeling a little . . . I don't know . . . *cynical*.'

'How come?'

Lucy looked up at her friend. 'Something my mentally unstable boss said the other day that really freaked me out.'

'What he say? You tell me and then we'll go over to your office and whack him one.'

She sighed. 'He's out of town, unfortunately.'

'What did the little prick say?'

Lucy liked that insult and tried it out to herself silently. *The little preek.* She'd have to remember to use it in the future. 'Well, he said it was obvious that I had a crush on Theo. That I looked pitiful because everyone could see that Theo was playing me for the money.'

Gia's mouth fell open. 'You didn't let him get away with that, did you?'

'I need to keep my job for five more months. Then I'm gone.'

Gia crossed and recrossed her legs, shaking her head. 'Look, Lucy. I don't know this man, but he sounds like he hates your guts or something. He's the one playing you, not Theo.'

Lucy nodded. Of course Gia was right. 'And there's one other little thing.'

'Shoot.'

'The last time I tried this whole sleeping-with-a-man thing, it didn't end so well.'

'I hear you, girlie.' Gia took a sip of her iced tea and nodded.

'Which was ten years ago.'

Gia slapped a hand to her mouth in a vain attempt to prevent the iced tea from exploding from her lips. She used a napkin to blot it from her chest, her tank top, the tablecloth. When a waiter arrived to fuss over her, she shooed him away. 'I'm sorry, but for a second I thought for sure you said *ten years*.'

Lucy sighed. 'That's what I said.'

'Oh my God!' Gia grabbed her hand. 'No wonder you look so stunned! You were practically a virgin! Are you all right?'

'I'm sure as hell better now,' Lucy said.

They both broke out into peals of laughter.

He watched her walk down the path from the parking lot, gym bag swinging in her hand, and felt that little jolt in his heart he got every time he saw Lucy after a weekend apart.

'Here's Lucy!' Buddy shouted. 'Here she comes!'

'Hi, boys!' Lucy tossed her bag down on the grass and went over to give Buddy a big hug. Then she kissed Theo on the cheek and grinned. 'Morning, coach.'

'Morning, Cunningham.'

This was a first. Lucy was wearing spandex bike shorts to her workout today. Maybe she'd finally gotten it through her head that yoga pants were a bit hot for summer in Miami, even at 5:00 a.m. Maybe she'd finally gotten it through her head that she looked great in spandex shorts.

'I like it,' Theo said, letting his eyes travel down Lucy's shapely legs. She didn't fidget with the shorts. She stood tall and straight, and on her face was a smile of great satisfaction.

'Thanks,' she said simply.

'You're quite welcome.'

Then she turned away and began stretching with Buddy.

Theo stared at her, half-listening to the

sound of their chatter and noticing once again how well Buddy and Lucy got along. Since the Summer Games, the three of them had trained together a couple times a week. Lucy seemed inspired by Buddy's company and was kicking some serious ass around the track lately.

'Hey, Lucy? How do you know if a girl likes you?' Buddy asked this as all three continued to stretch.

Theo watched Lucy smile and think about that question for a moment, grabbing her foot and bending to loosen her hamstring. 'Well, it depends on the girl, but I'd say if she finds ways to be near you, and smiles a lot, and asks you for your opinion about stuff, then she likes you.'

Buddy nodded. 'What if she grabs your face and kisses you on the lips?'

Lucy sputtered, then said, 'Uhh . . . ,' and shot a glance toward Theo for help. He couldn't give any, because this was all news to him.

'Somebody been kissing you, stud? How come you didn't mention that to your old brother?'

Buddy shrugged and did toe curls to stretch his calves. 'Never came up, I guess, and I was really asking Lucy.'

'Well, pardon me.' Theo jogged in place a

moment until everyone was ready to start off. They began at a slow, steady pace.

'Besides,' Buddy said, clearly amused at what he was about to say, because he was already snickering. 'You're the last person I'd ask for advice about girls.'

Theo laughed. Lucy laughed harder.

During the first two miles, Theo hung back and listened as Lucy and his brother talked about Buddy's upcoming senior year of high school. If Theo wasn't mistaken, Buddy went into greater detail when he talked to Lucy, especially about anything having to do with his social life. It was in the first two miles that Theo learned the name of the face grabber — Nancy — and that she was a recent transfer into the Miami Springs special education program.

'She doesn't have Down's syndrome. She's just slow,' Buddy said. 'But she's nice and she likes me and I love her smile.'

Theo watched Lucy ruffle Buddy's short hair. 'She sounds great, Bud,' Lucy told him.

The exchange reminded Theo of the way his mom used to deal with Buddy — with love but respect for his independence. She'd always worked hard to find the right balance of freedom and supervision he needed at every stage of his life. Theo could only hope that his mom would approve of how he'd taken care of Buddy in the last three years and wished like hell she was there to advise him through what was coming.

The obvious big questions were just around the corner for them: Could Buddy deal with Theo going back to med school? Would Buddy want his own place someday soon, and could he handle the responsibility? What kind of work would he enjoy that was within his ability? And what if — as this turn of events with Nancy made Theo wonder — Buddy decided he'd fallen in love? How much of it was even Theo's business?

'Yeah, and she's a good kisser, too,' Buddy said. 'I'll catch you two later.' He kicked up the pace just as Lucy neared the end of her jog.

Lucy tried to suppress her smile, but Theo figured that was like the clouds trying to keep the sun from rising. Why bother? Lucy's face was designed for that smile. It was who she was. And as she looked over at him to gauge his reaction to what Buddy had said, Theo had the strangest thought.

He realized that the woman at his side — the one with the sweaty red face and the sweet smile — had pried open his heart, one day at a time.

Lucy's smile grew, and it spread to her beautiful deep gray eyes and her adorable cheeks and Theo realized that maybe Jenna had been right with that comment about love. Maybe it just happens when it happens. Maybe the real thing shows up and doesn't give a damn what your calendar looks like for the next decade.

'Somebody is figuring out life,' Lucy said, catching her breath.

'Yeah. No kidding.'

Theo put them all through a round of calisthenics and stretching in the infield afterward, including push-ups — even Lucy had to do the boy kind — crunches, leg lifts, and some power yoga moves.

'We're renting tuxedos for your party,' Buddy said. 'Theo's taking me. He said he was allowed to take a date, but he'd rather take me.'

'Oh really?' She grinned at Theo, then moved to a spread-eagle position on the grass, reaching out toward her right toe. Theo watched her easily rest her forehead on her kneecap. He swallowed hard. Yes, he'd known from the start that she was flexible, but his interest was way beyond clinical at this point.

'Didn't want to bring a date, coach?'

She then stretched toward the center, and Theo watched her touch her nose to the grass. An overtly sexual image flashed through his brain, and it involved Lucy's limbs arranged in a similar fashion in her bed four nights ago, and he forgot the question.

'Huh?'

'I said . . . '

Lucy then turned to face the other leg, and Theo had to close his eyes.

' . . . how come you're not bringing a date?'

'I'm not allowed to date my clients, remember? Who are you taking?'

Lucy slowly raised her face from her left shin and smiled at him. 'I'm not allowed to date my trainer, so I asked Tyson, who turned me down in the nicest — but *strangest* — way imaginable. Any insight into that, Theo?'

'Nope.' *Ha!* He'd told Tyson that if he showed up with Lucy on his arm it would be the last night he'd be able to move that arm.

'So Gia's coming with me instead. She's helped me pick out my dress.'

'I bet you're going to look real pretty,' Buddy said. 'I think you're real pretty all the time.'

Lucy hopped up and stretched her arms up into the air, then pulled from side to side. 'Thanks, Bud.' She grabbed for her gym bag and put the strap over her shoulder, then briefly turned to look at Theo. 'Thanks for the workout. See you tomorrow at the gym, right?'

Theo had to think for a moment, because

he was mesmerized by this sure, strong, beautiful woman who stood in front of him. She was carrying herself differently these days, with a dramatically different kind of confidence. And she was behaving so casual about it all. It felt like she was distancing herself from him a little, forcing herself to be nonchalant and flirty with him.

It almost felt like she'd grown cynical, of all things.

Fine. He'd admit it — he didn't want *casual* from Lucy. He didn't want *flirty* or fucking *cynical*! He wanted it real and deep and true. He wanted the love thing. He wanted all of it.

He swallowed hard.

'The gym? Tomorrow? Theo?'

'Right.'

She kissed his cheek again, and in a breeze of Paradise Awaits, she was gone.

Buddy moved to Theo's side and put a hand on his shoulder. 'See why I don't ask you stuff about girls?'

★ ★ ★

Theo arranged to drive Lucy to the studio for their *WakeUp Miami* appearance, explaining that he wanted to take her to breakfast afterward to celebrate. And there was plenty to celebrate, as Lucy had lost another eight pounds and four inches that month. After the show, Lucy was mobbed by autograph seekers outside the station, and Theo found himself working crowd control with fans he could only describe as rabid.

At least fifty people wearing or holding WE LOVE LUCY T-shirts waited on the sidewalks. Most brought their own laundry markers and pressed them into Lucy's hand and asked her to sign. She signed her name over people's chests or their bellies or the shirt backs. One man, who introduced himself as a bakery truck driver from Homestead, wanted Lucy to sign his pants. She politely declined.

Theo couldn't help but laugh at the spectacle. Lucy was a star.

He drove her up to Miami Springs and watched the curious look on her face as he turned down into the residential area. When he pulled into his driveway, she frowned at him.

'Norton has been on my case. He wants you to autograph his fur.' Theo was relieved to hear her laugh, because she still seemed distant to him. They'd kept up their usual five-day routine and met for at least one lunch or dinner a week, but he'd spent most weekend nights at Flawless and was up to his eyeballs in practice tests. Lucy had said she understood his time constraints, but since that day at the track with Buddy she'd never warmed all the way to Theo again. She'd never again relaxed into that sweet and open and sexy woman he first encountered in the guest suite in Tampa.

Maybe the lust had left him overly optimistic. Maybe Lucy couldn't handle a sexual relationship on top of everything else they were doing. Maybe he'd been an ass to even expect her to.

As they walked toward the front door, Theo watched her scan the outside of his home. It was a normal enough place, he supposed. A four-bedroom single-story stucco house in a brick color with white trim, a kind of home that screamed middle-class South Florida. They walked inside and he tried to see it through her eyes. He knew that most everything in the house had belonged to his parents, picked out by his mother, whose style was understated but nice.

Lucy looked around. 'You boys live lush.'

He smiled at that. 'It's my mom's doing. She was into design.'

'She knew what she was doing.'

Lucy's eyes wandered to the fuzzy orange blob now sitting on the tile floor in front of them. Theo heard her giggle.

'This must be Beelzebub boy.'

232

Theo waited for the hissing to begin. And waited some more. But Norton just sat there and blinked at Lucy, his whiskers twitching, as if he was making up his mind whether to reveal his true personality or keep pretending he was something less than bad-to-the-bone.

Lucy crouched down and held out her hand. 'Hello, pretty kitty.'

Theo figured that would do it. Norton hated anyone commenting on his appearance. But the damn cat just sat there — no hissing, no spitting, no skittering away like he was running from the fires of hell. Lucy moved to pet him and he rose, flipped his tail, and wandered off.

Lucy stood up. 'Affectionate little bugger.'

'That was a veritable wet sloppy kiss coming from him, let me assure you. Come on back to the kitchen.'

Theo made a pot of decaf, started the oatmeal, and set the table out on the back porch. It had yet to get blistering hot, and he had to admit he wanted Lucy to admire his handiwork in the backyard. He took her on a tour of the rhododendrons and the firebush and the beautyberry, holding her hand in his.

'Jeez, Theo. When do you find time to work in the yard?'

He shrugged. 'One thing I've learned since moving back with Buddy is that a person can do what needs to be done with the time he has. It's a universal law I never really appreciated before, not even in med school.'

Lucy nodded. 'Do you ever take time to have fun?'

'I had fun in Tampa. I have fun whenever I'm with you, and I'm having fun again right now.'

He watched her blush, and he swore he'd never seen anything more attractive in his life. There was something so tender about Lucy. She tried to show the world she was tough, with that humor and determination, but the inner core of her was tender and easily bruised, and he felt privileged that she'd let him see that part of her. It was the part that connected with his heart, yanked on it, whispered impossible things to it.

He must have been staring at her oddly, because she asked, 'You OK, Theo?'

'Fine. Just thinking about mulch.'

'Ah.' She nodded, as if that made perfect sense to her. 'Is Buddy home?'

'Sleeping in. He's got a swim meet tonight. Want to come with us?'

Lucy shrugged. 'Don't think I can, but thanks.'

Theo gave her a sideways glance, noting the pleasant but cool smile she offered him. He admired the pretty cotton dress Lucy had worn that morning, something a little on the funky side that showed off her figure. She'd developed a real sense of what looked good on her, and Theo wondered if it was something Gia had helped her with or something that came to her instinctively.

He leaned in to kiss her, and she offered him her cheek. If that wasn't an indication that something was amiss, he didn't know what was.

'What's up, Lucy?'

'Nothing. Just tired, I guess.'

'Let's have it, Cunningham. Why have you frosted over so much in the last couple weeks?'

'Frosted over?' Lucy put her hands on her hips. 'What are you talking about, Theo? You're the one who's too occupied to hang out with me.'

So *that* was it.

Theo watched Lucy stroll back to the porch and sit in a chair at the small breakfast table, where she stared out at the yard.

'Can I help with breakfast?' she asked absently.

'I got it.'

As Theo served the oatmeal, yogurt, and a freshly made citrus salad, he wondered how he could smooth things over with her. In the throes of lust, like in the pool in Tampa, everything seemed fairly simple: Go for it, and worry about the consequences later. Well this was later, and the disappointed woman sitting across the table was the consequence.

This was what he thought might happen.

'I bet you anything that when I'm not around you make sausage patties and Belgian waffles.' Lucy leaned in and gave him her first real smile of the day. 'And don't you try to lie to me, Theo Redmond. I know you too well at this point.'

He grinned, realizing that entire statement was true. She did know him well by now, better than any woman since Jenna. And the truth was he did occasionally snarf down waffles and sausage.

'I hope my secrets are safe with you,' he said.

'Of course they are.' She patted his hand. 'Just like my secrets are safe with you — if I was allowed to have any, that is. Which I'm not.'

'Sure you are, Luce. You've managed to keep a few secrets from me just fine.'

She frowned a little and took a sip of her decaf. 'Like what?'

'Like what happened to you back when you were nineteen, back when you started putting on all the extra weight. I keep thinking of that, and it's like a line was drawn in your life

236

that year. One day you were active and the next day you weren't.'

Lucy's face went tight.

'You've never answered my questions about it. You just shrug it off like it was nothing.'

She did it again right then, gave a little shrug and avoided his eyes. It had been nearly seven months since they'd started this adventure, but they still had a long way to go, and his gut told him there was something big that Lucy wasn't dealing with and if she didn't, she wouldn't make it.

They wouldn't make it.

'It's an old story, really,' she said with a sigh. 'Girl meets boy, boy humiliates girl, girl checks into the Pepperidge Farm hotel.'

'Who was this jerk?' Theo was stunned by the intensity of the anger that just welled up inside him.

'He is no one that matters, Theo.'

'He matters to me.' *What kind of loser would do that to her?* 'Let's track him down and make him suffer.'

Lucy's laugh was soft and sad. 'I'd really rather not.'

Theo knew they were heading somewhere, but he also knew Lucy was at the wheel. It appeared she was done with her story.

Tears began to form in Lucy's eyes, a development that Theo was not prepared for.

He started to get up out of his chair and head to the kitchen for extra napkins, but she stopped him with a gentle hand on his arm.

'No mental breakdown today, I swear. It's Friday, and you know I only have craptacular meltdowns on Tuesdays.'

'Of course.' He stayed standing, aware that her tears didn't care what day it was.

'It's just that sometimes this whole thing seems like a fantasy to me. Do you know how long it's been since I was this thin and felt this good?'

'A long time.'

'Right after I was weaned and started on solid food, I think.'

Theo laughed.

'So, thank you.'

Theo was speechless. What he wanted to do was pull her into his lap and hold her and kiss her until they both couldn't breathe. But the signals she was giving off today made him rethink that plan.

'Then thank you, too,' he said.

'No sweat. I know the money's going to help with med school.'

Theo took a deep breath, moved his chair closer to hers, and sat down again. 'When my parents died, they left their investments and cash assets in a trust fund for Buddy and they left the house and all their belongings to me.

They were paying for part of my med school, and I was taking the rest out in loans, which I'll be paying back for many years.'

Lucy nodded.

'I can't touch a dime of Buddy's money. People with Down's syndrome are living very long lives now, but often with medical complications as they get older. I have no idea what he'll need in his life, or when he'll need it. That money is not mine.'

Lucy frowned. 'So what you're saying is that every pound I lose is a thousand dollars straight into your med school tuition?'

'That's a no-frills way to put it.'

'Yikes. I really shouldn't have eaten that pecan pie.'

Theo laughed. 'You said it was only half a pie.'

After a moment of quiet, Lucy cocked her head and smiled at him. 'I've never asked you — what kind of doctor do you want to be, Theo?'

'A physiatrist.'

'Do you mean a psychiatrist?'

Theo shook his head. 'No, Cunningham. I know the kind of doctor I want to be, and the word is *physiatrist* — physical medicine in a hospital setting, postsurgery rehab, mostly.'

'How long will that take?'

'After med school there's a four-year

residency and a one-year fellowship. At best, it'll be seven years until I'm done. I won't be out of training until I'm thirty-nine — old and gray.'

'Hardly.' Lucy smiled at him again.

'What I'm saying is that your dream is my dream, Luce. That's the way it works for us.'

Lucy fiddled with her coffee cup. 'I can't wait to break away from psycho Stephan and start my own company, you know? I want the challenge of making my own decisions. I want the chance to thrive or dive on my own.'

'You'll be getting that chance soon.'

Theo and Lucy sat for a long moment, looking into each other's eyes. Theo reached for her hand.

'Buddy is my hero. Did I ever tell you that?'

'No,' Lucy said.

'Yeah. God gave him a whopping disadvantage, but he's always made the absolute most of his gifts. I see being a doctor as my way of doing that.'

'OK.'

'You're the exact opposite of Buddy. Do you know what I'm saying?'

She looked surprised. 'Not really.'

'You've got everything, Lucy. Brains. Beauty. Wit. Determination. A good heart. And I can't tell you how cool it is to see you claim it all.'

She laughed, but it was a little sob of a laugh and it was clear the tears weren't going to stop this time.

'I'll get those tissues now.'

'Maybe that's a good idea.'

Theo returned with an entire box, which made Lucy giggle.

'I'm sorry I've been so busy, Lucy. I wish things were different, but this is how it is. I can only ask for your patience.'

She blew her nose and nodded. 'Patience is not my best virtue.'

'C'mere, Luce.'

He pulled her onto his lap and held her tight. Lucy put her arms around him and hugged him back, a hug full of affection and connection, and he felt the power of it — all the way down to his shoes.

The timbre of the embrace changed slowly. Lucy curled into him, relaxed against Theo's body. He held her softly, feeling her breathe, drawing her scent into him, reveling in the deep satisfaction he felt just having this woman in his arms.

'I really want to do this, Theo.'

'Hug me?'

'That, too.' Lucy pulled back to look down into his face. 'But I was referring to my goal. I want to succeed.'

'I know you do.' Theo grabbed a tissue and

wiped away a smear of mascara on her cheek. 'Maybe what we need is some serious-assed motivation. Are you with me?'

Her eyes widened. 'Sure.'

'Our challenge is another thirty-two pounds in twenty-one weeks. It's doable, but it's going to be tough. So pick something — something big and juicy and decadent — as your reward when you reach your goal.'

'I'm assuming Milk Duds are out.'

'They are.'

'Starting my own company, then.'

'Nope. Can't be work-related. It's gotta be a splurge. An adventure. Something you've always wanted. Something you can't wait to do.'

He could almost see the synapses fire behind the bright light of her eyes. 'All right,' she whispered. 'I want to go to bed with you again.'

Theo thought he would fall out of the chair. 'Uh . . . ' He ran a hand through his hair. 'Not a good idea.'

'Why not?'

'Because I don't think I can wait five months to make wild love to you again. I'm not sure I can wait five minutes. What else you got?'

She smiled and looked off into the yard in thought for a minute. 'I know!' Her face shone with delight. 'How about I arrange to go somewhere exotic where I can be pampered head to toe? I'm talking total sensory overload, Theo.'

'Go on. This is good.' His hand slid up her back, then caressed her between her shoulder blades.

'I want to loll around in abject luxury at some island resort, where a whole team of people tends to my every desire.'

Theo's hand strayed down to her lower back, where he spread his fingers wide and pressed in. 'Excellent. Maybe Fran could go with you.'

'That would be fun. Don't stop touching me.'

Theo let his hand slide down to Lucy's ass, packed tight in that little dress, and he grabbed a handful. Lucy's head wobbled backward. She breathed heavily. 'And I want cabana boys named Raoul to rub warm, fragrant oil all over me, from head to toe, all over my throat and chest and my legs and arms. I want — '

Theo pushed the chair back on the deck and it made a loud scraping sound. He grabbed Lucy's face and kissed her hard, then rose up and placed her on her feet, taking her hand.

'Where are we going, Theo?'

'*Shh.*' He stroked her hair as he led her inside. 'The name's Raoul.'

8

July

Office of Doris Lehman, MSW, PhD
'But how did you know it was love?'

Doris shifted in the modern leather and chrome chair and crossed, then recrossed her legs before she answered. 'How I came to love Mr Lehman has very little to do with how you might experience love with Theo.'

Lucy sighed and kicked off her new strappy little mules. She now wore an entire shoe size smaller than last November, and she'd just gotten her toenails painted a bright pink, her first pedicure since the Clinton administration. 'So you're not going to tell me?'

'The real question is one that only you can answer, Lucy.' Doris smiled kindly. 'So. Are you in love with Theo?'

'Oh God! I'm completely, utterly, nutso in love with that man! But how do I let go of the rope? How do I loosen my grip and fall into the water if I can't even see what's down in there? Piranhas? Sharp rocks? Toxic waste? I don't even know how deep the water is! I

244

could snap my neck like a twig!'

Doris raised an eyebrow. 'That was quite a metaphor.'

Lucy glared at the kimono kittens on the paper screen and swore she heard them tittering and snickering at her outburst. She was really starting to hate those little trollops.

'Actually, Doris, I was hoping this is where you tell me *what the hell I'm supposed to do with my life*!'

Lucy could hardly believe it, but Doris got up out of the therapist's chair, walked over to the love seat, sat down right next to her, and hugged her tight.

It felt nice. It felt safe. And Doris smelled like she'd just strolled out of the Hermès boutique in Bal Harbor.

'Everything's going to be all right.'

Lucy shook her head vehemently and wailed, 'He keeps asking me to tell him what happened to me ten years ago!'

'Here, sweetheart.' Doris shoved a tissue into Lucy's cupped hands, and Lucy realized that lately people seemed to be forever fetching paper goods in her company. She blew her nose and straightened up a little.

'I'd rather die than tell Theo Redmond about the Taco Bowl incident.'

'Why does telling him the truth frighten you so?'

'Because if he knows, that's how he'll see me! In his mind, I won't be *me* anymore. I'll just be the fattest Pitt State coed Brad Zirkle could find to have sex with!'

'Lucy — '

'I'll be the ugly chick Zirkle used to break his rushing slump!'

'Do you really think — '

'I'll be that pathetic porker everyone felt sorry for when the shit hit the fan and the ESPN camera crews descended on campus and people started getting expelled and fired! And I don't *want* Theo to see me that way! I can't *let* him! I don't want him to know I was the *Pitt State Slump Buster*!'

'He already knows who you are, Lucy.'

She shook her head.

'Perhaps Theo would prefer to form his own opinion based on the truth. Maybe he can handle it without running away.'

Lucy let loose with a loud sob.

'Theo has spent seven months getting to know you. This part of your past won't make him love you any less than he does.'

Lucy stopped crying and raised her head to stare at Doris. 'Love me?' She blinked and blew her nose. 'You think he loves me?'

Doris smiled sweetly. 'You know, Lucy, in addition to my weekly sessions with you, I've also grown to know Theo the way the rest of this city has. I see him with you on TV. I hear what he says and the way he says it. I notice the way he looks at you.'

Lucy sat up straight.

'He cares very much for you, Lucy.'

'I know he does.'

'He deserves to know.' Doris loosened her hug and stroked Lucy's hair. 'When the time is right, you might consider telling Theo that you've been in love with him for a long time now.'

Lucy sniffed. 'And I'm supposed to do this without Milk Duds? As if!'

Doris laughed. 'You know, being true to yourself takes courage, Lucy. Great joy always requires great risk, and even effort.'

'Yeah. OK. But I've always been more of a drive-through person.'

'Now, to answer your initial question, it felt like someone zapped me with an electric cattle prod.'

Lucy wasn't sure how her therapist got from joy to animal husbandry techniques but figured it might be worth clarifying. 'What are you talking about, Doris?'

She smiled and patted Lucy's knee. 'Every time I saw Irving — Mr Lehman — it was like I'd been struck by a very friendly little bolt of lightning and the atmosphere became clearer in the aftermath.'

'Oh.' Lucy was following her just fine now.

'You'll know when the time is right to tell Theo. You'll feel it.'

She imagined it would feel an awful lot like indigestion.

★　★　★

Journal Entry July 11

Breakfast: *½ grapefruit; 2 egg whites, scrambled; ½ whole wheat bagel*

Lunch: *3 oz tuna; 1 tbsp light mayo; 1 apple; 3 Ry-Krisp*

Dinner: *3 oz sirloin; 1 small baked potato; 1 tbsp light butter; 1 c steamed cauliflower*

Snack: *1 light yogurt; 1 c strawberries*

Affirmation for Today:
Light mayonnaise is like masturbation — it approximates the real thing but leaves you unfulfilled, ultimately leading to fantasies about diving face-first into a big-ass jar of the real stuff.

★　★　★

Veronica poked her head into Lucy's office. 'I've answered two crates of fan mail today, but I'm running out of storage room. Any suggestions?'

Lucy groaned. 'None.'

'Oh. And there's another package for you out front. A big one. You want me to open it?'

The anonymous delivery of junk food in bulk had become so commonplace that Lucy no longer even bothered mentioning it to Theo. Malomars. Oreos. Fritos. There was even a shipment of frozen Snickers bars on dry ice. Somebody with a significant disposable income thought it was funny to torture her like this.

'Sure. Go ahead and open it.'

'You don't want to know what's in it, like usual, right?'

'Absolutely.'

'You got it, boss.'

Veronica left and Lucy sat patiently at her desk, waiting. Eventually, her assistant returned, giving her a sympathetic nod.

'Frozen stuffed pizzas shipped directly from the original Pizzeria Uno in Chicago.'

Lucy's heart stopped. 'People can be so sick and twisted,' she hissed.

'Sausage.'

'I'm not strong enough for this.'

'It's OK, Lucy. I'll put them in Stephan's

office. He's the one who's been taking most of this stuff home anyway.'

★ ★ ★

'You like the dress?' Lucy was standing toward the entrance of the grand ballroom as the guests began to filter in. Tyson had been one of the first to arrive, and he'd come with Lola, who was already hitting on the bartender.

'Not my style, to be honest.'

'Oh really?' Lucy would have been offended if it weren't for the glint in Tyson's eye.

'No.' He shook his head, his eyes still scanning every detail of the item of clothing in question. 'That's the kind of dress that belongs on the floor, all wrinkled up, with the zipper broken and the sleeves torn. That dress isn't right for you at all. In fact, I think you should take it off right now.'

Tyson had remained her friend — her flirtatious, fun friend — even though they hadn't dated since she returned from Tampa. He'd seemed disappointed when she told him she couldn't keep seeing him, but he'd never lost that gleam in his eye or that smile for her. Tyson's playful attention made her feel appreciated, even while she wrestled with the more serious feelings she had for Theo.

Lucy was laughing when Theo arrived between her mother and father. The entire arrangement felt like a nonsensical wedding march — she stood with a guy she used to date waiting to receive her beloved, who was being escorted by her parents.

It briefly registered that her mother looked smashing in a shimmering blue dress and her father remarkably put-together in his rented tux; then Lucy's eyes returned to the real sensory delicacy at hand.

Seeing Theo Redmond in a white dinner jacket was like eating a DoveBar in an outdoor Jacuzzi while listening to Mozart and gazing at the aurora borealis — almost too many pleasures going on at once for the brain to absorb. His golden skin and sun-touched hair, his clear blue eyes, that killer smile, tall and lean and knock-you-on-your-ass delicious, all set in a framework of starched white dress shirt, austere black bow tie, creamy suit jacket . . .

'My, my, my.'

'Stay strong, Lucy.' Tyson shook his head. 'He's just a man — puts his jockstrap on like all the rest of us.'

She blew out air and looked up at Tyson. 'Must we discuss jockstraps tonight? I'm all dressed up and nowhere near the gym and I'd much rather just gawk at Theo.'

Tyson laughed. 'You're a goner, aren't you, Lucy? You really love Redmond.'

Lucy was saved as Tyson's gaze wandered toward the ballroom entrance, his champagne glass hovering in midair. 'Now who is *that* little lady?'

Lucy sought out the object of Tyson's inquiry. 'Oh. That's Veronica, my assistant. Be gentle with her. I need her able-bodied and alert at the office on Monday.'

'The able-bodied part's not going to be a problem,' he said, already moving away and toward Veronica.

Buddy came in next, right behind Theo, along with Dan and Gia. Mary Fran was on their heels — without Keith. Lucy hadn't actually seen her brother-in-law since Holden's baptism and was starting to think that Mary Fran had killed him and disposed of his body in the crawl space of their lovely redbrick Georgian in Buckhead. She'd have to remember to ask.

Then Stephan sauntered in with Carolina Buendia and John Weaver, who looked exactly as they did on the *WakeUp Miami* set, and it was obvious that the party was indeed getting started.

★ ★ ★

He'd picked a hell of a time to have this epiphany, but there it was, just a few feet away in the grand ballroom of the Mandarin Oriental Hotel. It was Lucy, breathtaking in that bare hint of a dress, and he was sure this would soon be one of the defining moments of his life. A moment that would change everything.

Theo put one foot in front of the other, his eyes on hers, and it all rushed into him — every other defining moment in his thirty-two years on the planet.

His brother's birth had been hard on his mom. Brian Joseph Redmond was born after eighteen hours of labor, and the doctors whisked him away and came back to explain to his distraught family that the baby had Down's syndrome. Theo was just sixteen, but in that instant he went from the focus of his parents' lives to their peer, an independent and grown person they relied on for help. He'd suddenly become his father's friend and ally, his mother's confidant, and a big brother to a beautiful and perplexing child.

Theo had observed how the soft-spoken doctor comforted his mom, held her hand, and gently told her the truth about Buddy. Immediately Theo knew that's what he was meant to do with his own life. He wanted a job that was real, important, healing. He wanted that mix of human connection and hard science. He wanted to be a doctor. Theo cornered the physician in the hallway afterward, talked to him for a good half hour, and his mind was made up. Everything he did after that was done in pursuit of that goal.

Another defining moment came when the dean of the med school came for Theo in the middle of assisting with a routine appendectomy. As Theo followed him into the hallway outside the operating suite, he already felt the weight of tragedy hanging over him — he just didn't know who was dead or how it had happened. When the dean put his hands on Theo's shoulders and said the words, 'I'm so sorry to have to tell you this . . . ' everything changed again.

The lunch date where Jenna broke up with him was another of those moments. As she laid it all out for him, Theo saw that he'd never really known the woman sitting across from him, that he'd been so enthralled by what the eye could see — her beauty and drive and smooth elegance — that in five years he'd never dug deep enough to know the person inside. Maybe he'd done that intentionally, knowing what he'd find would not be as pretty as the outer wrapping. But there it was — the truth — and the truth was, the woman he'd been convinced was his ideal life partner was really nothing but a cold mystery to him and he wasn't enough for her anymore.

Theo looked at Lucy again and his chest grew hot and he felt a smile spread across his face. He thought, *She's beautiful,* and then scolded himself for the inadequacy of those words. Yes, she was shockingly beautiful. She was luminous and alive and damn hot in that nothing of a dress. But she was also the bravest, funniest, best woman he'd ever known.

And the kicker was, she wasn't his Lucy anymore. She was everyone's Lucy. Now everybody could see what he'd seen in her from the very start — that she had it all.

Theo smiled a little broader, still walking toward her, his eyes still on hers, and something primal stirred in him. It was a dark need in his psyche he could identify only as possessiveness. Maybe that's why he'd been relieved to see Tyson leave her side just now.

It struck Theo as odd that he hadn't been able to spit it out — that he loved her. Because he really did. That was an oversight he intended to correct immediately, as soon as he was close enough for her to hear the words. He no longer gave a rat's ass about Palm Club policy — Ramona would just have to deal. He no longer minded the amount of gossip it would generate or that it was going to be a difficult seven years ahead of them. All that mattered was that he'd spend those years with Lucy.

And that was his epiphany — he wanted Lucy as much as he'd ever wanted anything. As much as he wanted to be a doctor.

'Hey, Theo,' Tyson greeted him on his way toward the door, stepping right in Theo's line of vision. 'You clean up real nice, bro.'

'You, too.' Theo peered around Tyson's shoulder to find that Lucy's family had gathered around her. Now he'd never get her alone . . .

'Theo, man, you'd better be good to that woman or I'm going to hunt you down like a dog.'

He laughed at that. 'Not to worry.'

'Hey, I'm being totally serious here, OK? Listen up.' Tyson pulled Theo over to a couple small formal chairs against a wall. 'Have a seat.'

Theo sat down and unbuttoned his dinner jacket. It was difficult to act suave when you were uncomfortable.

'Lucy Cunningham is completely in love with you, man. Do you realize that? She thinks you are the be-all and end-all. And that woman needs a man who can give her the works. Know what I'm saying?'

Theo tried to loosen his bow tie. It didn't budge.

Tyson kept going. 'The girl's so good-natured it's almost unbelievable — somehow, the world hasn't made her a hard-ass like so many other women out there.'

Theo ran a hand through his hair.

'She needs somebody who will spoil her rotten. Somebody who has time to savor her — yeah, that's it. Lucy needs a man to savor her, a man who has the time to enjoy her.'

Theo couldn't stand this conversation another second. He stood up, rebuttoned his James Bond wannabe jacket, and cursed himself for renting something so ridiculous.

He cursed himself for thinking Lucy would be satisfied with what he had to give her. She hadn't done so great in the last few weeks — how bitter would she become after a few years?

'Now, since I'm not allowed to have Lucy, I'm going to go peruse the menu. Check you later.'

Tyson strolled away, and Theo noticed his friend wasn't heading for the hors d'ouvres table but right toward the petite brunette in a black cocktail dress whom he knew was Lucy's assistant.

★　★　★

Lucy could feel it. All during dinner, as Theo sat at her side, he avoided looking her in the eye. He'd told her she looked lovely and kissed her cheek, but there was no *zing!* in the kiss. It almost felt as if Theo had put up an invisible *zing!* force field. He was all business, charming her parents right out of their seats, laughing and talking with Dan like they'd known each other forever, but it was all done in his capacity as her trainer, her business partner, nothing more.

She and Theo had been photographed and video-taped all evening, standing together, chatting, smiling at each other. All of it seemed hollow, and Lucy felt her heart sinking. Something was wrong. Something had happened since she'd seen him last at the gym, and it made her question everything she felt. It made her question her decision to tell him she loved him.

Stephan was finishing up his comments at a tasteful podium set up at the head table. She hadn't listened to a word he'd said, and now he was introducing Carolina Buendia and John Weaver, who smiled brightly and said they had a surprise for Lucy.

Carolina leaned into the microphone and announced that *WakeUp Miami* had heard Lucy wanted to reward herself at the end of her yearlong program and they'd decided to pick up the tab and send her to . . . There was a dramatic pause . . .

' . . . An all-expenses-paid week for two at the exclusive Caves Resort and Spa in Jamaica!'

The room burst into applause and Theo elbowed Lucy so she knew to stand up. She said 'thank you' over and over and acted suitably shocked and thrilled. Then sat back down.

She glanced around the table and locked eyes first with Mary Fran, who scowled at her, then with Gia, who raised her hands and her eyebrows as if to say, *What's your problem*, chica *girlie?*

'Lucy, why don't you come on up and say a few words?' Stephan glanced down on her with a fake smile frozen on his face. She had a bad feeling about this.

'This is a surprise!' She smiled, thinking that Stephan should have had the courtesy to warn her she would be speaking tonight. Not to do so was just plain vindictive.

Which was nothing new for him.

Lucy rose from her seat and began the walk to the microphone, feeling with precise discomfort how the dress clung to every nook and curvature of her body. She turned and faced at least 250 people, feeling a slight tremble rise from her toes to her lips. Her eyes darted to the video and still cameras trained on her and to the expectant looks of the faces of her family, friends, and Theo. The silence sliced through her brain and left her numb.

A voice called out from the back of the room, and Lucy recognized the reporter from the *Herald*. 'So, Lucy? What's the single most important lesson you've learned so far?'

Lucy wasn't prepared to be ganged up on by reporters like this tonight. One-on-one was fine, but she'd done nothing to prepare for a press conference. She'd been set up, and she glanced down at Stephan, who sat comfortably in his chair, a vacant smile pasted on his flushed, rounded face. Lucy noticed with a shock that the buttons were nearly popping off his tuxedo shirt. When had Stephan gained so much weight? She hadn't even noticed . . .

'What would you tell anyone out there trying to lose weight?' the *Herald* reporter tried rephrasing the question. 'The single most important lesson.'

Lucy turned toward the crowd and laughed. Something about this whole evening was just so damn funny — she was prepared to tell Theo she loved him and he was acting like she had bubonic plague; it now appeared Stephan had gained a pound for every two she'd lost; and the woman who'd been so afraid of cameras and reporters and attention was now glorying in it. The woman who used to wear a size 22 now wore a size 10.

'Take the risk,' Lucy said. 'Instead of sitting around listing all the reasons why you'll fail, take that first risky step.' She smiled down at Theo and back at the cameras. 'And it wouldn't hurt to step right into the Palm Club and sign up with one of their trainers.'

Stephan led Lucy away from the microphone after about fifteen minutes of questions and answers, which had apparently gone far too well for his taste. After coffee, the band began to play. Lucy danced an awkward salsa number with her father, who told her she looked cute as a button, and then accepted dances with Buddy, Dan, John Weaver, and Tyson. Theo burned up the dance floor with Lucy's mother, then Mary Fran, Gia, Veronica, Carolina Buendia, his boss, Ramona, and every other breathing female at the event. Except for Lucy.

She didn't understand why he was ignoring her. It was as if he was doing everything he could to avoid speaking to her or standing anywhere near her. Lucy headed over to the bar and ordered herself a margarita. Dan tagged along.

'You supposed to be drinking those things?'

'Mind your own beeswax, Danny.'

'Hey, I'm just looking out for you.' Dan put his arm around her. 'Lucy, you look amazing. I mean it. I don't think I've ever seen you so gorgeous. I am so proud of you.'

She accepted the compliment with a nod and the margarita with relief and began to snarf it down. When she came up for air she said, 'A lot of good all this gorgeousness is doing me.'

Dan's auburn eyebrows went askew and he whispered in her ear, 'Well, Theo's great. I like him.'

She sucked down some more candy-flavored tequila and felt good about it.

'I think he really digs you, Lucy.'

'Uh-huh.'

'He's hanging back. I think he's waiting for a sign from you. You might have to take the bull by the horns on this one.'

'Ha!' She looked up at her brother and laughed. 'And then take a seat in the stands and wait for him to unfurl the banner?'

Dan scowled at her. 'There is no banner here, Luce. This is not a college football stadium.'

'So you say.'

'Seriously. Talk to me. I thought you were completely over the Taco Bowl incident.'

'Nope.' More slurping. 'A girl doesn't just

262

get over that, Dan. It destroyed me, OK? I went on like it didn't, I think mostly to make it easier on Mom and Dad, but it nearly killed me.'

Dan's eyes got huge.

'I may be thinner, but I fight every damn day not to walk around seeing myself as the Pitt State Slump Buster!'

She obviously said it a little too loudly, because Dan shushed her and pulled her to an alcove.

'I had no idea, Luce.'

'Yeah, well. I've been lying for about a decade now and I'm pretty sick of it. When they unfurled that banner I wanted to die — there you go. The truth is out!'

Dan hugged her and tried to take the margarita out of her hand. 'Hey! Get your own,' she said. 'Wait. While you're getting your own, would you be a sweetheart and get me one, too?'

★ ★ ★

Stephan enjoyed Lola immensely. She was dull as a stump and talked about nothing but weight lifting and the line of protein supplements she was selling on the side. But she had two things going for her. All right, technically she had three things going for her

— a nice set of tits and a deep dislike for Lucy Cunningham.

'She makes me sick,' Lola said while dancing in Stephan's arms. He could not remember ever touching a woman who felt as solid as Lola. It was oddly exciting, almost taboo.

'I don't know what it is about her, but she just rubs me the wrong way. And Theo is so gullible that he's falling for her. I think it's gross.'

Stephan mulled that for a moment and wondered if Lola was just plain jealous. This could be a real boon.

'Why do you think they're doing so well?' he asked. 'You're the expert, so tell me — they're pretty much accomplishing the impossible, aren't they?'

'I really didn't think she had a chance in hell. It must be the money.' She looked up at him from behind her heavily mascarared eyes. 'Stephan, are you married?'

He placed his hand right on Lola's rock-hard rump, and he smiled. 'Haven't been for three blissful years. You?'

'Never. But I'm only twenty-six.'

'Of course. Let me buy you a drink.' He began to steer her off the dance floor.

'But it's an open bar.'

'Exactly.'

Lola giggled. Stephan looked down the front of her dress, wondering how he could use this dear girl to his advantage.

★ ★ ★

Is this the moment Dr Lehman had referred to? Lucy wondered. Because it was ten o'clock, she'd had three margaritas, and Theo had pissed her off something fierce by not even speaking with her the entire night! All these factors led Lucy to believe the timing couldn't be better, so, after a quick stop in the ladies' room to realign her body shaper and fix her lipstick, she stormed Theo's way.

He and Buddy sat at a table, and Buddy broke out into a huge grin and waved when he saw her approaching. Lucy waved back and smiled big, just as Theo turned to see who was coming toward them. His eyes flashed.

'Hey, Cunningham.'

She asked Buddy to hold her purse and grabbed Theo's hand. 'C'mon, coach. We're going to dance.'

This was precisely what Theo had wanted to avoid — Lucy's luscious body in that come-fuck-me dress, pressed up against him, her tipsy breath on his cheek, the scent of

265

Paradise Awaits pummeling his adrenal glands.

She snuggled close to him and it all came racing back — every damn time he'd ever had the pleasure to touch her, kiss her, be inside her. Lucy felt so good in his hands. So warm and soft and perfect, and she was nuzzling into the crook of his neck and making those little sounds of pleasure she made whenever she got nearly naked in his presence.

'Luce?'

'Mmm?'

She wiggled a little bit, and all her parts rubbed up against all of his and he had to bite down on the inside of his cheek. *Oh yes. Oh no.* She was lifting that lovely face up to his, and in those heels she was at just the right level . . .

'Lucy, just wait a — '

She kissed him. In front of everyone! Theo grabbed her by the upper arms and steadied her in front of him. She was toasted, more so than he'd realized at first, and he knew he'd better get her out of there. She could probably use some air. So could he, for that matter.

Theo took her by the hand and swooped down on the table where Buddy now sat with Lola and Stephan, and Theo made a quick note at how odd that little grouping seemed,

266

then said, 'We'll be right back.' He grabbed Lucy's purse and acknowledged Mary Fran's look of concern as they passed her.

'We're going for a walk — we'll be back in fifteen minutes,' he assured Lucy's sister.

They took the ornate elevator down, and Theo tried not to look at Lucy, who was leaning back against the glass wall, holding on to the brass handrail, her head lolled back.

She was a knockout. That dress was the most provocative thin strip of fabric he'd ever seen on a woman's body. It did wonders for her, or she for it — he didn't know which. All he knew was that the color seemed to melt into the peachy hue of her skin, so the general effect was that she looked sparkly but naked, and that was about as blistering hot as it could get.

She hiccupped, then giggled and opened her eyes.

'I've got something important to tell you, Theo.' Her voice was husky and low, and when she looked at him with those gray-blue pools of femaleness he felt sort of drunk himself, though he'd had exactly nothing to drink the whole evening.

Lucy moved close to him on unsteady feet. Theo could hardly believe it, but she slapped a hand directly on his ass and squeezed.

'For seven months now, I've wanted to just

walk right up to you in the middle of the Palm Club and put my hand on your booty,' she slurred.

The elevator dinged as they arrived at the ground floor. He grabbed her elbow and escorted her across the marble foyer toward an exit that led to the pool and beach. The doorman assisted them with the revolving door and finally they were outside. It was powerfully hot — hot like July in Miami is hot — and Theo turned Lucy toward the beach. She leaned into him as he steered her through the hotel's elaborate poolside, gardens, and walkways.

'Theo, listen . . . ,' she hiccupped. 'I have to tell you something. It's soooo important.'

Lucy snaked a hand up along the back of his dinner jacket, over the collar, and into his hair. She pressed one of those sparkly round breasts against his side. She smelled like sin, and his head was spinning.

She put her lips to the side of his face, then left a little string of kisses down his jaw and back up to his ear, all while she stumbled along next to him.

Theo had no idea where he was taking her or what he was going to do once he got there, but somewhere in the back of his caveman brain all he wanted was Lucy in some type of reclining position, where he could get at her.

He realized that made him scum. Because Lucy was drunk and Tyson was right — Theo couldn't give her what she needed. All night the reality of Tyson's comments had hammered in at Theo's head. He'd tell her he loved her, only to disappoint her. Why even go there? Why hurt her any more than he had to? Why hurt himself?

How the fuck was he supposed to spoil a woman while he was in med school and residency? Why would he want to set himself up for another defining moment, when the woman he loved sat across a lunch table and told him he wasn't enough for her, that she'd found someone who could do the job better?

He looked down to see Lucy lift each of her pretty feet and slip off her sandals, her hands resting on his shoulders. He placed the shoes on a hotel beach chair, along with his own shoes and socks, and held her hand as they walked in the sand.

The air was thick with humidity and there wasn't another soul on the Mandarin's private beach. He was already starting to sweat in his jacket. Lucy stumbled in the sand and he caught her, delighting in the sound of her giggle.

'Are you OK, Lucy?'

'God, no. I'm drunk and I love you, Theo.'

She'd whispered it, and with the sound of

the waves he wasn't sure he'd heard her correctly. But then, *dammit*, she said it again, turning her face up to his.

'I love you so much it hurts, Theo. I had to tell you. I just can't keep it in anymore.' She hiccupped. 'I've loved you since that day I choked on my Milk Duds. Do you remember that day?'

Theo smiled. 'I'll never forget it.'

'OK, so that day, when I woke up on the floor and you were kissing me . . . ?' She frowned at him. 'You remember that part?'

'Oh yes.'

'Well, I fell in love with you right then. And I love, love, love you now. And I'm going to kiss you, you big, gorgeous, studly — '

When Theo slammed his lips onto Lucy's soft, sweet mouth, he couldn't think of a good reason to ever stop kissing her. He couldn't think at all. He couldn't remember what it was that he wanted to tell her.

The kiss said everything, anyway. It told Theo that Lucy just broke through a dam in her heart and the love was pouring out of her and it was all for him and he was sucking it down because he wanted it. He was dying for it.

He was dying for Lucy.

He brought his arms around her and pulled her as close as he could. She tilted her head to the side for him, giving him leeway to kiss her like a crazy man, and he lifted her, tossed her up in the air for the second it took him to relocate his hands on her butt, where he held her aloft.

'I love you, Theo. Did you hear me? This is the part where you say, 'I love you, too,' and then tell me the night in Tampa was the most wonderful night of your life, and every night since has been perfect, and you want to sleep with me every night from now on!'

He put her down and set her aside long enough for him to remove his dinner jacket, because he was sweating and because he wanted to have something under them when he pulled her into that reclining position he'd envisioned a few minutes earlier. He took her hand and led her closer to the surf, where he spread out his coat.

He lay down on it and propped himself on his elbows.

'Come here, Lucy.'

'What are we doing?'

'Come here and I'll show you.'

Lucy knelt at his side, then crawled over him, hiking her dress up enough that she could straddle him.

'You are incredible.' He stroked his hands over her knees, then her thighs.

'I just told you I love you, Theo. I've loved

you for a long time.' She frowned at him, her hair slipping from its fancy little twist. 'Did you hear what I just said?'

He was stalling for time and he knew it. He grabbed her head and kissed her hard and crushed her to the front of his body and waited until he felt her relax, simply surrender to the force they created together, what they'd always created together.

Their mouths fought and pushed and then soothed. Their tongues wrestled, then caressed. Theo's hands were all over Lucy's body, and she was a delight under his touch — female and hot and sexy — and he was losing his mind over this woman. Lucy Cunningham was a revelation to him, a woman he dared to picture as his companion and lover. Maybe even his wife someday. If only things were different.

'Answer me!' She pushed up and away.

Theo reached out and cupped her left breast. Paradise indeed. She swatted his hand away.

'Oh my God,' she said. Theo watched her face stiffen in horror. 'You're pulling out the banner!'

'What?' He continued to stare, mesmerized by her sparkly, perfect breasts.

Lucy scrambled to get up, and as she did so, Theo saw the first slash of lightning in the sky above them.

'Lightning, Lucy. We'd better go back inside.'

'There's always lightning with us, you bastard!' And with that, she started to run. She could really make tracks these days, and he had a hard time catching her, given that she'd had a decent head start.

Theo grabbed their shoes, then put on his jacket as he ran behind her along the boardwalk and poolside. The rain started coming down in a hard sheet, and they were soaked by the time the doorman let them back in, no small amount of amusement on his face.

'Thanks,' Theo said, brushing sand from his jacket.

'Enjoy your evening,' the doorman said, smiling.

The ride back up in the elevator was an interminable hell. Lucy's chest heaved, her hair and dress ruined, as a little puddle formed under her bare feet. Theo held out her sandals. She snagged them without looking his way.

'My life isn't what you want or need, Lucy. I can't give you what you deserve.'

She swung her face around and her eyes were clear and bright, not a tear to be seen.

'You are worse than any of them.'

'Lucy — '

'I thought . . . Everyone thought . . . Even Doris thought . . . ' Lucy shook her head and squared her shoulders. 'Go to hell, Theo.'

'You mean more to me than I can say.' Theo knew that was lame, but it was accurate, and it was the best he could come up with in the circumstances.

Lucy laughed. 'We're done, Theo. I'm getting another trainer. I can't spend time with you anymore.'

'Don't, Luce.'

'It's not fair to me.' Her lips were trembling and her jaw was set rigid. 'You sleep with me. You tell me you want me. But you don't love me. I just told you I loved you, for God's sake, and you said . . . You said *nothing*!'

Theo opened his mouth, but there was no air and nothing happened except a drop of rainwater fell from his brow onto his cheek.

'How sad is this?' Lucy slumped back against the elevator wall and let go with a bitter laugh. 'The fat girl thinks she's good enough for the golden boy, but she's wrong again.'

Theo's body went numb. 'You are not a fat girl, Lucy. You're a beautiful woman. And I'm not a golden boy — I'm just a guy. Whatever this is really about, whatever it is that you won't tell me, just get over it.'

274

She nodded at him, her mouth rigid. 'I'm going to get over it, Theo — don't you doubt that for a second. But not with you.'

The elevator arrived at the ballroom level and the doors opened. Lucy stepped ahead of him, and as they passed a small reception table Theo reached for her arm.

'There's a reason I can't say what you want to hear, Lucy.'

She scanned the foyer, as if to search for something to throw at him. She grabbed an abandoned goblet of red wine and tossed the contents onto his James Bond dinner jacket.

He watched Lucy disappear with Gia and Mary Fran. Theo found Buddy sitting alone at the table where he'd left him.

'Come on, Bud. The night has officially been shot to hell, thanks to me.'

Buddy followed him out the double doors and to the bank of elevators. When one didn't arrive immediately, Theo charged through the fire door and began racing down the stairwell.

'Why are we taking the stairs?'

'Think of it as part of your training.'

'That would be going up, not down.'

'Just come on, Bud.'

'What happened to you and Lucy? She looked very sad.'

'We got caught in the rain.'

'Are we running away?'

'Not really.'

'That Stephan guy is a bad man. He hates Lucy. Lola is a mean lady, too. She called me a 'tardo' like I didn't know what it meant.'

'*What?*' Theo looked behind him to see Buddy struggling to keep up. He stopped. 'Are you all right?'

'I'm OK, but Stephan kind of scared me. He asked me questions about you and Lucy — like how often you kissed her and our address and if Lucy ever came over to our house. Where are we going?'

'Back upstairs.'

Theo took the stairs two at a time and slammed open the fire door, checking quickly to make sure Buddy was right behind him. 'Stay out here just a moment.'

He knew he must look like a crazy man, wet and disheveled and angry as hell, but he didn't care. He found Lola and Stephan canoodling at a table in the corner, Lola practically in his lap.

'Is there something I can help you with, Stephan? My brother mentioned you all had a nice little chat.'

Stephan jumped up from his chair so fast that Lola got knocked sideways. 'I have no idea what you're talking about.'

Lola hit Stephan in the arm. 'Sure you do! The retarded kid!'

Stephan closed his eyes and shook his head slowly. Lola put a hand over her mouth a second too late, and Theo realized he had never seen Lola drunk before. It was scary.

'We had a friendly exchange is all.'

Theo got up close in Stephan's face. 'What are you up to, Sherrod? What do you have against Lucy? She's working her ass off for you — I just don't get it.'

Stephan laughed in his face. 'I have nothing against her. She's doing a fine job.'

Theo frowned. 'Then why try to embarrass her like you did tonight? Why give her such a hard time at the office?'

'Is there a point to this conversation? If so, I don't see it.'

Theo put his nose right up to Stephan's. 'Here's my point, dickhead — if you do anything to harm Lucy or ever speak to my brother again, I will unleash my inner psycho killer on your ass. Do you see the point now?'

Lola gasped and Stephan stepped back, trying to hide his shaking hands. He forced a laugh. 'I must say I've enjoyed your heroic charge in here, defending Lucy's honor and all, but do you realize that girl thinks you care for her? Do you know she thinks you *love* her?'

Lola laughed.

He did love Lucy. That was the hell of it.

And as Theo raced through the ballroom, he knew he'd hurt her in his effort to spare her. How could he have done that to her? How would she ever trust him again?

★   ★   ★

Theo squealed out of the parking garage and drove in silence the fifteen minutes to Miami Beach. He double-parked in front of the Palm Club, keyed in the security code, and ran with Buddy back to the trainer lounge.

'Here. Hold this.' He handed Buddy the club's digital camera, then clicked the power button.

'What are we doing, Theo?' Buddy looked like he was ready to cry, so Theo stopped racing around and looked him in the eye.

'This is for Lucy, Bud. She's the most wonderful woman I've ever known, and I just hurt her really bad. I don't know how I'm ever going to make it up to her, but I know that right now I've got to do this one thing and I need your help. Will you help me?'

Buddy nodded. 'I guess. But why are we doing this?'

Theo rubbed his knuckles on Buddy's hair. 'I have a feeling that someday I'm going to need to prove what I learned tonight — do you understand?'

Buddy pouted. 'No.'

'OK. Here's the deal. I know Lucy, right?'

Buddy nodded.

'And one day, when we're done with our project and I figure out a way to make my life work with her in it, she's going to ask me for proof that I came to my senses before she lost all the weight. It will be important to her.'

Buddy nodded slowly. 'You're going to finally tell her you love her?'

Theo stopped what he was doing and stared at Buddy. 'Just give me a couple minutes and then take my picture.'

Theo dug through the supply closet, Buddy staring at him like he'd lost his mind, which, in a way, Theo supposed was a correct diagnosis. Then he riffled through the desk drawer until he found a wide-tipped Magic Marker.

'What are you *doing*?' Buddy asked impatiently.

Theo held up the sign to inspect his handiwork. It was truly the work of a man on the brink, but so be it. It got the point across.

'Nice job,' Buddy said, giggling. 'Do you want to smile for this?'

'Sure. Why not?' Theo smiled and Buddy snapped the picture. Then they both went to the computer, down-loaded the image, and printed it out on photo paper.

It was a color shot of Theo, standing in a sandy white dinner jacket splashed with red wine, holding a sign that read simply: I LOVE LUCY.

★ ★ ★

Tyson was a natural at this. He worked the camera like a seasoned politician, spinning the truth with such panache and charm that the hosts of *WakeUp Miami*, along with the entire studio audience, were hoodwinked.

'Theo sends his regards, but he's feeling so under the weather that he thought it was best not to expose anyone to what he's got.'

Yeah, Lucy said to herself. *He's got shit for brains; that's what he's got.*

Lucy kept her eyes on her shoes. She was able to remain like that, lifeless and out of focus, for several long minutes while Tyson regaled everyone with tales from his college football days and his aspirations to be a TV sports announcer.

Lucy didn't mind one bit that he was using this appearance as one giant job interview. It was fine with her. Anything was fine with her.

Then it was time for the weigh-in, and it surprised her just how little it bothered her that Tyson was doing the weighing.

'Great job, Lucy!' Tyson said. 'Another

eight pounds and one and three-quarter inches!'

The audience began whooping and hooting and chanting, 'Go, Lucy! Go, Lucy!'

And all she wanted to do was go home, put on her pink sweatpants, and eat.

9

August

Journal Entry Aug 4

Breakfast: *2-egg-white omelet with ¼ c low-fat cheddar, ½ c onion, pepper, and tomato; one slice whole wheat toast; 1 tbsp no-sugar-added apple butter; decaf with splash of skim milk*

Lunch: *3 oz broiled salmon; 1 c steamed broccoli; 1 c salad with 1 tbsp oil and vinegar; ½ c brown rice*

Dinner: *A Wendy's Triple with everything; a large fry; a large Frosty*

Evening snack: *1 qt butter brickle ice cream; 1 box of ginger snaps*

Affirmation for Today:
I seem to be drawing a blank.

★ ★ ★

Lucy woke up the next morning, looked in the mirror, and said out loud, 'Get your shit together, quick.'

She refused to even attempt to wear anything without elastic embedded somewhere in the waist and found a pair of khaki crop pants that would do fine for the day. She had no pressing appointments.

Then she shoved her feet into a pair of slides and yanked a white cotton twinset out of her closet. She tied a paisley silk scarf around her neck for color, ran a brush through her hair, and smeared some coral pink gloss over her lips. That would have to do. It was all she could handle that morning.

There would be no breakfast. The idea of food made her wish she were dead. In the hours between 6:00 p.m. and 10:00 p.m. of the previous day, she'd violated every promise she'd made to herself and to Theo. She'd even violated the only sensible rule of dieting she'd ever run across, the sage advice of the Muppets' Miss Piggy, who recommended never eating anything bigger than your head.

Lucy was fairly certain that if piled together, all that junk she binged on the day before would be bigger than anyone's head. Perhaps even Theo's.

And who cared what promise she'd made to Theo, anyway? He was out of the picture.

This was all *her* problem now, and she'd just have to deal with it alone.

Lucy drove to work, and though she didn't intend to eat for the rest of her life, food called out to her all the way to the office. Doughnuts whispered her name from their evil glass display cases. Croissants and muffins beckoned to her from bakery windows like prostitutes in the doorways of French Quarter brothels. Fast-food drive-throughs shouted obscene lies about the relief to be found in a bacon, egg, and cheese biscuit — or two.

Lucy told herself she would make it through this day. She *would* get around to calling Tyson about scheduling workout sessions. She *would* stick to a sane and healthy food plan.

She would not allow Theo's rejection to stand in the way of her dreams. She could do it without him. She'd show *him*.

★ ★ ★

Stephan traced his fingers down the ridges of Lola's abdominals, agog at the carved perfection of the woman now stretched out on his bed. He had to admit that she wasn't the most passionate female he'd ever been with, in fact she was rather lifeless, but, with all the lights on, it was fun in a visual kind of way.

'You're pretty out of shape, Stephan,' Lola said.

He flinched and sucked in his gut.

'You should schedule some sessions with me out of bed,' she continued, propping herself on her side as she smiled at him. 'We'll focus on trimming body fat and adding definition. In the meantime, you should cut down on your refined carbs and try some of the protein powder I was telling you about.'

What the hell was this? He hadn't asked her for her advice!

'I hate to say this, but the nutrition plan Theo and Lucy are using seems to work. Have you checked out their Web site? Hundreds of people are now following their program. It's, like, amazing.'

Stephan felt his blood pressure build.

'Stephan?' Lola sat up cross-legged, and he was fascinated at how the only things that seemed to roll or crinkle on her body were three tiny creases of darkly tanned skin around her waist. No fat. Anywhere. He wondered if that might be unnatural.

He rolled over onto his back and stared at the ceiling for a few moments, then put a hand over his eyes. When had it gotten so complicated? All he'd wanted was to reward himself for working so hard all these years, have a little fun. So he'd been siphoning some profits to a bank in the Caymans. So what? A lot of businesspeople did it. But now he'd gone and pissed off Murray Goldstein, who was threatening to sic the feds on him.

It was all Lucy's fault. She'd gone out there and worked her ass off — literally — and now his ass was in real danger of being sent to prison or ending up in a watery grave at the bottom of Biscayne Bay. He didn't know which was worse.

At this point, it wasn't even about stopping her from losing weight anymore. The damage had been done. Now Stephan just wanted to make her pay.

'Here.' Stephan hoisted himself up off the bed and leaned over toward the nightstand drawer. 'I have a little something for you, Lola. Just to let you know how special you are to me.'

He watched with satisfaction as Lola opened the jewelry box and gasped at the platinum toe ring.

'It's great!' She wasted no time placing it on the second toe of her right foot. Then she hugged Stephan tight, which made him feel amorous for the third time that day, which could have very well been a record.

Lola ended the hug and spent a few

moments admiring her newly festooned toe, then let her gaze return to Stephan's. It really was a pity she didn't have a pretty face, but he figured a man couldn't have everything.

'You know, Stephan, Lucy hasn't shown up at the gym for at least a couple weeks.'

Now they were getting somewhere — a little platinum apparently greased the skids. 'Really now?'

'I think she and Theo had a huge fight.'

This was welcome news. 'Do you think Lucy's losing her momentum?' he asked.

'Maybe. But I know Theo, and he doesn't like quitters. He'll do everything he can to convince her to come back.'

'So you like the toe ring?' Stephan enjoyed watching the eager nod of her head and wondered just how much of this game Lola was cognizant of.

'I love it!'

'Why don't you poke around a little at the gym and find out what you can about Lucy? You know, if she's gone off her diet and has stopped exercising completely, stuff like that. Maybe we can leak it to the press — bad publicity is better than no publicity at all.'

Lola gave him a little frown. 'I don't like Lucy much, but you *really* don't like her, do you? I mean, you act like you *hate* Lucy Cunningham.'

Stephan smiled. 'Let's just say she won't be getting a raise this year.'

★ ★ ★

'Whatever happened to the picture?' Buddy jogged along at Theo's side, the sweat soaking through his T-shirt.

'I sent it to myself registered mail that next morning, so it has the date on it. I'm waiting for the right time to show it to her.'

'She's still not coming to see you at the gym?'

'No. And she won't answer any of her phones. She won't return e-mails.'

'I'm sorry, Theo.' Buddy shook his head. 'That was a real nice picture, too.'

Theo laughed. The picture was pretty stupid. But it was the best he could do at the time. At least it would get the point across, and he knew that someday Lucy would find the humor in it.

At least he hoped.

'Buddy, let me ask you something.'

'Sure.'

'Have you thought much about how you'll feel if I get back into med school?'

Buddy raised the hem of his shirt and swiped at his sweaty face, not answering right away. 'I'll be OK, Theo. I'm growing up. I want you to be happy. When's your big test?'

'Next Friday.' Theo patted his brother's shoulder and knew they needed to wrap up their morning run. They'd gone through the Miami Springs residential neighborhood this morning instead of the track, because Lucy wasn't joining them.

'I miss her a lot,' Buddy said.

'I miss her, too.'

'You've got to get her back, Theo. She's the nicest lady who's ever loved you.'

Buddy was right again. Lucy was the nicest lady who'd ever loved Theo. In fact, she was the most of everything of any woman Theo had ever met. And if he'd already lost her, he'd never stop kicking his own stupid ass.

'Do you worry that you don't have time to love her? Is that what's making you so dumb about this?'

Buddy's question nearly knocked the wind out of him.

'Is it because of *me*, Theo? Do I take up too much of your time?'

'Oh God, Buddy. No.'

''Cause I won't be living with you forever, you know. I want my own apartment after I graduate, and I want to get a job and maybe even get married one day. I worry that you'll just sit around being lonely.'

Theo nudged his brother to turn left at

Pinecrest so they could head back toward their place on DeLeon. 'I won't be doing much sitting around, Bud. I won't even be doing much sleeping. Not for a lot of years.'

'Yeah, but even busy people get lonely. I worry that you'll be sad, wishing you still had Lucy. So you'd probably better get her back now.'

Theo stopped running, and Buddy came to a halt in front of him. He looked at his amazing brother — someone who was determined to carve out a life for himself without a single guarantee of success — and wondered why he couldn't be just as courageous.

'You look surprised that I have these plans, Theo.'

'Not surprised. Proud.'

Buddy put his hands on his hips and smiled, his eyes squinting through his thick glasses. 'I think Lucy makes you even happier than Jenna. Lucy loves you back. I don't think Jenna did.'

Theo gulped the air and stared at his brother. 'You're right, Bud. You're right about everything.'

Buddy gave Theo a friendly slap on his back, and the two jogged the few blocks back to their house in silence. As they stretched in the driveway, Norton padded across the grass to sit near them, cleaning himself. Occasionally he would glance in their direction.

'I hope you don't mind, but I'm taking Norton with me when I get my own place. But you and Lucy can visit.'

Theo broke out in a huge smile. 'You can count on it, Bud.'

★ ★ ★

'It's been two hours. Give the guy a break, Lucy.'

Veronica slipped in Lucy's office door and stood with her arms crossed over her chest, tapping her toe.

'I don't want to see him.'

'He's such a nice guy.'

'Is there anything else? Or was this just a 'Theo Redmond is still in the building' update?'

'He's been hanging out in the lobby three days now.'

Lucy chewed on the end of her pen, hearing and feeling her stomach rumble. She'd basically been starving herself the last few days, trying to make up for overdoing it the previous week. But she felt exhausted, shaky, and about as cranky as she'd been in ten months. 'What's he doing out there?'

'Studying. He said his test is Friday. He

said he took the whole week off to study.'

Lucy cringed. *And to sit around in the Sherrod & Thoms lobby.* She was ashamed of herself — if Theo didn't do well it would be all her fault. If he didn't reach his dream it would be . . .

His dream! Maybe he was here about the money! Maybe that's all he wanted.

'You can send him in,' Lucy said abruptly.

Veronica let her head swivel around in surprise. 'Huh?'

'Send him in. Let's get this over with.'

Theo popped in a moment later and shut the door behind him. He sat down in one of the chairs in front of Lucy's desk and threw a heavy-looking backpack on the other.

As he glanced around her office, Lucy realized Theo had never before been here. She wondered if he liked the pale yellow walls and the combination of primitive and modern art. Then she reminded herself she didn't care what he liked.

He smiled at her. 'How are you, Luce?'

What kind of a greeting was that? Like she could answer that question truthfully!

'Fine, thanks.'

One of Theo's eyes squinted and his smile grew a bit crooked.

'And how are you, Theo?'

'Tired and nervous about tomorrow. And I

miss you, Cunningham.'

Why did he have to be so direct? So . . . Theo?

'I suppose you want to talk about the money.'

He said nothing and didn't move, and she took that as his way of letting on that he was embarrassed about it, but that's exactly why he was here.

'I've thought it over,' she went on, 'and I think the equitable thing would be to have Ramona pay you for the seventy-two pounds, through last month, and then the rest should go to Tyson.'

Theo still said nothing.

'I know that's not all the money you'd hoped to have for med school, but it's still a lot.'

Theo finally stopped staring at her, and he looked down at his hands, the fingers spread wide over his knees. It was then Lucy noticed he wasn't wearing his usual white Palm Club polo and the blue trainer shorts. He was wearing the white linen slacks he'd worn to the victory dance in Tampa, with a dusky blue cotton button-down. And the way he sat, with his head bent and his strong shoulders sloped, he looked tired. Weighted down.

She remembered how she'd summed him up when they'd first met. She thought he was a pretty-boy jock with an empty head and not a care in the world. She'd been so unfair to him. And completely wrong.

Maybe she was wrong again.

'Theo — '

He cut her off when he raised his head and shot her a look of fierce anger and hurt. That face was too beautiful and kind to carry the force of those emotions. It surprised her.

'I only meant — ' Her phone rang. She could see by the numbers on the display that it was Gia, calling from her cell.

'You wanna go to lunch?'

Lucy held the phone to her ear while she watched Theo begin to seethe.

'Uh, well — '

'Yes? No? What's the story with you, *chica*? You busy or what?'

'Gia, I'm sorry, but I can't today. I'm just kind of — ' Her second line began flashing, and this time it was Mary Fran's cell.

Lucy abruptly ended the call with Gia and answered her sister.

'I've reached the end of my rope. I'm going to talk to an attorney on Friday, and I'm really leaving this time.' Mary Fran said all this without any kind of greeting.

Theo continued to fume. The man had a temper! And he seemed perfectly content just to sit there in the chair and boil over until

Lucy broke down and said something to him.

'My flight gets in at ten thirty Saturday morning. I'm bringing all the kids.'

'Whaa — ?'

'Shoot! Hold on just a second.' Mary Fran put her hand over the mouthpiece and screamed, '*Don't you dare put that in your sister's nose!*' Then she was back. 'I have to go. Ten thirty, don't forget.'

'Mary Fran, this really isn't a good time for me.'

'Dan told me all about it. We'll talk. I promise. Love you.'

Click.

Theo picked up his backpack and held it in his lap. He looked like he was about ready to produce a few choice words to go along with the seething just as Lucy's phone rang again.

Perfect. *Her mother.*

'I'm so sorry, Theo. Just a second.' She picked up the phone. 'Hi, Mom.'

'I hope I am not disturbing you, but Gia just called me to say you're in a funk.'

That was quick.

'I'm worried about you.'

'I'm fine, Mom.'

'That's not what Dan told me. According to him, you haven't been fine for a decade. Why didn't you come to me about this?'

Theo was making moves like he was going

to stand up and leave. She wasn't sure if that was a good thing or a bad thing. She mouthed to him, *I'll just be a minute.*

'Are you listening to me, Lucy?'

'I never really envisioned having this conversation over the phone, Mother.'

'Well, I'd say the phone is better than never at all. Let me get your father on the other extension. Bill!'

Oh, Jesus.

Theo stood up. 'We've managed to really screw this up, haven't we, Lucy?'

'Wait. Just wait a — '

'Hello. This is Bill Cunningham.' Her father was on the line.

'Bill, for God's sake, this is Lucy, not a telemarketer. We are discussing that thing I told you about.'

'Which thing? You tell me about a lot of things in the course of a day, Maggie.'

'Lucy's thing. Her feelings about what happened at Pitt State.'

'Oh, sure. Gotcha.' Lucy's father cleared his throat. 'Now Lucy, you didn't have to pretend with us. You could have told us that it hurt like the devil. You didn't need to protect us.'

Theo tossed the backpack onto his shoulder and turned to go. Lucy stood up behind her desk. '*Wait!*' she whispered.

'No, I think we should talk about this now,' her mother said, her voice getting wobbly. 'You really shouldn't have been worried about anyone but yourself! We could have found help for you right then, before things got so out of control. Maybe you wouldn't have gotten so heavy.'

Lucy rolled her eyes, then saw that Theo thought the eye-rolling was for him. *Not you,* she mouthed.

'Maggie?'

'Yes, Bill?'

'Hang up the phone so I can talk to Lucy alone.'

'Do you really think that's a — '

'Just hang up the damn telephone so I can speak with my daughter.'

Click.

'Hi, pumpkin. How are you doin'?'

Theo's hand was on the doorknob.

'Quite crappy at the moment, Dad.'

'Does this have to do with that trainer of yours? I noticed at the party how you look at him. Lucy, I don't want to see you hurt. Are you sure he's the right kind of man for you?'

Her dad noticed the way she looked at Theo? He noticed *anything*?

'You know, sweetheart, we love you for being you, not because you're getting all gussied up on TV. You don't have to do any of this.'

Theo shook his head, exasperated.

'I know I don't have to, Daddy. But I want to.'

'Then do it, but only if it makes you happy. No more sadness, pumpkin.'

'Thanks, Dad.'

'And your mother's right. You didn't have to try to spare us anything, Lucy. What happened to you back in school was not your fault. You did nothing wrong, well, except for having sex out of wedlock, but I'm not an idiot. I know all my children have done that.'

'I can see you don't have time for this. See ya, Lucy,' Theo opened the door.

'Dad — ?'

'So don't ever hold back from us again. You got something to say — you just come right out and say it. Are we clear on that?'

Lucy heard a rush of air on the line and knew that her mother had picked up. 'I'm sorry, but I just couldn't stand it! Are you all right, Lucy?'

'I'm good, Mom. Dad helped me out a lot.'

There was a pause. 'He did?'

'Yes. And now I have to get back to work.' Theo was out the door. 'Thanks for the call, Mom. And thanks for the chat, Dad. I love you both.'

'We love you,' her mother said.

'Don't be a stranger,' her father said.

She hung up the phone and tried to reach Theo before he got in the elevator, but she was a second too late. So she cupped her mouth in her hands and yelled into the closed doors, 'Good luck on your test tomorrow!'

And Lucy turned around thinking to herself how funny it was that a person can spend an entire decade making a huge unscalable mountain out of something that can be taken care of in a five-minute phone call.

★   ★   ★

It started with a few postings on the TheoandLucy.net message board. In between ongoing commentary on the nearly nude beaded party dress Lucy had worn the previous month and the pros and cons of the low-carb lifestyle — a subject that got so nasty and personal that it required intervention by the site moderator — a few fans began to speculate about what had happened to Theo.

Some claimed the flu to which he'd allegedly succumbed was really something much more serious, such as mad cow disease or meningitis. One fan claimed to have seen

Theo hospitalized. Then another came up with the theory that Lucy and Theo had a terrible argument and had broken up and that Lucy was now engaged to marry Tyson. Yet another speculated that Theo couldn't handle Lucy's celebrity and jealousy had driven him underground.

But when Theo opened the Sunday *Miami Herald* one morning to see their gossip column chock-full of the same drivel, he nearly spit out his coffee. The subject of Theo and Lucy was more than just one item among many — it was the entire column, and it featured three photographs and quotes from, of all people, Lola DiPaolo and Stephan Sherrod.

'They can't stand the sight of each other anymore,' was one of the statements attributed to Lola. And Stephan was quoted as saying, 'As much as I hate to admit this, it looks like Lucy has lost her commitment to this project. It's sad, really. She was starting to come out of her shell.'

Then Theo carefully examined the photos the newspaper had selected and felt the bile start to rise in his throat. He hated that what he and Lucy may or may not be feeling for each other was up for public commentary. He hated that he'd put himself in this situation. He hated the thought of how hurt Lucy would be when she saw this.

The first photo was of Lucy's initial TV weigh-in, and Theo was shocked at her appearance. He'd not forgotten where they'd started, but the sight of Lucy at that size no longer registered in his brain. It didn't even look like her. The second photo showed them running at the high school track back in May. The third photo showed them dancing at the Mandarin, Lucy pressing her cheek against his chest in the seconds before she raised her face to him. Theo was relieved to see the photographer somehow missed the actual kiss when his eyes strayed to the photo caption. It read: *Who's in training now?*

Theo studied that photo, and his skin began to tingle in awareness. Anyone looking at that picture would recognize his bliss. His eyes were closed, his chin rested on her hair, and a goofy smile had spread across his face. His arms held her with a tenderness so sweet it shocked him.

And the way Lucy pressed up against him, her elegant neck turned so that she could snuggle into his shoulder . . .

He and Lucy looked like lovers in that picture. Theo supposed the whole world could see it, just as he did right then. And maybe it was that simple. They were lovers, and it was time to dive headfirst into the concept. *It is what it is,* as Tyson would say.

'What'cha reading, Theo?' Buddy opened the sliding glass doors and joined him at the back porch table.

'The paper.'

'You got the baseball standings?'

'Here you go.' Theo tried to keep his face hidden so Buddy wouldn't see how upset he was.

'What are you upset about?'

Theo laughed. 'Nothing. Just still real tired from the test.'

Buddy nodded and poured himself a bowl of cereal. 'When will you know if they'll let you back in?'

'A few weeks, Bud.' And Theo knew it was going to be the longest few weeks of his life.

★　★　★

Tyson had called her at home the night before and asked her to wear a jog bra and spandex running shorts for their workout in the morning. When Lucy asked if he had something particular planned, he said, 'No. I just want to watch you move in them.'

So Lucy showed up at the Palm Club in her favorite pink sweatpants and a baggy T-shirt, and as she made her way across the gym Tyson shielded his eyes as if from a glaring sun.

'Ouch! You sure know how to torture a man, Lucy.'

She laughed and reached up to rub a hand over his shaved head. 'Sorry, but spandex and me were not on speaking terms this morning.'

'Yeah? How much damage you think you've done in the last couple weeks?'

'I'd say a few pounds and a whole lot of backtracking in the attitude department.'

'You're going to be fine.' Tyson tugged on her ponytail. 'I thought today we'd do some free weights on the stabilizer ball, with some power lunges and squats, and then maybe we'd hit the bags a little. You know, something an engaged couple like us might do.'

Lucy shook her head and tried to laugh, but her heart wasn't in it. It seemed she'd learned a new lesson about celebrity — that anything was fair game. You couldn't put yourself out there for public consumption and then tell the public what they could and could not consume. They simply consumed whatever part of your life they were hungry for at the moment — whether it was what you wore, what you said, how you danced, or your state of mind. It was all theirs for the taking.

This was an experience quite unlike her

last encounter with fame, which was wholly unintentional. The only thing people wanted to know back then was how it felt to be used. Anything else was not interesting.

'Can we do something else for cardio?' she asked Tyson. 'I'm really not in the mood for brutality today, if you don't mind.'

Tyson shot her a wily smile. 'I'm not sure what's left without spandex or brutality, unless we do the six o'clock spinning class. You up for that?'

Ugh. Lucy hated those cycling classes. If she ended up in hell after this life, she was sure the devil would greet her at the door, then escort her to her own personal Reebok stationary bicycle, her pain in the ass for all eternity.

'Fine.'

'Have you spoken to Theo lately?'

Lucy's answer was a groan of frustration. When Theo left her office the week before, he'd looked disgusted with her. She couldn't blame him — she was disgusted with herself. She accused him of only caring about money. She was angry at the world, and overeating and not exercising, and not going to her appointments with Doris.

Who'd want to be in the same room with that kind of bundle of joy?

'Just push me until I'm exhausted today,'

she told Tyson. 'Suffering is a path to Nirvana, right?'

Tyson laughed, punching in a fifteen-minute warm-up on the elliptical trainer. 'Need some tough love today, baby girl?'

'Sure do.'

'You've come to the right man.' Tyson leaned over and planted a cheerful kiss right on Lucy's lips, just as Theo walked into the cardio room.

'You two set a date yet?' he asked drily. Then Theo disappeared into the trainer lounge.

'Dayum,' Tyson whispered, shaking his head. 'I picked a bad time to start kissing you again.'

Lucy stared at the closed door to the lounge and kept pedaling. 'Kissing can be more trouble than it's worth.'

'Hmm, well I gotta go in there and talk to him.' Tyson studied her on the machine for a moment and asked, 'You gonna be OK on your own for a few? You're not going to eat some Danishes or something while I got my back turned, right?'

Under normal circumstances, Lucy would have laughed at that comment. But these weren't normal circumstances, because it seemed that with each new day, things got more twisted up between Theo and herself, and the truth was that without him, she didn't want to face this fifteen-minute warm-up, let alone the next few months. Lucy had come to rely on Theo's calm conviction, his steady presence, and his smile, and now that she no longer had them, she missed them so much it hurt.

She loved Theo *and* she needed him — like she'd never needed anyone in her life. Lucy pedaled and took a deep breath, wondering how she could have let things get so out of hand.

★　★　★

When Tyson entered the room and cleared his throat, Theo could already hear the apology coming. So he stopped his friend before he could start.

'It's cool, Tyson.' He kept his back to him. 'Thanks for being good to Lucy and picking up where I left off with training — just watch her form on the bench press, because she has a tendency to torque her elbows, and don't let her in the same room with a pecan pie.'

Theo heard Tyson collapse into a chair.

'Well, it ain't cool. You two need to talk to each other. That woman loves your sorry white ass, Theo, and for the life of me, I don't know what the holdup is. Why can't you tell her you love her, too? Because it's plain to everyone that you do.'

Theo turned around and studied all six-feet-five of Tyson Williams, sprawled out on one of the small metal chairs. He was wearing a half smile, clasping his hands behind his bald head. 'It's all your fault,' Theo told him.

Tyson gave his head an exaggerated shake, then focused in on Theo. 'What the *hell* did I do now?'

'That night at the Mandarin you said she deserved to be savored. Spoiled! *Enjoyed!*'

'All right. I said that. So what?'

'I was on my way over to tell her I loved her — and you fucked with my head!'

Tyson sat up in the chair and leaned forward, elbows to knees. 'How you figure that, Redmond?'

'After you said all that, I figured I don't have the time to do any of those things now, let alone when I get back into school and then into my residency.' Theo smacked a pile of mail onto the conference table. 'I wondered how I was going to savor Lucy on two hours of sleep a night. How I was going to spoil her if I hardly ever saw her. How I would find a way to enjoy her when my life is going to be reduced to studying, working, wolfing down hospital cafeteria food, and fantasizing about what it's like to sleep in my own bed.'

Tyson shifted uncomfortably.

'I've seen what medical school and residency do to relationships, Tyson, and it sucks. I don't know if it's fair to ask Lucy to start something right when my life's about to get even more fucked up than it is.'

'I know you want to be a doctor.'

'I do. It's what I'm supposed to do with my life. Simple as that.'

Tyson studied his hands and said softly, 'Is this about Jenna?'

'*What?*' All the jagged energy rushing through Theo's body slammed to a halt at the sound of her name. 'Jenna has nothing to do with Lucy.'

Tyson looked up and smiled. 'C'mon, man. I was with you through the Jenna shit, remember? She betrayed your ass, and I saw how you took it.' Tyson got up from the chair and moved closer to Theo, then sat on the edge of the table. 'You swore you'd never let a woman in as far as you'd let Jenna, remember? You told me you'd never let a female become that important to you again.'

Theo let out a startled laugh.

'And listen, Theo, I think losing your parents and Jenna like that made you kind of crawl up inside yourself and hide behind all your surface business. I remember you said — '

'What are you, my therapist?' Theo laughed in earnest now.

'I'm your friend, Theo. I'm making sure you're not walking around thinking that Lucy is another Jenna.'

Theo stopped laughing. 'Lucy isn't Jenna.'

'See? I'm damn good at this.' Tyson smiled.

'I just don't want to hurt her.'

'And you don't want to leave yourself open to being hurt.' Tyson shrugged. 'It makes perfect sense. All I'm saying is you can't blame this mess you're making with Lucy on your med school shit alone.'

Theo collapsed into a chair and rubbed his forehead, because Tyson's words were making more sense than he cared to admit.

'Have you talked with her about this? Have you really told her about how Jenna fucked you up? How it felt to lose your parents? How scared you are about going back to school?'

Theo raised his head and blinked at Tyson. 'Maybe not everything.'

'Then do it, Redmond. I think Lucy is the kind of woman who can handle most anything if it's given to her straight.'

Theo walked over to the large tinted window of the trainer room and watched

Lucy bounce up and down on the elliptical trainer in her pink sweatpants, ponytail swirling.

Lucy is not Jenna. Theo smiled to himself, sensing Tyson coming up behind him.

'Lucy's cool.'

'She is.'

'If you really love her — even if you're in med school or law school or in training to be the king of the fucking world — you gotta be straight with her and give her whatever you can.'

'Even if it's an hour a day?'

'Hey, if *you* know and *she* knows that you got one hour a day for her, then that's what you give her. But you give her your full attention for that one hour. You see what I'm saying, Theo? You make the most of that hour. Then you give her another hour the next day.'

Theo turned his head and smiled at Tyson. 'You're on a roll, aren't you?'

'And if you ever find yourself with a whole day, you give her that whole day. And you tell her that you can't wait for the next whole day you get to spend with her.'

That's when Theo began to laugh. He laughed loud, and Tyson joined in. Then Tyson said, 'What's so damn funny?'

'You. You're funny. Since when did you get

to be an expert on how the female species thinks?'

Tyson smiled so big he obviously enjoyed having the opportunity to answer that question. 'We all have our fields of expertise, Theo. Your life's work is going to be medicine. My life's work is women.'

Theo studied Lucy again, now trudging along in earnest, the pink sweatpants a blur. 'I think I'll just concentrate on this one woman.'

'She's a good one.'

'But those sweatpants have got to go.'

'No shit.'

The two of them watched Lucy without comment for a moment, and then Tyson asked, 'So what's your plan?'

Theo smiled at him. 'I'm going to get her back.'

Tyson nodded, then raised his eyebrows hopefully. 'If you fuck up, feel free to delegate my way again.'

Theo laughed and smacked Tyson on the shoulder. 'Not going to happen.'

★ ★ ★

Office of Doris Lehman, MSW, PhD
'It concerns me that you missed several appointments and didn't return my calls.

311

What's going on, Lucy?'

'Well, let's see.' Lucy got comfortable in the peach damask and refused — absolutely refused — to look at the annoying geisha girls. They'd have to wait for the next patient to harass, because she wasn't giving them the satisfaction today.

'I've been following a very hectic schedule, Dr Lehman, doing things like telling Theo I love him and getting rejected, eating, working, worrying, crying, eating, obsessing about Theo rejecting me, eating, trying to figure out my whacked-out boss, eating, thinking about Theo, lounging around, taking phone calls from crazed family members, eating. Other than that, not much.'

Doris finished taking notes, and Lucy would have given anything to see what she'd just written. She guessed it would be along the lines of, *Patient sarcastic; in relapse with food; rejection issues have surfaced.*

'What happened with Theo?'

'Banner City, I'm afraid.'

Doris cleared her throat. 'I have a very hard time believing he unrolled a bedsheet painted with derogatory statements about you. Where did you choose to tell him how you felt? What were the circumstances?'

'The party three weeks ago.'

'Ah, yes. I saw photos in the *Herald*.'

312

'I made an error in judgment — I really expected him to tell me he loved me, too. Isn't that rich? Instead, he said something about his life not being what I needed or deserved — some crap like that.'

Doris recrossed her legs and blinked at Lucy a few times. 'That might have been a sincere response. Maybe he fears he's not good enough for you.'

Lucy's mouth hung open.

'I'm merely suggesting that Theo might believe you'd find something about him or his lifestyle unacceptable.'

Lucy shut her mouth and took a deep breath. 'Uh-huh. Like the fact that he's smart, witty, gorgeous, and fun to be with? You mean those annoying traits?'

'Perhaps he's concerned about how you would handle him being in medical school. Did that cross your mind?'

Lucy frowned. 'You mean he's worried he won't have enough time for me?'

'Exactly, Lucy. Maybe it wasn't a rejection at all but his attempt, albeit an awkward one, to tell you he wasn't sure he could give you everything you need.'

'But all I need is him.'

Doris smiled. She put her clipboard down on the floor near her feet and leaned in, lacing her fingers together as she, Lucy hoped, came up with a plan to fix everything. It was times like these that Lucy didn't mind the copays.

Doris shook her head and laughed. 'I'd love to lock the two of you in a room for a few days without diets or scales and certainly with no family or TV cameras. Just the two of you, free to be yourselves. I wonder what would come to the surface?'

Then Doris made a preposterous suggestion.

'Have you considered inviting Theo to go with you to Jamaica when this is all over?'

Lucy swallowed hard. Alone with Theo? In paradise? With nothing to do but enjoy each other's company?

'I've already asked Fran. She can't wait to go.'

Doris nodded. 'I think she'd understand if you made other arrangements.'

★ ★ ★

'What really happened between the two of you?' Carolina Buendia flapped her eyelashes and glanced at the camera, as if to warn viewers that now was not the time to go for a coffee refill.

'Oh, crap,' Theo said. He leaned back in his kitchen chair and clasped his hands behind his head, sprawling his legs out in front of him.

'We've all seen the newspaper and the Web site — everyone is talking about it,' Carolina continued. 'Was there a relationship between the two of you outside the gym that went sour?'

The look on Lucy's face made Theo queasy. He wasn't sure if she was going to break into tears, laugh, or rip poor Carolina to shreds with her sharp tongue. As Theo watched Lucy's eyes go wider and wider still, he contemplated rushing downtown and busting through the studio doors to save her.

'That's quite flattering,' Lucy eventually said. She looked at Carolina without flinching. 'The truth is that Theo and I have a wonderful working relationship, but nothing more.'

Groans of disappointment rose from the audience. Theo sat up straight in the chair.

'Then why has he suddenly disappeared? Why is Tyson here?' John Weaver asked. 'Not that we don't love you, Tyson.'

Theo's friend shrugged and laughed nervously.

'This is really Theo's business and not my story to tell, but I will say this . . . ' Lucy looked right into the camera and smiled. 'Theo has a lot going on in his life. He's hoping to return to medical school, and he recently took the entrance exam. He studied for months and months.'

'Oh, crap,' Theo said again. It's not that he was hiding it, but he wasn't exactly advertising it, either. What if he didn't get accepted? Now the whole Miami-Dade TV market could share in his humiliation!

'Whatcha watching, Theo?' Buddy shuffled into the kitchen in his briefs and a white T-shirt, his glasses askew. Mornings had been far more leisurely since the predawn workouts with Lucy had come to an end.

'Never mind. I see.' Buddy plopped into a chair. 'Her hair looks pretty today. Her earrings are nice.'

Theo returned his gaze to the television and tried not to listen to the ongoing discussion of his personal life. Buddy was right — Lucy's hair looked pretty. The way it seemed to swing right along her shoulders made Theo think she might have gotten it trimmed. And the dangly earrings were new. She was wearing a cute skirt and a top he'd never seen before. Same with the sandals. All of a sudden, it really bothered him that he'd missed out on so many of the details of Lucy's life.

Once Carolina and John seemed placated as to why Theo had been a no-show, it was

316

time for Lucy's weighing and measuring. She walked toward the scale tentatively. She was frowning and her head was bowed. Tyson whispered something in her ear that earned a sweet little smile, but Theo could tell she was thoroughly panicked.

Tyson tapped the scale and stopped. Then he began tapping the other way — not the way anyone wanted it to go. The studio audience gasped and went silent.

Theo wished he were there with her. He should be right there with her! Because Lucy's lips were starting to tremble and her cheeks got splotchy and Tyson said softly, 'Looks like we've had a setback this month — a gain of six pounds.'

Lucy took a deep breath. Then, right there on live television, she mumbled, '*Fuck this!*'

She stormed off the set, leaving Tyson and the *WakeUp Miami* hosts speechless. Someone in the control room made an executive decision to cut to a commercial.

'I don't think girls are supposed to use those words on TV,' Buddy noted, pouring himself a glass of orange juice.

10

September

By eight that evening, Mary Fran was once again crying in the bedroom, having made Lucy swear she would not leave the apartment for any reason, not for a second.

Yes, this was a fitting end to one shitty day, and as Lucy rummaged through her pitifully stocked kitchen cabinets, she wanted to crawl in behind the brown rice and garbanzo beans and hide.

This day alone, she'd turned down fourteen requests for print or broadcast interviews, including two from major national magazines. Her weight gain was the subject of newspaper columns, radio call-ins, conversations at bus stops. She knew it would be just hours or minutes before some halfway-bright reporter somewhere put two and two together and figured out she was the Lucy Cunningham of Pitt State Slump Buster fame.

Plus, her boss had gone missing. Not that this was a tragedy, but it was inconvenient, because Friday was payday.

And she hadn't had anything to eat since

her breakfast of yogurt and a banana.

All these things conspired to make Lucy cranky and fidgety, and she moved to the refrigerator, where she stood in front of the open door, tapping her foot.

She gave up. There was only one thing she truly wanted, one thing that could save her. It was hot and filling, and in all the time she'd been in Miami, it had never failed to relax her, soothe her.

She would call Luigi. A twelve incher would be just right tonight.

But as Lucy picked up the phone she had to laugh at herself — she couldn't remember the number for Luigi's Pizza! It had once been No. 1 on her speed dial, but she'd deleted the number last November, and at the time it felt like getting closure on a soured relationship. And now, nine months later, she was crawling back to him and even had to stoop so low as to look up his number in the book.

Her fingers trembled but managed to hit all the right buttons on the keypad. Luigi answered. Lucy froze.

'Hello? Anybody there?'

Lucy eventually spit out her order — a large stuffed crust sausage with extra cheese — and it sounded like the lyrics to a bittersweet love song from her past.

'Lucy? Is that you?'

Good God! She couldn't even order a pizza with impunity. 'Hey, Luigi, how have you been?'

'Great, great, but you shouldn't be eating pizza no more, Lucy, especially with the weight gain. I hate to turn down a sale, but you're lookin' too good to eat my pie.'

Though Lucy stood at her kitchen counter, she knew she was really standing at a crossroads. She could agree with Luigi, open a can of garbanzo beans, and feel good about herself, or she could lie.

'It's for my sister,' she said.

'She likes the sausage and extra cheese just like you, eh?' Luigi didn't even try to hide his amusement.

'Yes, she does.'

'You need anything to drink with that?'

'Do you still carry ice cream?'

It was Luigi's turn for silence. After a couple of seconds he asked, 'Your sister like butter brickle same as you?'

'Yes. As a matter of fact, she can't get enough of the stuff.'

'It comes to eighteen ninety-five. Twenty minutes. And you're breakin' my heart, Lucy.' He hung up.

It was done.

Lucy poked her head into the bedroom to

check on Mary Fran, who was now sleeping, thank God. The twins and Holden were with Mom and Dad for the night. This time, it seemed Mary Fran had finally followed through on her threat to leave Keith for good. She and Lucy had talked most of the evening, and as far as Lucy could see, the problem with Fran and Keith was a continuing failure to communicate.

Mary Fran said they'd tried counseling, but after Keith missed one appointment because of a last-minute business trip, they never got back on track. Mary Fran said she'd hired a nanny for two half days a week to give her some alone time but found it only made her lonelier. So two days ago, when Keith called to say he'd be another week in Houston, she hit the wall. Mary Fran left him. And she ran to Miami, the city where she'd come so many times to sleep or dance away her heartache.

Lucy left the bedroom and shook her head, realizing this was a far cry from the wild single-girl lifestyle Mary Fran had once pined for. She flopped down on the couch and surfed aimlessly through the channels, allowing her mind to rehash all the latest weirdness in her life.

Stephan had been missing for four days now — just gone. Though he sometimes left town for weeks on end, he always gave them a heads-up. But this time, nothing. No one could track him down, and Lucy had the misfortune of pulling the short straw to call his ex-wife. Upon hearing Stephan was nowhere to be found, she'd laughed. Everyone at the office agreed that if he didn't show up tomorrow, they'd have to bring in the authorities.

Also that day, Tyson called to inform her that Lola DiPaolo had been canned. Apparently, Ramona had warned Lola to keep her mouth shut after she made those mean-spirited comments to the *Herald*, but just that morning she'd phoned into a morning radio show to repeat the same drivel — that Lucy was no longer even trying. Ramona canned Lola the minute she showed up for work. Good riddance to her.

Lucy clicked away at the remote control, eventually stumbling onto an *Andy Griffith Show* marathon. The pizza came, and she whispered her thanks to the delivery boy so Mary Fran wouldn't hear. Lucy put away the ice cream and returned to the couch, the box balanced on her knees. She studied the red, green, and white map of Italy and the cute little illustration of the pizza guy holding out a steaming pie pan. She opened the lid and feasted her eyes on the sight

— twelve inches of crisp white heaven topped with spicy sausage and a homemade tomato sauce, smothered in a velvet veil of melted mozzarella. It had been far too long.

Lucy managed to eat the entire pizza while watching Sheriff Andy Taylor orchestrate the budding romance between Goober and Flora, the new diner waitress. During the episode where Opie befriends a hobo, Lucy ate the pint of butter brickle. And while Opie searched for his lost baseball in the haunted Rimshaw house, Lucy lay on her side moaning.

'Lucy? Are you out there?' Mary Fran's voice sounded stuffy, like she'd been crying again.

Lucy managed to get up off the couch and fought back dizziness as she raced to the bedroom door, noting the empty pizza box on the counter as she went. She'd have to find a way to get rid of that.

'I'm here, Frannie. You want a cup of tea?'

'No. Nothing. I just wanted to make sure you're still here. Please don't leave the apartment.'

'No problem.'

'Do I smell pizza?'

It seemed more untruths would be required, and Lucy had to wonder if pizza was worth repeatedly lying to family members and small businessmen. 'I nuked a Weight Watchers pasta bowl. Want one?' She winced when she heard herself say it.

'No thanks. I'm going back to sleep.'

Lucy turned to shut the door, but Mary Fran's soft voice stopped her. 'Wait, Luce.'

'Sure.' Lucy leaned against the doorjamb and cradled her stomach.

'Thank you for everything.'

'No problem.'

'Can I talk to you for a minute? I . . . I want to apologize for something.'

Lucy straightened up. 'For what?' She moved to turn on the lamp, but Mary Fran asked her not to. 'This will be easier for me to talk about in the dark,' she whispered.

'All right.' Lucy waited. In the indirect light from the kitchen, she watched Frannie push herself up to sit cross-legged on the bed.

'First, I want to apologize for not being a very good sister to you lately, or ever, really. I've been so focused on my own problems that I haven't been there for you when you needed me.' Mary Fran studied her hands, her voice choked with sadness. 'I know things aren't great with you and Theo, and I haven't helped you at all. I'm just making things worse by showing up here and crying. I am sorry.'

Lucy was dumbstruck. In all her life, Mary Fran had never been this frank. Lucy cleared her throat. 'It's all right.'

'No, wait — it gets worse.' Mary Fran blew her nose in a tissue and hung her head. 'I need to admit something awful to you. It's really been weighing on my mind lately and I need to just tell you.'

'OK.' This sounded ominous.

'I've always been jealous of you, Lucy. There's this mean and nasty part of me that was always glad you were heavy, because being thin was the one thing I had that you didn't. I am ashamed to tell you this.'

'*Whoa.*' Lucy's knees gave out and she landed on the edge of the bed.

Fran looked up at her, and Lucy could see more tears welling in her eyes. 'I think I've been feeling a little threatened by your weight loss success. I don't know what's wrong with me. I'm sure you hate me now.'

Lucy sighed. It seemed they were doing some house-cleaning tonight, so she'd better do her share. 'I've always been jealous of you, too.'

Mary Fran frowned. 'Because I was thin?'

'Well, yeah. Thin and pretty and popular. Everyone always compared me to you. 'The Cunningham girls — the pretty one and the fat one.''

Mary Fran laughed. 'I always thought it was 'the Cunningham girls — the brilliant one and the ditzy one.''

They laughed, and Mary Fran reached out for Lucy and they threw their arms around each other. Lucy held Mary Fran's little body tight to her as they rocked back and forth. Eventually Lucy pulled back and stroked her sister's short hair. 'We're both ditzes, Frannie.'

'You don't hate me?' The sincerity in her sister's expression touched her.

'How could I hate you? Do you hate me?'

'God, no.' Mary Fran fell forward on the bed and stretched out. 'I don't know what I would've done if I didn't have you to come to these past months.' She turned to look at Lucy. 'It's really scary, discovering I may have made a mistake when I married Keith. I've got so many decisions ahead of me.' She smiled sadly. 'But I'm going to figure out my life. I promise.'

'I know you will. You're strong. And I'll always be right here for you.'

'You're strong, too, Lucy.' Mary Fran rubbed her eyes and rested her cheek on the pillow. 'And I'm so proud of you. So proud of everything — '

In seconds, her breathing was deep and slow and Lucy leaned over and kissed her cheek. 'I'm going to figure out my life, too,' she whispered.

Lucy closed the bedroom door behind her, and her eyes immediately went to the pizza box on the counter-top. It dawned on her that if she and Frannie had gotten around to that conversation an hour earlier, the pizza wouldn't have been so appealing. As usual, expressing her feelings felt more satisfying than stuffing them down with food.

With a sigh, Lucy pulled out the plastic kitchen garbage pail and shoved the pizza box and ice-cream carton inside. But wait. What if Mary Fran opened the lid to the trash can? She'd be found out. And going to the garbage chute was out of the question, since she'd promised Mary Fran she'd stay in the apartment. So how would she get rid of the evidence?

Lucy picked up the garbage bag, the colors of Italy plainly visible under the thin plastic. She got a pair of scissors from the drawer. She cut the box in half, then fourths, then eighths, and kept going until she had a nice stack of little tomato-stained cardboard squares. She shoved them inside the ice-cream carton, replaced its lid, and shoved the pint back in the trash bag. Then she returned to the couch.

A few minutes later, Lucy realized that

wouldn't work, either. What if Mary Fran saw the ice-cream container? Was ice cream any less damning than pizza? What if the lid fell off the ice-cream container and Mary Fran saw all those little cardboard cutouts? She'd think Lucy was off her nut!

Lucy ran back into the kitchen, where she stood in the center of the room and plotted how to remove all evidence of her binge. Surely this was how ax murderers felt in the aftermath of their crime. Her gaze drifted to the sink, and inspiration hit her.

By the end of the episode where Barney Fife gets his first new car, the sink of hot tap water had done its job. One quick stir with a wooden spoon and Lucy was satisfied the cardboard had disintegrated into an unidentifiable blob of gray pulp. She had begun to scoop the amalgam into a fresh trash bag when the doorbell rang.

'*Where is she?*' Keith stood in the harsh hallway light, his tie askew and his hair wild. 'Mom said she's here.'

Lucy crossed her arms over her chest and blocked the door. 'She's sleeping.'

'I have to see her.'

Lucy was suddenly afraid something bad had happened. 'Is everything all right? The kids — '

Keith barged right past her. 'The kids are

fine. But I'm not. I get out of a meeting this afternoon and I get a voice mail that my wife is leaving me. I get dumped via voice mail.'

Keith spun around, obviously looking for the door to Lucy's bedroom. 'Where is she?'

Lucy pointed, watching her handsome Brooks Brothers brother-in-law jog through her tiny kitchen. He suddenly stopped, staring at the mess in the sink, dripping down the cabinets into the trash bag.

'What the hell is *that*?'

Lucy grimaced, forcing her mind to spring from its pizza-induced stupor. 'Uh. Papier-mâché?'

Keith looked her up and down. 'You look great, Luce. Whatever it takes.'

Lucy spent the next few moments desperately trying not to eavesdrop on the conversation taking place in her bedroom. She turned up the volume on the episode where Aunt Bea makes the metric ton of pickles, its plot line meshing with Fran and Keith discussing work, sex, economizing, family dinners, Holden and the twins, and whether they should downsize and sell the manse in Buckhead so that Keith could get a less demanding job.

Lucy even heard Fran say something about going back to work part-time.

Moments later, Fran and Keith exited from the bedroom holding hands. Keith looked in shock but calmer, and Frannie looked happier than Lucy had seen her in months. Her smile was so wide it pushed up the pink apple of her cheeks. In his free hand Keith held Fran's overnight bag.

'We're checking into the Four Seasons tonight. I'll call Mom and let her know.' Fran walked to the couch and kissed Lucy good-bye. 'Thank you, sweetie. We'll talk more tomorrow.'

Lucy watched them wait for the elevator. She sighed with vicarious bliss when Keith cupped Fran's head in his hands and kissed her mouth hard. Lucy closed the door and gave them privacy.

She'd just finished scraping the sink clean when there was another pounding at the door. She figured Fran had forgotten something.

But it was Theo.

★ ★ ★

He knew the timing wasn't perfect, but when would it ever be? Lucy had been expertly avoiding him at the gym and cleverly returned his calls when he was with clients, so it appeared she was making a good-faith effort to communicate, only he knew she wasn't.

Theo hoped to God he wasn't waking her up — it was after ten. And he really hoped he wasn't walking in on some kind of date. He didn't think he could handle that. All he knew was he had to see her, try to break through this impasse and make sure she was OK.

Because he had a feeling she wasn't OK at all.

Theo put the gift behind his back just as Lucy opened the door. The expression on her face nearly made him laugh — she looked like a kid who'd been caught doing something *reeeeally* bad.

One quick scan revealed that she was wearing his favorite ensemble — the pink sweatpants and a baggy T-shirt.

'Hey, Luce. I hope I'm not disturbing you.'

She said nothing, but her eyes got wider.

'Can I come in?'

'Of course. Sure. Sorry.' She opened the door for him and Theo looked around, smiling at how it always looked like such a girl's place from top to bottom — green plants and nice furniture, a spotless kitchen with place mats and a centerpiece on the dinette table. Then he smelled tomato sauce.

'Italian for dinner tonight?'

Lucy's eyes got huge. 'Can I get you

something to drink, Theo? What brings you downtown?'

That look in her eyes told him he was right about the Italian — maybe takeout lasagna or pizza — and he asked for some iced tea if she had it. She said she did and motioned for Theo to have a seat in an overstuffed chair.

'How've you been?' she asked from the kitchen. 'How'd the test go? When do you find out?'

Theo stared at the back of her head — that ponytail — and the sweet, strong ledge of her shoulders, the graceful neck. He'd missed her so much that he found it hard to breathe.

'The test was eight hours long, in two four-hour sessions — anatomy and physiology, histology, pathology. I'd forgotten how it felt to think so hard my brain got sore.' She handed him a glass of iced tea and he drank gratefully.

'That's a lot of ologies in one day.'

'Yeah, I think that was the point — they wanted to remind me what I was in for.'

Lucy snuggled up on the end of the couch and tucked her feet under her. He saw a flash of pink toenails before they disappeared under pink sweatpants. He smiled at her.

'When will you know, Theo?'

'Soon.'

'You'll get back in. They'd be stupid not to let you back in.'

Theo shrugged. 'Even giving me this test was an exception to the rule. I have no idea what they'll decide.'

Lucy rested her chin in her hand and smiled at him. 'So what's up?'

'I've missed you, Luce. I saw you on *WakeUp Miami* last week.'

She nodded. 'Ah. Not my best work.'

'You need to get back in the gym with me.'

Lucy's eyebrows knit together and she sat up, then tucked her arms around her waist, as if protecting herself. 'I am sorry about that crack I made about the money. I know that's not the only thing that's important to you.'

Theo laughed. He'd had a fairly amusing conversation with Tyson just the other day about how, if Lucy's proposed formula was applied, Tyson now owed him six thousand dollars for the weight she'd gained under his tutelage. 'Thanks,' he said. 'So you'll work with me again?'

Lucy sighed and grabbed herself tighter. It almost looked like she was fighting off a stomachache.

'I think I have to. Tyson is great, but it's not the same. I need to get back in the rhythm I had with you, or I'm going to blow this completely.'

Theo set the iced tea on a glass end table and reached behind him. 'I brought you something. Buddy and I thought it was just what you needed.' Theo handed her the tissue-wrapped square. 'A little something to keep you focused.'

'Peanut brittle?'

'Better.'

Lucy pulled away the paper and Theo watched as she held the Special Olympics creed in her hands, reading, saying nothing. He saw a tear plop onto the shiny brass surface of the plaque.

'It was supposed to inspire you, Luce, not make you sad.'

She looked up at him and grinned. 'Thank you, and please tell Buddy I said thank you.'

'Will do. It was his idea. He misses you almost as much as I do. Even Norton seems out-of-sorts.'

Lucy laughed. 'And you, Theo? How are you?'

Theo just loved this. The cadence of this whole conversation with Lucy felt so damn good it amazed him. Being with her felt like home, like peace, like where he was meant to be. 'I'm nothing without you, Luce.'

'Clearly just a shell of a man.'

'I'm even having trouble with my hair gel.'

Lucy placed the plaque on the coffee table

and curled back up in a ball, chuckling. Theo reached his hand toward her. Tentatively, she took it.

Lucy shook her head slowly, her ponytail gently swooshing over her shoulder. 'I've really dropped the ball these last few weeks, Theo. All our hard work — '

'We'll just start from here. It's just a place to start.'

Lucy's beautiful face twisted with disappointment. 'With my gain last month, I've got thirty-four pounds to go in twelve weeks. We're probably not going to make our goal.'

'Hey, sweetie . . . ' Theo moved to the edge of his chair and leaned closer, cradling her hand in both of his now. 'If you don't lose another pound from now until December, you still would have made it.'

She nodded, giving him a brave smile.

'That goal was just a gimmick, Luce. An even number that sounded good. You don't have to go there if you don't want. You are healthy and fit and beautiful right now. You're ready to take on the world.'

Lucy nodded. 'I rock.'

'You do.' Theo wanted to put his arms around her and smell her hair and feel her warm skin against his. He wanted to love her, soothe her, make her laugh. He wanted to kiss her.

'The important thing is we make the most of the time we've got.'

Lucy laughed softly. 'Is this Theo-the-Trainer or Theo-the-Philosopher talking?'

He grinned. 'Both, Luce.'

'I'm in.'

He was up out of the chair and on the couch before he realized he was moving.

'Theo — '

'Look, I've got to tell you something. Will you hear me out?'

Lucy giggled. 'I think I should charge a per-confession fee this evening.'

'A what?'

'Nothing.' She smiled at him. 'I'm all ears, Theo.'

'No, you're not.' Theo's gaze strayed to Lucy's pretty forearms, wrists, and hands, then to the hollow at the base of her slim throat, to her shoulders, breasts, thighs, hips . . .

'Does your confession have to do with lust?'

'No.' Theo looked up quickly. 'I mean yes! I mean — ' Theo brought his arm up over the back of the sofa and stroked her shoulder. 'That night at the Mandarin — '

'Theo, look. I'm aware my feelings for you don't come at a great time, and I also know women have this annoying habit of falling for you — '

'Are you done yet?' Theo brushed his fingertip down the curve of that beautiful, sweet face.

Lucy swallowed and nodded.

'I don't care about any other woman. Just you. Only you.'

Lucy's lips parted and her eyes became huge. 'What exactly are you saying?'

'The night of the party wasn't *my* best work, Lucy. I blew it. I wanted to tell you I loved you, but I was so screwed up in my head that I couldn't. It was a disaster and I apologize.'

Theo drew his thumb along her bottom lip and watched her turn in to his touch. 'I saw you standing there in the ballroom and the force of your beauty and strength just about knocked me over. It was like everything had come to the surface for both of us, right at that instant, and I was in awe of you, so crazy about you, and so afraid.'

'I scared you? I hadn't even had my first margarita at that point.'

'I'm walking toward you, ready to strip bare my soul to you, and Tyson picks that moment to tell me that you deserve to be savored, enjoyed, and spoiled. Do you know he goes around talking about you like that?'

Lucy beamed. 'That's really nice of him.'

'He was right, you know. And all I could

think was that I wouldn't have time to spoil and enjoy you and if that's what you deserved, you'd be better off with someone who could.'

Lucy shook her head. 'That's why you acted so weird all night?'

'I didn't want to let you in and then lose you. I'm sick of losing people, you know? When my parents died, the only thing that kept me going was how angry I was, and how much Buddy needed me. When Jenna left me last year, it was the same shit all over again.'

'Oh, Theo — '

'I thought I could keep my heart safe if I crammed my life so full that there was no room for anyone new to squeeze in. But you squeezed in anyway.' Theo smiled. 'You found a crack and you pushed through. Does this make any sense to you?'

She nodded softly. 'It does.'

'I never meant to play games with you, Lucy. But when I'm with you, I seem to lose my head. Plus I have a hard time keeping my hands to myself.'

At that, her head popped up and her eyes widened further.

Theo stroked her cheek again and put his mouth to her ear, whispering, 'I want to feel you and bury my nose in you and kiss you all over. You draw me in, make me weak.'

Lucy looked to her left and then to her right and said, 'You talkin' to me?'

'Yes, you,' he said, laughing. 'And ever since you started ignoring me, I haven't been able to remember the reasons why I shouldn't be with you, just the reasons why I should.'

'What reasons are those?'

Theo got to his knees in front of the sofa. He smoothed her forehead and ran his fingers through her hair. 'That you're everything I've ever wanted. I need you in my life.'

Her reaction wasn't what he expected. Lucy winced and leaned over, clutching her sides. 'Are you all right?'

She peered up from her crouch and nodded.

'Was it something you ate?'

'You might say that.'

Theo opened his arms, and Lucy fell in to him, pressing against his chest and sighing in contentment. He sighed, too. She was back where she belonged, in his arms and in his life.

Theo put his lips on her hair and held her tight. 'Now that you know how I feel, I want you to take off your clothes and make me glad I'm a man.'

She giggled and brought her lips to his throat, flicking her tongue across his skin. 'You're so suave, Theo. No wonder the

339

women throw themselves at you.'

'So it worked?'

Lucy laughed. 'Will this disrobing be for professional assessment purposes only?'

Theo reveled in the feel of her warm and soft kisses on his throat and face. He closed his eyes and wallowed in the scent of Lucy. 'This is all horribly unprofessional.'

'Good. Then kiss me.'

He obliged, grabbing her with one arm and pulling himself up to the couch, falling over her, pressing his body down into her, cradling her head as he kissed and nibbled and probed and generally lapped her up.

'You taste so good, Luce. You feel so damn good to me — ' Theo's hands moved along her back and onto her hip and up into the front of that T-shirt, and all he could think about was getting his palm on a breast — one of those round, warm female breasts that he'd missed desperately.

Lucy had her hands inside his shirt as well, up underneath the cotton, her fingers splayed over his chest, her mouth meeting his and giving back every bit of what she received. Lucy was hot and sweet and Theo knew he had waited far too long and made far too much of a very simple reality — this woman was what he wanted. He loved her.

'Let me love you, Lucy.'

'I thought you'd never ask.' She pushed up to a sitting position, then threw herself at him and knocked him back into the couch cushions, covering him with her heat and her smell and the silky sweet kisses and sexy little moans he didn't think he'd ever be able to live without.

He yanked on her T-shirt and pulled it over her head. He grabbed the waistband of those revolting pink sweatpants and pushed down until they cleared the mounds of her butt, which he then grabbed onto with both hands.

'Let me feel you. Let me look at you. God, yes, I need you so much, Luce.'

Lucy popped up and sat on his thighs. She smiled down at him as she reached around and unhooked her bra, shrugged out of it, and tossed it to the floor. Then she reached up and dragged the ponytail holder out of her hair.

And there she was, naked from the hips up, all pink and soft and sexy, and those eyes were sparkling and daring him and Theo wanted this woman so much he thought he'd bust.

He brought his hands up and cradled her breasts, watching with fascination how the large dark pink nipples puckered and elongated from the gentle touch. He stroked his fingers across the pale freckles on her chest, then across the beat of her blood as it pulsed through her carotid artery, thinking such a profoundly simple thought — that a human body could be exercised and molded and trained, but it was the spirit inside that made a person who she was.

And he'd always loved the person inside this body.

Theo rose up and brought his mouth to her left breast and suckled on her, felt her move back and forth on his thighs, heard her moans grow deeper and louder.

'Do you think we could possibly ditch these butt-ugly pink sweatpants, Luce?'

She nodded enthusiastically and rose on her knees and shimmied the pants down, then reached behind her and pulled them off her calves and feet, tossing them to the floor.

Lucy was now just wearing a pair of lacy underwear, not a thong but not granny panties, either, and Theo could see her like never before. Her hips were smooth and curvy and her belly — the one they'd worked on for ten months — was soft and rounded and vulnerable, and he stroked her there, spread his hands over her, and she rolled her head back and groaned. She was simply beautiful.

He let his hands travel downward, and he cupped her mound through her panties. Her head flew upright.

'Wait,' she gasped.

'For how long? And why?'

Lucy grabbed his wrist and held his hand still. She looked down at him. 'I'll be right back.'

'Oh jeez, Luce. Not this again.'

She was already off him, and he watched her as she ran into her bedroom. Before she could change her mind, he ran in there after her, catching her just as she slipped a slinky little camisole over her top. He came up behind her and nuzzled the back of her neck, all while he slipped off her panties.

'I want all of you.'

'You can have all of me. I'm just not ready for you to see it all, not all at once.'

'I adore you. I want to see every inch of you.'

'Someday soon. I promise.'

'Maybe that could be *my* reward at the end of all this, Lucy,' he joked. 'We reach our goal and you get Jamaica and I get your totally naked body to look at as I please.'

She turned in his arms, a thoughtful look on her face. 'Maybe we really should use this as our motivator. No sex until we've reached our goal. I would be positively *driven* to succeed.'

She placed her hand on his shorts and

slipped the belt free, unzipped the zipper, and reached inside his boxers. 'Think about it,' she whispered, stroking him until dark splotches danced in his vision. 'You're the expert on motivation, aren't you? Didn't you say I needed a reward that was decadent, luxurious, something waiting for me that I wanted more than anything?'

'Forget it.'

'It's just twelve weeks.'

'No way.' Theo slammed his lips down on hers, stroked the bare flesh of her bottom and her thighs, reached around between her legs, touched the hard little button between her pussy lips.

'I'd be ready to explode by then,' Lucy gasped.

'I'm ready to explode now,' he said, pushing her down onto the bed.

'Let's flip a coin,' she suggested.

Theo couldn't believe they were having this conversation. Lucy was on her back, her legs open, her sex exposed, and she was suggesting they flip a coin to determine if they'd proceed.

As Theo ripped off his shorts, he rooted around in his pocket for a quarter. Lucy sat up on the edge of the bed, holding the coin and staring at his hard cock.

'I've missed you,' she said, momentarily

distracted. 'OK. Heads or tails?'

'I want head *and* tail,' he said.

Lucy laughed. Theo didn't.

'All right,' she said with a sigh. 'Heads, we hose like rabbits for the next twelve weeks. Tails, we torture each other for motivation and after the last weigh-in you get me naked, no delaying on my part, no more excuses. Ready?'

This was insane. 'No.'

Lucy flipped the coin and smacked it down on the back of her hand. She peeled her top hand away. 'Tails.'

'Fuck that.' Theo rolled with her on the bed and they laughed and in between kisses and guffaws they agreed that it would be just this once . . . then they'd go on the clock.

They did everything they could think of in the next five hours, and Theo got his head and his tail, and at four in the morning Lucy walked Theo to the door.

'I'll see you at the gym in an hour, Cunningham. Don't be late.'

She snickered, straightening the camisole. 'Be nice to me today. I can hardly move.'

Theo stared at her. 'I can't go twelve weeks without you, you know. The coin flipping was amusing, but you can't really be serious about this no-sex policy.'

Lucy shifted her weight and leaned against

the hall table. She brought her eyes to his and said thoughtfully, 'Theo? What if I said the sacrifice would keep me focused?'

'You're serious.'

'Think about it. I love you and want you and need you, and I have millions of people watching me make this last push toward my goal. What if sexual tension spurs me on? Think of what I would do to get my hands on you again.'

Theo felt his eyebrows rise high. 'Spinning classes?'

'You're not that good.'

Theo laughed. 'My goodness, Miss Cunningham. You're a shark.'

Lucy gave him one of her sweet, wonderful smiles. 'No. I'm just a practical woman. You'll be my carrot on a stick. You'll be my Miller time.'

'I won't last four days.'

'I'll wear my pink sweatpants a lot.'

'That'll help.'

'Be brave. Be strong.'

'I'll see you in less than an hour now, Cunningham.' Theo kissed her cheek, and as he turned to leave he picked up a small slip of paper from the foyer table. He turned and frowned at her.

'What?' she asked.

'Did you order pizza last night?'

Lucy's jaw fell open and her eyes got huge. 'How the *hell* did you know? Did you taste it on my breath?'

Theo smiled and shook his head. 'The only thing I tasted on your breath was paradise, babe. But here's your receipt.'

★ ★ ★

'She's not fat enough! She needs to be fat! You promised she'd stay fat!'

Stephan winced at the sound of Murray Goldstein's New York bellow, wondering how he could gently point out that technically, he'd promised no such thing. He'd only promised that Lucy would fail to meet her goal, making the Palm Club look bad, and that would, in turn, stop Murray from losing customers to Ramona Cortez.

That's all he'd ever promised. Not that that wasn't bad enough.

'She's attractive now! You're ruining me!'

Stephan felt the sweat break out on his upper lip and wiped it off with a shaking hand.

'I'm done with you. You put a stop to this *right now* or you have seaweed growing out of your eye sockets. Your choice.'

He supposed it was a blessing to know the truth about his fate instead of worrying about

347

it. At least Murray had not used the expression 'sleeping with the fishes.'

It's a good thing he'd taken the time off to prepare for his escape. He'd acquired a fake Canadian passport. He'd rented a house in the Caymans. He was ready to go at a moment's notice.

Stephan reached for his ibuprofen but found a Snickers bar instead and unwrapped it. He finished it in three bites and added the latest wrapper to the pile in the trash can. He really should cool it on the carbs. Maybe Lola had been right.

'Are you listening to me, Sherrod? Your time is up.'

Stephan hung up on him and had begun to root around for another Snickers when he felt someone's presence in his doorway. He looked up to see Lola DiPaolo, which shocked him for two reasons — she'd never come to his office before, and he wasn't used to seeing her with clothes on.

She frowned at him. 'Have you been eating candy bars?'

'Huh?' He looked down at his hand and shoved the Snickers back in the desk drawer. 'Of course not. What are you doing here?'

Lola closed the door behind her and made herself comfortable in one of the chairs facing his desk. 'That fat bitch got me fired.'

Stephan smiled. 'So I heard. But I think you helped yourself out a little, there.'

'It's not fair!'

Stephan nodded. 'Look, Lola, I have a meeting. Is there something I can do for you?'

She huffed, and looked quite hurt. 'I want you to give me a job.'

Stephan nearly choked. 'Uh. Doing what exactly?'

'I'll help you with your Lucy problem, maybe see if I can find a way to pop her balloon. If I weren't out of a job, I'd do it for free, of course.'

Stephan nodded. Maybe Lola really did understand how this game was played. 'And your salary would be in platinum toe rings or cash?'

She smiled. 'How about a little of both?'

* * *

Journal Entry Sept 16

Breakfast: *¾ c oatmeal; ¼ c raisins; 1 c skim milk; decaf*

Lunch: *3 oz turkey breast; 1 oz light cheese; 2 c salad and raw veggies; 2 tbsp olive oil and red wine vinegar; ½ c brown rice*

Dinner: *3 oz grilled red snapper; 1 c steamed broccoli; ¾ c couscous*

Snack: *1 c light yogurt; 1 c raspberries*

Affirmation for Today:
Whoever penned the phrase 'being thin feels better than anything tastes' should be forced to eat nothing but rice cakes for all of eternity.

★ ★ ★

Office of Doris Lehman, MSW, PhD

Lucy decided she'd lie down today. She kicked off her shoes, stretched out on the love seat, and propped her head on an armrest. She crossed her feet at the ankles.

'I am ready to be analyzed,' she said.

Doris laughed. 'How's the celibacy thing been working out?'

Lucy closed her eyes and sighed deeply. 'Well, since the pizza night we've been pretty good. A few kisses here and there. Theo rubbed my back one morning after a hard workout and it got a little out of control.'

'Oh? What happened?'

'He started rubbing my front, too.'

'I see.'

'Then he followed me into the ladies'

350

locker room and threw me down on the bench.'

'Oh my.'

'Yeah. Scared the cleaning lady half to death.'

'But is it motivating you?'

Lucy opened one eye. 'Doris, I'm so damn motivated I can't see straight. I'm so motivated that I'm starting to think both Andy Taylor *and* Barney Fife are sexy.'

★   ★   ★

As Lucy walked toward the scale, she crossed her fingers. She crossed her toes. She crossed her eyes.

She knew this was a moment of reckoning. That morning's *WakeUp Miami* audience was overflowing out into the street. The TV station had to hire off-duty Miami police officers for crowd control. Lucy saw some of her steadfast fans out in the studio audience waving signs and wearing their autographed T-shirts, and she really didn't want to let them down. She didn't want to let Theo down. Most of all, she didn't want to let herself down.

In the moment it took to reach the scale, the last few weeks raced by in her mind. She'd worked harder than she'd ever worked in her life — running, cycling, free weights, abs, glutes, pecs — it was a blur. Her food had been sane and healthy. Her journal was accurate and full of positive thinking — OK, most days. And Theo was back in her life. They were a team again.

'Go, Lucy! Go, Lucy!' the audience shouted.

Theo held out his hand and she took it, stepping onto the scale. She blinked and focused on the audience, then abruptly laughed — Luigi the pizza guy was in the second row! He waved and shouted and she waved back, exhaling deeply, knowing that the air in her lungs didn't weigh much, but surely it weighed something.

At least Theo's fingers were tapping the right way. At least she hadn't gained again. The crowd was getting a little rowdy, and John Weaver asked for quiet.

Tap, tap, tap. Tap, tap.

'You rock, Cunningham,' Theo whispered to her. Then he faced the cameras. 'Lucy's lost the six pounds she gained last month, plus an additional four. Lucy weighs one hundred and fifty-four pounds today.'

The cheering was so loud that her ears hurt. Theo helped her down and hugged her hard. She started to cry — from relief, from happiness, and because Theo had his arms around her for the world to see, and they reached just fine.

11

October

It was a glowing evening in suburban Fort Lauderdale, and the Cunninghams' backyard was overflowing with guests. The reason for this get-together was Lucy's parents' thirty-fifth wedding anniversary, and Dan had come down from Pittsburgh and Mary Fran and the kids were there and — total shocker — Keith came, too. Lucy noted that he was laughing a lot and seemed more relaxed than she'd seen him in years. Mary Fran was working part-time and Keith had quit his sales job and started a consulting group with a former colleague. Money was tight, but Frannie said he was home at least three nights a week for dinner. There had been no dancing on bars in quite a while.

Milling around the backyard were Theo and Buddy plus Aunt Viv and Uncle Martin, whom Lucy hadn't seen for several months. Everyone seemed to get along fine, and the party was in full swing when Dan came over to sit next to her.

He fidgeted with the sleeve of his shirt and

stared down at the grass. 'I don't think I do it for Gia anymore. I think the novelty has worn off.' Dan raised his eyes to his sister's. 'She hasn't returned my calls. She doesn't swing by Pittsburgh on the way back from New York. I guess I was deluding myself.'

Lucy didn't know what to say. She'd never seen Dan so sad or even so serious. She herself hadn't talked to Gia much, so she had no idea what was going on in her life. 'I know she's traveling a lot, Dan.'

He shrugged, giving her a weak smile. 'Who'd a thunk in the first place, huh? I mean, how many other residents at Pittsburgh Children's Hospital have ever dated a supermodel?'

'My guess would be zero,' Lucy said, patting his hand.

'You got that right.'

Lucy smiled at her brother. 'You're great, Dan. You'll find somebody. It'll happen.'

Dan wagged an eyebrow. 'Word's gotten around, though. The women back home are trying to figure out what ole Danny's got that Gia Altamonte wanted. My stock has gone up dramatically.'

Lucy and Dan joined Theo, Buddy, and Keith in a game of volleyball. Then Lucy went to chat with Viv and Martin for a while, then helped her mom make the salad. When

Lucy carried it out, Theo said he had an announcement to make.

'Only Buddy knows about this.' Theo smiled at his brother and continued. 'I thought I'd use this opportunity to tell everyone that I did get readmitted to medical school.'

Aunt Viv screamed and made her way as fast as she could to Theo and hugged him. Uncle Martin followed, slapping Theo's back. Lucy smiled at Theo, so proud of him she could scream, too. Instead she kissed his cheek and whispered, 'You rock, Redmond.'

'The downside is I have to pick up in the middle of my second year. I start classes January tenth.'

Lucy saw the disappointment in Theo's eyes — he had to repeat a whole year — but he was smiling.

'I thought long and hard about it, but I've decided it's worth it. I'm back in.'

Lucy's dad went inside and rustled up a bottle of champagne. They were in the middle of toasting to Theo's success when the phone rang.

'Hold that thought just a moment.' Her dad ran into the kitchen to answer it. Everyone waited for him to return, but it took several long minutes, and when he did make it back, he was frowning.

'Who was that, Bill?' Lucy's mother stopped her conversation with Viv and Martin and waited for him to answer, but he just continued to frown. 'Bill?'

His eyes found Lucy, and he began to walk toward the lawn chair where she sat. Lucy swallowed hard. Something was wrong.

The twins chose that particular moment to stop screaming and it got very quiet as everyone watched Lucy's dad come closer. He knelt down at her feet and placed a hand on her knee.

'Pumpkin, that was a young lady from *WakeUp Miami* — one of their producers.'

'OK. What's up?'

Theo had moved up behind Lucy, and she felt his hand on her shoulder.

'Well, it seems somebody's put a bee in their bonnet to do a special show about you this month, and they want your mom and me to come on TV and be interviewed.'

Lucy's pulse began to drum. 'What kind of special show, Dad?'

'The girl said they're calling it, *This Is Your Life, Lucy Cunningham*.'

Her body went stiff. She tried to remain calm. 'Oh really?'

'Pumpkin, I'm so sorry to have to tell you this . . .' Her dad craned his neck and sought out her mother, who gasped before he could finish his sentence. 'They've gone and tracked down Brad Zirkle and he's coming to do the show.'

Lucy was out of the chair in a flash, running up the back steps to the kitchen. Without breathing, without thinking, she grabbed her purse and keys off the counter and stumbled through the living room and out the front door to her car. She was inside and driving before the first sob hit her.

Theo was right behind her, but Dan grabbed his arm before he made it out the front door.

'Get her to tell you what happened,' he said.

'I've tried!' Theo said, exasperated. 'Would somebody please just tell me what the hell — '

'She has to do it, Theo. It's her story.'

Theo jogged for his car, Dan still at his side. 'Can you get Buddy and my aunt and uncle home?'

'Sure.' Dan prevented Theo from closing the driver-side door. 'Do not let her run away from this any longer.'

Theo let out a bitter laugh, shut the door, and drove to the end of the residential street, where he barely caught the flash of Lucy's red Toyota as it went around the bend. He ran a stop sign to catch up with her.

He immediately called her cell phone and got her voice mail. He checked his gas gauge and cursed himself for not filling up before he arrived at the Cunninghams'. He had a quarter tank and no idea where Lucy was headed.

He stayed behind her on southbound I — 95, and for once he was glad there was a decent amount of traffic — at least she wouldn't be pulling a *Starsky and Hutch* on him. He stayed close behind, heading toward Miami.

The fourth time he tried, she picked up her cell.

'Where are you going?'

Her voice was very small. 'I don't know.'

'Drive to my house. It's closer than the city.'

'No.

'Then go to the gym. Park wherever you can.'

'All right.'

She hung up, but Theo was relieved that at least he'd heard her voice and he knew where they were going. He was on empty when she took the Miami Beach exit. He was running on fumes by the time he found a place to park. He jogged down Washington Avenue and caught a glimpse of her rounding the corner of Second Street, heading toward the strip.

'Lucy!'

She ignored him. Theo caught up with her and did a quick check to make sure she still had all her limbs. Lucy looked straight ahead, marching toward the beach.

'Are we going swimming, Luce?'

'No.'

She stomped across Ocean and walked up the sidewalk to the beach entrance. She took off her sandals and dangled them in her hand.

'Tell me. Whatever it is, now's the time. Who's Brad Zirkle and what did the son of a bitch do to you?'

'I'd like to be by myself.'

Theo laughed. 'Not this time, sweetheart.' He grabbed her by the shoulders and spun her around. Lucy looked past his eyes toward the South Beach strip, already buzzing with the early dinner crowd. 'Lucy. Look at me.'

Her eyes slowly focused on him, and her mouth began to tremble.

'You've been by yourself long enough. Now you're with me, and you're going to tell me what happened to you. *Right now.*'

She nodded almost imperceptibly, her eyes still on his.

'Hey! It's Lucy and Theo!' A woman with two sunburned kids stopped on their way back from the beach. They stared, their arms full of beach toys and their mouths open in surprise.

'This isn't a good time,' Theo said, taking Lucy's elbow.

The mother pushed her two children on ahead. 'I understand.' She smiled at Theo. 'Good luck to the two of you.'

Lucy and Theo headed down the gentle slope of the beach to the surf. Theo put his arm around her waist and pulled her tight. The waning sun lit up her footprints in the wet sand and Theo knew it was a strange time to notice this, but Lucy had the cutest feet and the prettiest little toes.

'I was very athletic in high school, but somewhat overweight, as you know. I wasn't particularly appealing to the most popular boys.' She looked straight ahead up the beach.

'Go on.'

'So when I got to Pitt State, it was a chance for me to reinvent myself. I really thought I could change myself — that I could leave behind the 'fat chick' label.'

'OK.'

Lucy stopped and turned toward Theo, the breeze lifting her hair off her shoulders. 'Do you know what scares me the most about telling you this?'

He smoothed her hair back with his fingers. 'What?'

'That you'll hear this and you won't ever see me the same way again.'

He cocked his head to the side. 'How could that happen, Luce? What is there left that we haven't seen in each other?'

Lucy half-laughed and half-sniffled as she resumed walking. 'You want to know why I started gaining weight the second part of my freshman year? It was to avoid men. I wanted to become completely invisible to men.'

'Why did you want to do that?'

She pressed her palms into her eyes and stood still on the sand. When she looked at him, Theo saw no tears, just fierce determination.

'I'm a slump buster, Theo,' she said. 'No, wait — I'm *the* famous Pitt State Slump Buster: Lucky Lucy, the fat girl who helped Brad Zirkle end his six-game rushing slump. The fat girl who thought she had a *relationship* with Brad Zirkle, only to learn she was being used, and she learned this in a packed stadium during a nationally televised game, no less!'

Rage thundered in Theo's ears. 'Say *what*?'

'The fat girl whose public humiliation brought down the entire Pitt State athletic department and caused the team to forfeit

361

their Taco Bowl berth to their arch-rivals, the Purdue Boilermakers. Does this ring any bells?'

Theo was struck by the tone of Lucy's voice. She sounded like a TV news anchor giving background to a faraway tragedy. He wondered how many thousands of times she'd repeated that cold summary in her own head.

'So? Does that sound familiar to you?'

He nodded. 'I knew I'd heard Zirkle's name before — I watched that special on ESPN. I can't believe that was you.'

Theo reached up to touch her face, but Lucy backed away and crossed her arms over her chest.

'It was me, all right.'

'Start from the beginning.'

Lucy took a deep breath and stared out over the ocean for a moment, then focused on Theo. 'I met Brad in a geology class in October. He sat by me a couple times, was very nice, and I kept wondering why in the world he was acting interested in me. I was a freshman. I was overweight — around one seventy-five, probably about what I weighed back in May. I wore a size fourteen.'

'That's pretty average size, Lucy.'

'I realize that now.'

'Go on.'

'So he was very sweet to me. Told me he'd seen me on campus. He asked me to have lunch with him at the student union. The thing is, he wasn't very interesting, Theo. I didn't really like the guy all that much, but I was blinded by the fact that the senior football star *Brad Zirkle* wanted to be seen with *Lucy Cunningham*! It just boggled my mind. The girls in my dorm were flipping out with jealousy.'

'And then what happened?'

'The next week, he asked me out on a real date — took me to see a rerun of *Aliens* and then out for ice cream. He kissed me good night.' Lucy shook her head and laughed. 'I should have listened to my gut instinct right there.' She looked up at Theo. 'I *hated* his kiss. His mouth was all slimy and cold and his lips were too thin and . . . and . . . the feel of his tongue creeped me out.'

The anger sat hard and icy in Theo's gut. He didn't know how much more of this he could take. But he'd asked her to tell him, hadn't he? 'Go on.'

'So when Zirkle asked me out a second time, what did I say? I said *yes*! Duh! And why?' Lucy wiped her wet cheeks with the back of her hand. 'Because I wanted the dream to continue. I wanted so bad to believe he liked me, found me attractive — '

Theo reached for her and Lucy pushed his arm away.

'On our next date he took me to a Prince concert, but it wasn't called that back then because Prince was going by that unpronounceable symbol. Anyway, he took me to his fraternity room after, and we drank a bottle of Chardonnay. I pretended to be interested in his stories about football. I got pretty tipsy. I decided what the heck.'

'Oh, Luce.'

'I had no idea that this was all a setup. That a bunch of his teammates were outside the door listening, verifying that I was a legitimate, bona fide slump buster.'

'Shit.'

'Hey. It worked. Brad rushed for two hundred and eleven yards the next game. Broke the school record.'

'And your heart.'

Lucy stopped talking. She let her eyes drop to the sand, and Theo watched her stand still for a long moment.

When she finally had the courage to look up, she saw deep hurt and raw pity on his face, and she hated it. 'Don't you dare feel sorry for me, Theo.'

'I don't feel sorry for you, sweetheart. I want to fight for you. I want to fight *with* you. I want to fucking *kill* that guy for treating you like that. He deserves to die.'

Lucy blinked. 'Well, thanks. Nobody's ever offered to commit a felony to protect my honor. It feels kinda nice.'

Theo was suddenly hit by a horrifying thought. 'That wasn't your first time, was it? *Please* tell me you didn't give your virginity to that asshole.'

Lucy laughed. 'Nope. I gave it to a different asshole my senior year of high school — a tortured punk poet type who wore lots of black and a Mohawk. He's now a mega-millionaire software developer, I understand, but I digress. So, no. I wasn't a virgin the night I ended up in Brad Zirkle's fraternity room, but I wasn't exactly the campus harlot, either. But I sure remember . . . I remember . . . '

Lucy couldn't finish the sentence, and the tears ran down her beautiful face and Theo stood helpless in the sand in front of her, the water lapping at his feet. 'Don't stop. Tell me everything. Get it out.'

'I . . . I just remember how badly I wanted to look beautiful for him that night.' Lucy shook her head as the tears continued to pour. 'I worked so hard on my hair and was so careful about what I wore. I thought I looked pretty. I thought he found me attractive. I had convinced myself that I was . . . that I could be . . . oh my God . . . *desirable*.'

Theo was on her in a second. 'I'm so sorry, baby. Oh, Lucy.' He wrapped his arms around her and pulled her tight. She fit so close against his chest and smelled so good and felt so damn right. He stroked her hair and felt her start to shake all over. 'It's OK. Let it go.'

'Not here.' Her body went stiff. 'I can't let it go here. Not in public.'

'C'mon, then. Let's run.'

Theo pulled Lucy by the hand and raced across the sand. They ran barefoot across Ocean Drive and down the two blocks to the gym. She had no problem keeping up.

A couple of teenage girls yelled out, 'Hey! It's Lucy!'

She and Theo bounded up the stairs instead of taking the elevator, and they raced by the receptionist, who didn't even have time to say hello. Lucy was still crying, and Theo was literally dragging her through the cardiovascular studio, and for some reason all he could think about was that first morning she came in here, more than ten months ago, and how she choked on her Milk Duds and he had to save her and now everything had changed, but she was still choking, and he still hadn't saved her. At least not yet.

Theo opened the door to the kickboxing gym and flipped on the far bank of lights toward the back of the room. Lucy stood in dirty bare feet on the red exercise mat, gasping for breath.

Theo frowned at her. 'You're wearing a skirt.'

She looked down, curious as to why he'd suddenly taken an interest in fashion. 'Well, yeah,' she said.

'You're going to have to take it off.'

'*What?*'

'Take off your skirt, Luce. Otherwise, you won't have free range of motion in your legs, which you're going to need when you start to kick the living shit out of Brad Zirkle.'

'*Hello?*' Lucy was worrying that Stephan Sherrod's mental instability was contagious, and Theo had somehow caught it, while she watched him run to the side of the room and grab one of the kickboxing dummies — the one with the padded blue head, shoulders, and torso of an opponent who stood about six feet tall. Then he ran over to a cabinet and pulled out two thick rolls of gauze tape and returned to her side.

Theo shook his head in disgust. 'I guess I'll have to do it myself.' In one hard yank, her nice chino skirt was at her ankles, and Lucy was shocked. 'Step out,' he ordered. 'Right now, Cunningham.'

Lucy did as she was told, then held out her hands in front of her, palms up. Theo wrapped them quickly, testing to make sure the bandages weren't too tight, and then stepped behind the dummy.

'Lucy Cunningham, I'd like you to meet Brad Zirkle.'

'Oh no. I can't possibly do this.' Lucy shook her head and made a beeline for the door. She hadn't progressed two steps before Theo snagged her skirt from the floor and unceremoniously stuffed it down the front of his shorts.

'I know you, Lucy, and you're not going anywhere with your butt on display, so I'll make a deal with you.'

Theo looked fiercer than she'd ever seen him. She wasn't sure if she appreciated that comment about her butt, even though it was 100 percent accurate. 'What's the deal?'

'Simple. You tell our buddy Brad Zirkle here everything you've ever wanted to tell him — right this fucking minute — and I'll give you back your skirt and you can go home. Deal?'

'I can't do this.'

'*Why not?*'

The panic was so sharp that it poked at the soft lining of her throat. Her chest hurt. She couldn't breathe. There was hardly any air to say the words . . . 'Because I'm terrified.'

'Of what?'

'Of starting.'

'Why?'

And that's when it happened — something broke loose inside her body, and Lucy could feel it claw at the walls of her lungs. It burned. It hurt. It hurt so much, but she just couldn't stuff it down anymore . . . she didn't have the strength any longer . . . and it felt like barbed wire as it came out of her mouth . . .

'*Because I might never be able to stop!*'

'That's it, sweetheart. Let it out.'

Lucy threw herself at poor Brad Zirkle with such ferocity that Theo briefly questioned his brilliant plan. As she began to punch, he realized the most important thing was that she not hurt herself.

'Watch your form, Cunningham.'

'Fuck my form!' Lucy punched so hard, it knocked Theo back a full step.

'Listen, Lucy. This is going to be Brad Zirkle talking from now on — not me — until I tell you otherwise. Are we clear on this?'

'Crystal.' Ole Brad got a killer ax kick to the gut.

'You were fat and ugly.'

'No! I was *not!*' Two uppercuts to the jaw,

followed by a side kick that would have broken a whole lotta ribs on a real man. 'I was average size, you jerk! And I was pretty — '

Smack!

'And smart — '

Slam!

'And I was way too special for scum like you! I just didn't know it at the time!'

Lucy was breathing hard and crying even harder.

'Nobody thought you were attractive.'

'That's not true!' Lucy's foot slammed brutally into the dummy's chest, and she panted for air.

'Nobody liked you.'

'That's such bullshit! I had a lot of friends! So many people liked me!' She jabbed Brad right in the nose.

'You are not attractive now.'

'Fuck you, you stupid, mean-spirited loser!' Her fists were flying, and the sweat was pouring off her face. 'I am drop-dead gorgeous now — more beautiful than I've ever been in my life! And stronger! And I'm going to — '

Thwack! went a roundhouse kick to Brad's kidneys.

'Kick — '

Wham! went the right jab to Brad's eye socket.

'Your — '

Theo peeked around to enjoy the spectacle of Lucy finding just the right balance on her left foot to support a big ole juicy hook kick, which was executed perfectly . . .

'Ass!'

And connected with Theo's left brow bone.

The pain was instant, and it was monumental. Right away, Theo knew there would be a lot of blood.

'Oh my God! Theo!'

He was sprawled flat on his back on the mat, the bank of lights swimming in and out of his vision. He felt the blood start a warm trickle down the side of his face and he opened his good eye to see Lucy hovering directly over him, crying so hard her tears were running down his own cheeks.

'I think I might need ice,' he groaned, watching as Lucy raced out the door without her skirt. He nearly laughed, but it hurt too much.

Theo endured the indignity of Lucy's ministrations and the litany of Tyson's questions — which seemed to focus on why Lucy was kickboxing on the weekend in a pair of leopard-print underpants — as he drove them to the emergency room.

Lucy sat with Theo while he waited for the plastic surgeon on call to arrive, and she held his hand while the local anesthesia kicked in. She couldn't stop apologizing.

'Your face, Theo! Your beautiful face!'

The surgeon was finishing up the last of six delicate stitches just above Theo's left eye when he broke out laughing. 'I'm sorry.' The surgeon snorted, handing the supplies to the nurse. 'I've just got to tell you, Lucy — some women threaten it, but most don't actually kick their man in the head.'

Theo chuckled out of the area of his mouth that wasn't numb. 'She had some anger issues she needed to let go of,' he slurred.

Lucy sighed. 'I'm never going to live this down, am I?'

'Good luck to the both of you,' the surgeon said as he left the room. 'And go easy on the guy, Lucy. Med students need understanding lovers.'

Tyson drove them back to Theo's house, still doing his best to get all the details about why Theo had Lucy's skirt shoved down the front of his shorts. Buddy was staying at Martin and Viv's house, so after Tyson left, it was just the two of them. Lucy made sure Theo was comfortable on the couch and got him his pain medication and a cool drink.

She sat next to him. He reached out for her hand. She stroked his hair. All the while, Norton stayed in the dining room doorway, glaring at them with distrust.

'How bad does it hurt, Theo?'

'Not so bad. It'll heal up real quick.'

'But you'll always have a scar.'

'We all have them. Mine's just going to be more obvious than some.'

'Will you ever forgive me?'

Theo leaned his head back against the sofa cushion and sighed. 'There's nothing to forgive. We got the job done. That's what matters.'

Lucy nodded in silence, then laid her head down on Theo's lap. 'I feel empty inside. That's the only way I can explain it.'

Theo stroked her hair.

'It's very calm inside me. It's like I hacked up a giant hairball that's been giving me indigestion for years.'

Theo laughed softly. 'Maybe that's Norton's problem.'

'Nobody's ever done something like that for me. Thank you, Theo,' she whispered. 'Thank you so much.'

'You're welcome, baby. Will you stay with me tonight?'

Lucy raised her head and frowned at him. 'The whole left side of your face is swollen. You can only see out of one eye — granted, that might be the best way to see me naked for the first time, but . . .'

Theo laughed and said, 'We still have a few weeks left before the big payoff, but I need you to sleep with me tonight, keep me company. It's the least you could do after kicking me in the face.'

Lucy took him by the hand and looked at her watch. They'd spent nearly four hours in the emergency room and it was close to midnight. 'Let's get you to bed, then.'

Theo led her to the room at the end of the hall and then to a queen-size four-poster mahogany bed. He unceremoniously removed his shorts and shirt and stood by the bed wearing nothing but a pair of pale blue cotton boxers and a fine down of chest hair. Lucy tried to swallow, but there wasn't enough moisture in her mouth to get the job done. She licked her lips.

'I never asked you, but was this your parents' room?'

Theo nodded. 'Does that bother you?'

Lucy stared at the nearly naked man in her direct line of vision and knew that nothing could bother her at the moment. Nothing mattered but that a gorgeous and barely clothed Theo Redmond was about to climb into bed with her.

'What clothes should *I* take off?' Lucy's hands had already started to tremble, and she'd already begun to analyze the quality of the light coming from the bureau lamp. Not too harsh. About a 60-watt bulb. A wide white shade that diffused the glow. It would probably be all right.

'You know my preference.'

She watched Theo climb in between the sheets and prop himself up on the headboard with a groan. The man was in severe pain, but he still wanted to see her naked. This was good news.

Lucy unsnapped the waistband and pushed the skirt down over her hips, smiling to herself with the memory of how Theo had ripped it from her body a few hours ago. She'd always think back on that moment fondly.

Then she pulled her pink scoop-neck T-shirt over her head and stood before Theo in a cream and black leopard-print bra and panty set. Theo's good eye had popped quite wide.

'Lucy — don't move.' Theo adjusted his position against the headboard and hissed with pain.

Lucy gasped. 'Are you OK?'

'Do you have any idea how I'm going to ravage that body come December?'

She smiled. 'Tell me.'

'I'm not going to let you out of my clutches for at least a week, and clothes will be strictly forbidden. You'll have to do dishes naked, work naked, scramble eggs naked, dance naked. I'm picturing naked kickboxing, skinny-dipping, all-nude Andy Griffith marathons . . . '

'Being naked in front of Floyd the barber isn't a turn-on for me. Can I borrow a T-shirt to sleep in tonight?'

Theo laughed, gesturing to the middle drawer of the bureau. Lucy selected a well-worn but clean Special Olympics T-shirt and pulled it down over her head. She reached up her back, unhooked her bra, and pulled it through an armhole.

'I've always loved to watch women do that. There just isn't an equivalent for men.'

Lucy smiled, clicked off the light, and climbed into bed next to Theo, her trainer, her business partner, her lover, her hero.

Theo scooted down and opened his arms. Lucy rested her head on his chest — that not too hard and not too soft place that smelled like heaven to her. Theo caressed her shoulder.

'Everything you told Zirkle tonight was dead-on correct, you know.' Theo traced his fingers up and down her arm. 'You are beautiful. You are strong. And you are smart. But you left something out, my sweet Lucy.'

'I did?'

'Mmm-hmm. You're one hell of a brave woman.'

She nodded, feeling Theo's soft chest hairs brush against her cheek. 'That'll come in handy when I see Brad Zirkle again, won't it?'

'I'll be right there with you.'

'You can't do this for me.'

Theo laughed at that, hard enough that Lucy's face got tossed around on the surface of his chest. 'Think of it like the military press, Luce. I'm not going to do any of the work for you, but I'll be there, just in case you need me.'

Lucy rubbed her cheek against Theo's warm skin and waited until his breathing became slow and deep and his hand slid away from her shoulder.

When she was sure he was asleep, she whispered, 'You are the love of my life, Theo Redmond.'

★ ★ ★

Office of Doris Lehman, MSW, PhD
Though he'd known for a week that he was coming along to Lucy's appointment, it still surprised Theo to find himself there, on a little pinkish couch, looking at weird Japanese girls on a paper screen.

'You don't have to do the show, you know,'

Dr Lehman told Lucy. 'You have a choice.'

'I choose to confront Brad Zirkle and be done with it.'

Doris squinted in Theo's direction, and he rubbed his palms on the top of his slacks. He had the vaguest feeling that the therapist didn't like him all that much. Maybe all therapists were like that. Theo promised himself that he'd never need therapy of any kind.

Doris eventually returned her attention to Lucy. 'Do you know what you're going to say?'

'I'll come up with something — and I promise they won't have to cut to a commercial this time.'

'Would you like me to come?'

Lucy scrunched up her brows and pondered that. 'You're welcome to, but I'll be fine.'

Doris nodded, then looked to Theo. 'So, how exactly did you come up with the idea to assume the identity of Brad Zirkle in order for Lucy to vent her anger?'

Theo glanced sideways at Lucy, checking to see if this was a trick question. But Lucy just smiled amenably. Theo didn't know whether the throbbing in his head was from the now rainbow-hued slice on his brow or simply the stress of being trapped in a small room with two women and a paper screen decorated with little anorexic Japanese chicks.

He shrugged. 'It seemed like the thing to do at the time. Lucy was obviously ready to let it out, so I let her take it out on me.'

Doris smiled at him. 'Yes,' she said. 'It certainly appears you did.'

Lucy reached over and grabbed Theo's hand. He squeezed her fingers tight and smiled. And when he looked back toward Doris, the therapist had a thoughtful expression on her face.

Mercifully, the session soon ended, and Theo shook Dr Lehman's hand and waited while Lucy hugged her good-bye. He was half out the door when the two women broke into hoots of laughter, and Theo could have sworn he heard one of them say something about biscuits.

He asked Lucy about it in the car, but she pleaded doctor-patient confidentiality.

⋆   ⋆   ⋆

The entire hour of the *WakeUp Miami* show was to be dedicated to the story of Lucy's life, and she was supposed to be sitting alone in a producer's office while her family and anyone else they'd hauled in for this freak show were left to mill about in the green room.

Lucy sipped at a Styrofoam cup of black coffee and tried not to obsess about what she'd decided to wear to her own execution (a tailored suit jacket and matching slim skirt in a rich brown that looked great with her hair) or what Brad Zirkle would look like after all this time (she was hoping for fat and bald and poorly dressed) and what strange conversations might be taking place in the waiting room down the hall.

She was contemplating another trip to look out the window toward the MacArthur Causeway when the office door creaked open and Gia's lush head of hair appeared.

'There you are, *chica*!' She ran over to the desk chair and threw her arms around Lucy and whispered, 'God, I've missed you! You look mahvelous! I'm not supposed to be in here — it's like it's your wedding day or something; they don't want anybody to see you before!'

Gia looked beautiful as always, but there was something different about her, and Lucy studied her closely until it dawned on her — it was Gia's eyes. She looked radiantly happy.

'What have you been up to?' Lucy asked her, patting the desktop for Gia to have a seat. 'I haven't seen you in ages.'

'Oh, Lucy. Work has been crazy, you know? I got a shoot scheduled for next month in Sydney.'

Lucy smiled. 'Wow!'

'And that's not all, and I'm afraid to tell you about this other thing because — '

'Of Dan?'

Gia jolted and pursed her luscious lips. 'Yeah. Because he's your brother and he's great, but he's just not — '

'Right for you?'

Gia smiled and shook her head. 'Yeah. I just ran into him in that green room, you know? And he was so sweet and we talked and I told him I was sorry for not being direct about it, but we're cool now. I really like him, Lucy, but he's more friend material, you know?'

'I know.'

Gia sighed. 'But I met someone in New York last month. He's incredible. You'll love him. I brought him home with me.'

Lucy felt her eyes go wide with surprise. 'Like a puppy from the pound?'

'Ooh, girlie, listen to me when I tell you that this man is no puppy!'

The door opened. It was Theo. 'You're not supposed to be in here, Altamonte. Get back to the green room.'

Gia got up and acted all huffy as she strutted to the door. 'But it's OK for you, Theo-dorable? You're allowed? How come you're allowed? Who crowned you king?'

Lucy laughed.

'Just go back to the green room.' Theo turned Gia in the right direction and then grinned at Lucy. He'd obviously gone for a more formal look today himself — a white cashmere knit sweater and a pair of charcoal gray pleated slacks, plus a discreet little bandage applied lengthwise along his stitches. Lucy had indeed gotten used to seeing Theo's charming face, but it didn't mean she appreciated it any less.

'Are you looking at my bruise?' He lightly touched his brow. 'I probably shouldn't stand too close to you on the set — we'll clash.'

Lucy smiled at him. 'Hi, Theo-dorable.'

He checked behind him in the hallway, then closed the door. In a flash he was leaning on the armrest of Lucy's chair and kissing her, his lips warm and soft and more demanding than she'd felt since before she'd kicked him. He was apparently gaining back the use of his facial muscles.

'You doing OK, Cunningham?' He left little kisses all over her forehead. 'You up for this?'

She nodded. 'I am.'

'Well, he's here, baby. Brad Zirkle is down the hall. They put him in a separate room.'

Lucy felt a hot rush of fear move through her, but it didn't stay long, and its passage only gave her a burst of energy. 'I'm ready to rumble.'

Theo laughed and pulled her to her feet, then hugged her hard. 'No kicking. No punching. No cussing.'

'You're no fun anymore.'

He chuckled, releasing her and holding her by her shoulders. He leaned his forehead against hers and whispered, 'I can't wait to show you just how fun I really am.'

There was a knock on the door, and it was time.

★ ★ ★

'It's time to WakeUp Miami!' Lucy was an expert at this by now, and she gestured broadly toward the set and the band took it as their cue to start up and the crowd went crazy. The audience today was a sea of white T-shirts with red hearts and lettering that proclaimed: *We Love Lucy!*

Lucy had already spotted a few guests of note in the studio that morning. Doris sat in the second row, engaged in nonstop conversation with Tyson. Stephan, Maria, Barry, and Veronica were in the back left section, and Lola was sitting by herself in the far right corner, looking pissed.

The producers of this extravaganza had apparently decided that chronological order wouldn't be dramatic enough, so John Weaver and Carolina Buendia brought out everyone but Brad Zirkle, including family members, to childhood teachers, to friends from junior high and high school, to Lucy's first boss in Pittsburgh. In between there were softball teammates and a Girl Scout leader and a horse trainer and Gia Altamonte and even Buddy.

Lucy was thirsty and hot and her stomach was in knots when they took a final commercial break.

'Don't go away, Miami,' Carolina cooed. 'When we come back, we'll have a shocking surprise confession that Lucy may want to hear . . . ' She patted Lucy's knee. 'And then what we've all been waiting for — we'll get the skinny on this month's weight loss! Can she do it with only one month to go? Don't go away!'

During the break, the makeup technician blotted Lucy's damp forehead and let her take a swig of water. Theo stood at the edge of the set, his arms crossed over his chest, his face serious. She gave him the thumbs-up sign and he winked at her.

When Brad Zirkle walked onto the set, Lucy felt her head swim and her vision fail — then she remembered to breathe. He sat down in the chair right across from her, his eyes focused on his shoes. He wore an expensive business suit and a red-and-white-striped dress shirt with cuff links and a silk tie. He held a little blue book and a piece of folded notebook paper in his hand. Lucy had to admit he looked just the way he did in college, except better.

So much for fat, bald, and poorly dressed.

Her glance darted to Theo, but he didn't notice — he was staring at Brad Zirkle like he wanted to eviscerate the man. She hoped he remembered his own advice regarding acts of violence and curse words.

Lucy sat still while the producers ran an old video montage of the events of a decade ago — the bedsheet unfurled with the painted words, *Thank You, Lucky Lucy Cunningham — Slump Buster*; her father yelling at reporters from his front stoop; Lucy hounded by ESPN cameras as she walked between classes; the dean announcing that the coach, athletic director, and assistant athletic director had been fired and four athletes expelled.

385

John Weaver asked her how it felt to see that.

Lucy said, 'Like it happened to another person.'

As Brad cleared his throat and started to speak, Lucy was amazed at how loose her body felt, how relaxed and comfortable she was at this moment of truth. Her heart beat quietly. Her hands lay still in her lap. She stayed focused.

She wondered briefly if this meant she'd had a mental breakdown, but it didn't feel like illness. It felt like health. It felt like strength. It felt damn good.

Brad began to read from a prepared statement, telling Lucy and the entire Miami-Dade TV-viewing area that he'd always been ashamed of his behavior that day and that his life since then had been a series of relationship and job failures, including a struggle with alcohol.

'Oh my God,' Lucy whispered, searching out Doris in the second row. She shrugged and gave her a sympathetic smile and Lucy went back to listening to Brad Zirkle explain how his twelve-step recovery required that he apologize to Lucy for his behavior.

Is there nothing people won't do on television?

'I take full responsibility for what happened.

It was wrong and cruel, and I am so sorry, Lucy. You did not deserve to be treated so badly.'

Suddenly the camera zoomed in tight on Lucy's face, and Carolina and John looked at her expectantly and Lucy realized this was her chance, her opportunity for the ultimate words of revenge.

What came out of her mouth instead was a huge sigh of relief.

'Thank you for your apology, Brad,' she said. 'You hurt me a lot, and I'm sad to hear that you suffered, too.'

Brad fell back into his chair like he'd been pushed.

Lucy went on. 'Someone once told me that at the end of the day, the most important thing is that you make the most of what God gave you. I guess you and I are both trying to do that now. Everybody deserves a second chance.'

'Thank you, Lucy,' Brad said.

'But don't you dare ever hurt anyone like that again.'

'I won't.' Brad wiped a tear from his cheek.

Carolina cried next. Then Lucy's mom broke down in her chair at the back of the set, followed by Mary Fran and Gia and most of the females in the studio audience, and that's when Lucy thought for sure she heard

Stephan Sherrod's voice shout out something about being a dead man.

After the next commercial break, Theo led Lucy to the scale. She started laughing with joy before he could even settle on the number, which turned out to be 148, a loss of six pounds for the month.

Lucy had no idea how much a decade of rage and shame weighed, but she knew she'd unloaded a few of those pounds just moments ago, when she'd forgiven Brad Zirkle.

12

November and December

Journal Entry Nov 19

Breakfast: *1 banana; ¾ c Kashi; 1 c plain yogurt; decaf with skim milk*

Lunch: *3 oz grilled chicken; 2 rye flat breads; 2 c salad with a whole cucumber; 2 tbsp oil and vinegar*

Dinner: *3 oz grilled salmon; 1 julienned zucchini; ½ c brown rice*

Snack: *Another banana*

Affirmation for Today:
Only three weeks of celibacy left. Soon I will be fucking Theo's brains out on a regular basis and can stop subconsciously selecting phallic-shaped fruits and vegetables.

★ ★ ★

Lucy figured this was the worst-case scenario: in a few weeks' time, she would step up on that medical scale on the set of *WakeUp Miami* and not have lost another pound. That would still mean she was eighty-two pounds and forty-one inches smaller, eighty-two thousand dollars richer (at least on paper), and on her way with her sister to a luxury spa in Jamaica for a week of pampering.

As far as worst-case scenarios went, that wasn't so bad.

'Hey, Lucy? Is there anything else that needs to go?' Veronica poked her head into Lucy's open office door and blew a wayward strand of hair out of her face. She looked cute in a pair of overalls and flip-flops, and she'd been a real trouper, helping with everything that needed to be done in order for them to be in the new office by the end of the week.

Lucy took one last look around at the pale yellow walls and sighed. 'That's pretty much it, I guess. How about Maria and Barry?'

'Barry's unhooking his computer now. Maria's already over there working with the phone people.'

'Did the detective call with any news this morning?'

Veronica made her fish face. 'Not since

yesterday. They still think our fearless leader went AWOL and took Lola DiPaolo with him.'

Lucy shook her head. She didn't like leaving Stephan like this, but how were you supposed to give your two-week notice to an invisible man? All of them had left letters of resignation on Stephan's desk, should he ever show up to read them.

Though dozens of audience members had confirmed that Stephan loudly proclaimed that he was a dead man before running from the TV studio — the last time anyone saw him — Miami Police detectives were operating on the theory that he'd not met with foul play but flown the coop for financial reasons. The IRS was snooping around Sherrod & Thoms right along with the detectives.

Police also believed that Stephan and Lola had some sort of relationship. Lucy could only imagine the profound nature of their pillow talk.

Lucy took one last look around her little office and smiled — she was moving up in the world. Her new suite was in a high-rise on Biscayne with a view of the bay. The lease was hefty, but she didn't think that would be a problem. Every one of Stephan's longtime clients had happily jumped ship with her. The publicity she'd received in the last month had also helped her close deals for seven significant new accounts, including the Lucy Chef gourmet food chain Barry had been courting.

Slump Buster Advertising was officially open for business.

'What're your plans for lunch, Lucy?'

Lucy turned to answer Veronica when her lunch plans — all her plans, really — suddenly materialized in the doorway.

'Hey, Cunningham.'

Theo leaned up against the door frame in a pair of jeans, a ribbed polo shirt, and sneakers. He'd let his hair grow in the last couple months, and Lucy thought it suited him. He looked less like Malibu Ken and more like himself — funny, warm, sexy, and hers. All hers.

She felt the smile as it spread across her face. When she looked at Theo these days, she was astounded at the depth of her love for him, her trust in him, and how, with his help, she was living in hope for her future instead of fear of her past.

'Does Japanese sound OK to you?'

'Delish.'

'So is this the end of an era?' Theo glanced around the empty office.

'Thank God,' Veronica said, popping her

gum. 'Let's get out of here before he comes back.'

Theo held Lucy's hand as they walked through the downtown lunch crowd. He kept shooting her sideways glances and smiling. But he was unusually quiet.

'You look like you got something to tell me.'

'Nope.' He squeezed her hand harder. 'But I like your shoes. You've got the cutest little toes.'

Lucy laughed. 'Yeah, and now I can look down and see them.'

'Hey, Lucy! Way to go!' A threesome of young businessmen gave her the thumbs-up as they walked by. One of them whistled. Lucy felt herself blush. It was safe to say that being on the receiving end of whistles, hoots, catcalls, and kissy noises had been a fairly recent development and that she loved every minute of it.

'Don't you go getting a big head.'

'Ha. I think you'd be more worried about me getting a big butt.'

'Nope. Didn't even enter my mind.'

Lucy let her head fall back and she took a deep breath of the warm Miami air. She was about to tell herself that things could not possibly be better, but she knew that was a lie. Because things were definitely about to get better with Theo.

She had big plans for the man walking next to her. In just two weeks, their yearlong venture would be done. She'd no longer be his client. He'd already given his notice, so Theo would no longer even be a trainer at the Palm Club.

They were just going to be two regular people who'd decided to become lovers.

And as soon as she and Mary Fran got back from Jamaica; the boy had better watch out.

★ ★ ★

Office of Doris Lehman, MSW, PhD
'It feels like I'm saving myself for marriage.'

Doris chuckled. 'Well, in a way, you are, Lucy. You've had limited physical intimacy with Theo these last two months, and a deep friendship and trust had room to form. You're both entering into this with expectations for a committed relationship.'

'He's never really come right out and said, 'I love you, Lucy.' He said he's 'crazy' for me. Does that count?'

Doris smiled, very nearly looking like she was suppressing a laugh.

'Did I say something funny?'

'Have a little faith, Lucy.'

'What's that supposed to mean?'

'It means that some things are worth waiting for.'

While Lucy mulled that over, she let her gaze wander over to the pint-size geisha gals in their pint-size outfits. She was going to miss the little floozies. And she was really going to miss Doris but didn't know if it was appropriate for former patients to ask their former therapists to become their friends.

'When I marry Theo, I plan to ask Isaac Olorio to design a gown for me with a kimono theme. I've decided that would look really good on me. You're invited to the ceremony.'

Doris coughed and tapped her chest. 'So you're already planning your wedding, are you?'

Lucy smiled. 'Have a little faith, Dr Lehman.'

★ ★ ★

The big day arrived, and the irony was that Lucy didn't even care what the scale said — that was just the final detail. The cameras had been with them at the Palm Club the day before as Lucy completed her fitness evaluation for aerobic capacity, flexibility, and strength, and then she happily walked around in a tankini and let Theo submerge her in the hydrostatic tank. The numbers were being kept secret, like the results of the Miss America Pageant or the Academy Awards, until today, which cracked Lucy up.

Carolina Buendia appeared particularly agitated that morning, and she grabbed Lucy's arm before the show began and pulled her off into a corner of the set.

'I wanted you to know how remarkable you are and how much I admire you. I wish I were as brave as you . . . I . . . ' Her fingers shook as she expertly blotted away tears without smudging her mascara. 'It's just that I've struggled so much . . . I've had . . . Oh *God* . . . '

'Carolina! Lucy!' one of the producers shouted for them from the front of the set. 'We need you both out here — four minutes to air!'

Carolina didn't really need to say anything more, and Lucy stopped her. 'It's OK. I had a wonderful therapist, and she does it all — compulsive eating and bulimia and anorexia, too. Do you want her number?'

Carolina nodded and took a steadying breath. 'Please don't say anything to anyone. The media would have a field day with this.'

Lucy just smiled.

It was a relaxing show, and she and Theo

joked a lot and video was played of Lucy's year of progress. When they showed a clip of Lucy's first workout, it was a challenge for her to watch. The woman in the snug pink sweatpants was her but not her. Yes, it was obvious that she'd been a mess on the outside. But Lucy knew that mess originated on the inside, where no one could see. And it felt wonderful not to be that angry, lonely, ashamed woman anymore.

With a drumroll from the band, Lucy stood in between Carolina and John while Theo broke the seal of the envelope.

'In fifty-one weeks, Lucy Cunningham's percentage of body fat has gone from sixty-nine percent to fourteen percent, from a dress size of twenty-two to a size eight.'

The audience gasped.

'Her waist was forty-two inches; now it's twenty-eight. Her hips were fifty-one and a half inches; now they're thirty-eight inches.'

Carolina asked the studio audience to hold their applause, and Theo continued.

'This is really amazing — her upper right thigh once measured thirty inches around, bigger than her waist is now. That same thigh is now twenty-one inches around.'

'Holy shit!' John Weaver's hand slapped up to his mouth the instant after the words slipped out.

Lucy giggled, glad this FCC fine wouldn't be her fault.

Theo tucked the envelope in his shorts pocket and addressed the camera. 'Now, before Lucy gets on the scale, I want everyone out there to remember that if she doesn't hit one hundred and thirty pounds today — and chances are she won't — that does not mean she didn't reach her goal.'

The crowd nodded and manufactured a variety of supportive sounds.

Lucy knew he'd said that for her benefit. He still planned to see her naked, no matter what the scale said.

They came pretty close. Lucy's final weigh-in put her at 139 pounds, for a total loss of ninety-one pounds.

She'd take it.

★   ★   ★

Lucy and Mary Fran's flight to Jamaica left Miami International the next morning at seven. Lucy had decided to surprise Theo at his house the evening before. They had agreed to wait until she got back from Jamaica, but she couldn't do it. She wanted him now. She didn't want to wait another second.

She pulled into the driveway of his house

on DeLeon and gingerly got out of her Toyota, trying not to get her panties all twisted up. She was wearing only a trench coat tied at the waist, a pair of three-inch heels, and some very slippery and very crotchless lingerie Gia had brought her from Paris. It took Lucy several attempts to figure out which holes were intended for her legs, but once she'd done that, the effect was shocking.

At least she hoped it would shock Theo.

She'd come by this evening because she knew Buddy was at an away track meet and wouldn't be back until late. It was the perfect opportunity.

Lucy went to the front door and knocked. There was no answer. She peered into the garage and saw Theo's car tucked inside. Maybe he'd gone on another run, though they'd done five miles together that morning. She thought she'd check around back, just in case he was working in the yard, and she was suddenly struck by an idea — why not just ditch the coat? Why not just go for the full effect? If she was going to shock Theo, why not just go ahead and shock the man all the way?

Lucy giggled as she untied the belt. By God, she was desirable and beautiful, and she was going to flaunt it! She'd be thirty years old in a few days and she'd never flaunted jack shit! She'd worked awful hard to get this flauntable body, and soon she'd be past the flaunting age! If she didn't do it now, when would she?

Lucy draped the trench coat over the fence, then scurried inside the gate before anyone could see her from the street.

And then Lucy halted, frozen, in her underwear — because Theo was standing in the middle of his backyard with what appeared to be a very attractive woman in his arms.

Theo must have sensed Lucy's presence, because his head popped up, and he saw her. He blinked. Blinked again. Then his mouth gaped open and his arms fell to his sides and he took two steps away from the woman, who seemed to be a bit unsteady on her feet.

Of course, the woman noticed Theo's shock, so naturally she looked over her shoulder to see what he was staring at with such astonishment. And logically, she did what any woman would do under the circumstances. She screamed bloody murder.

So did Lucy.

Lucy bolted out the gate and threw on her L.L. Bean trench coat and cinched the belt so tight it nearly cut off her circulation. Then she paced in the driveway, trying to get her brain to wrap around everything that had just happened and what it meant.

'Lucy. Uh. This is not exactly what you might think.'

She whipped her head around and saw Theo standing at the open gate with the woman at his side and OK, Lucy had been wrong. The woman wasn't very attractive — she was drop-dead beautiful!

'This is Jenna Tolliver, my old friend from medical school I told you about, the one who got engaged a while back.' Theo took a step closer to Lucy. 'She's going through a rough patch and came by to talk, Luce.'

Jenna stepped forward and held out her thin, pale hand. 'Hello, Lucy. It's a pleasure to meet you in person. I've been watching you all year.'

Well now, wasn't that pleasant of her? But all Lucy could wonder was how does a woman greet a potential rival when the rival knows her body fat percentage and the circumference of her thighs and had just seen her in a pair of baby pink crotchless French-cut boy shorts trimmed in black lace with a matching demi-bra? What was the appropriate response in this situation? Lucy was fairly certain it didn't involve shaking the woman's hand!

'He's mine. Hit the road,' was the response

Lucy settled on, which she could not *believe.* The awkward silence that followed was cut short by Theo's snort, followed by his loud laughter. Jenna began to giggle.

Norton chose that moment to exit the backyard and sit next to Lucy's feet, which were planted wide apart on the driveway. It was as if the cat was choosing sides, and Lucy decided she'd never forget his loyalty to her at this crucial moment.

Jenna came closer to Lucy, which sent Norton spitting and skittering away. Then the beautiful woman invaded Lucy's personal space by kissing her on the cheek. She gave her a stiff smile. 'Good luck to you,' Jenna said, walking by. 'Have fun in Jamaica.'

Lucy watched Jenna get into the Acura parked at the curb, then drive away. She turned her attention to Theo.

He didn't look a bit guilty. Of course, he was busy staring down the deep vee in her raincoat while a crooked smile spread across his face. Lucy adjusted the lapels and sniffed. 'So? Tell me what I'm misinterpreting here.'

Theo's smile grew wider. 'Can I see those underpants again?'

'No!' Lucy hugged herself and made sure the coat was closed from shin to chin. 'The moment has been ruined.'

'Her fiancé dumped her, Luce.' Theo

shoved his hands in the pockets of his jeans. 'He strung her along for nine months, told her he was getting a divorce, then didn't follow through. She was pretty devastated.'

Lucy nodded. 'And she came to you for advice?'

'Yeah. And a shoulder to cry on.'

'I saw that part.'

'Jenna doesn't mean anything to me anymore. She hasn't for a long time. You are what matters to me.'

'That's good to hear. Well, I need to go home and get packed. I just wanted to say good-bye.'

Theo moved close and caressed the side of Lucy's face. She felt the heat of his touch warm her skin and she automatically turned her mouth into his hand. It was a reflex. Theo's pinkie stroked along her bottom lip.

'You know, Luce, that outfit you're wearing is the way a woman says hello, not good-bye.'

'Ha. Well, maybe it was a see-you-later. Just try to be good while I'm gone, OK?' Lucy kissed Theo hard on the mouth and turned to get in her car.

'Are you going to pack those undies for Jamaica?'

Lucy laughed. 'I don't think Mary Fran would be as appreciative as you.'

'Right.' Theo held open the car door for

her. 'Is she at your place now?'

Lucy scowled at him. 'Yeah. She's packing. Why?'

'Just tell her I said to have a nice trip.'

Lucy shook her head, then looked up at Theo, leaning on the car window, relaxed and long and handsome and sweet and smiling at her like he loved her.

She knew he loved her — even if he couldn't say it. It was all over his face. She was so sure of it, it didn't even bother her that she'd just seen him hugging his ex-girlfriend.

Well, not much anyway.

'You're going to miss me, aren't you?'

'So much, Lucy.' Theo leaned down and kissed her one last time. 'Until then, baby.'

Theo watched Lucy drive down his street, and as soon as she made the corner he pulled out his cell phone.

'Mary Fran? You've got to make sure she packs the bra and panties she's wearing tonight. This is critical. Do you understand what I'm saying?'

'What bra and panties? Where is she? I don't have any idea what she's even wearing — and how do *you* know?'

'Just do it, Fran. Stick them into her bag when she's not looking. Did all my stuff fit in your suitcase?'

'Good Lord. Yes, Theo.'

'Just do this one little thing for me, and I swear I'll owe you for the rest of my life.'

He heard Mary Fran sigh. 'All right! Jeesh! What I won't do for my sister!'

Theo clicked his phone shut and smiled. This was going to be so much fun.

★　★　★

The check-in line at the airline counter snaked through a three-tiered maze, and Lucy was getting impatient. It wasn't like they were going to miss their flight, but she hated waiting.

'Do you have to use the ladies' room?' Mary Fran asked for the second time. 'Because I can stay here with our luggage if you want to run to the ladies' room.'

'Not particularly. Do you need to go?'

'No. But you go on ahead.'

'I don't need to.'

'But you might by the time we get to the front of the line, right?'

Lucy had never known her sister to be so concerned about her bladder habits. Mary Fran was acting weird all around this morning. Downright anxious. 'Have you suddenly developed a fear of flying or something?' Lucy asked.

'What? No. Of course not. But I think you should use the ladies' room.'

So Lucy did, and when she returned a few minutes later it didn't seem they'd made much progress in the line, but Lucy did notice her luggage was partially unzipped and Mary Fran seemed much less antsy.

About a half hour later, they finally made it to the counter, and as a matter of course, the ticket agent asked Lucy if her bags had been in her possession the entire time she'd been in the airport. Before Lucy could respond, Mary Fran shouted, 'Yes! Of course!' and Lucy decided that as soon as they were in their first-class seats, she was ordering her sister a big-ass Bloody Mary.

They chatted amicably all the way through security and began their walk toward their gate. Lucy noticed quite a clamor up ahead and wondered if someone famous might be on their flight that morning. The closer they got to the gate, the more familiar some of the faces became.

'Is that *Mom* I see up there?' Lucy turned toward Mary Fran, who had suddenly become Theo. 'What the — ?'

Theo grabbed her and kissed her hard and that's when the camera lights clicked on and Lucy realized that *they* were the famous people and that everyone there — Mary

Fran, Dan, her parents, Buddy, Uncle Martin and Aunt Viv, John Weaver and Carolina Buendia, Tyson, Barry, and Maria and Veronica, and even Doris Lehman and her husband (*God* was he good-looking for an old guy!) — had all been in on the surprise.

And the surprise was that Theo was going to Jamaica with Lucy.

Lucy and Theo finished their interview with Carolina, signed autographs for other passengers, and hugged everyone good-bye. Just as they were about to head down the gangway, Doris Lehman handed Lucy a small plastic Baggie, and inside was a solitary homemade biscuit.

'Bon appétit,' was all she said.

★　★　★

Theo didn't think he'd ever be able to move again. His exhaustion began deep in his solar plexus and radiated to the very last hair on his head and the small nail on his small toe. He was soaked in sweat, breathing hard, and happier than he'd ever been in his whole life.

All because of Lucy, the not-quite-naked nymph now sprawled out right next to him on the king-size bed, a luxurious canopy of white gauze overhead.

'You rock, Cunningham,' he said in

between gulps of air. He let his head roll to the side, laying a cheek on the mangled bedsheets so he could look right in those beautiful eyes.

'Tired yet, coach?'

'Hell no. I'm not even warmed up.'

'I can't tell you how relieved I am to hear you say that.' Lucy jumped on top of him again and started kissing him some more, and Theo wrapped his arms around her and squeezed so tight he heard something pop.

'Hey! I'm not choking on Milk Duds at the moment! Lighten up!'

Theo laughed and rolled with her until their intertwined feet brushed the floor and they were nearly falling off the bed.

'I want to see you completely naked.'

'I'm working up to it.'

Theo laughed. 'You swore, Lucy. And I've been naked for at least two hours. Or maybe you haven't noticed.' He loved how Lucy's eyes flashed and her cheeks flushed.

'Oh, I've noticed.'

Her sweet, soft hand stroked his cock, and Theo could hardly believe it, but he was already responding to her again. Maybe there was something to be said for going without sex for months at a time, though he hoped to God that period of his life was gone for good.

'Do you like this?' Lucy whispered, looking

into his eyes as her hand caressed him to full length and breadth once more, then dragged her tongue along the underside of him.

'I love it — I love everything about being with you.' Theo arched his head back and groaned with pleasure, and suddenly her hand was gone and so was her tongue.

Lucy had gotten up. She stood on the floor over him, wearing a little blue tank top thing and nothing else. Her hair was messed up and her skin was pink and her lips were wet and she was a vision — a vision of lusciousness and lust and paradise. It was a good look on her.

Lucy reached over and flicked on the bedside lamp. Theo had no idea what time it was — probably about seven in the evening — but the shadows had already started to fill their comfortable bungalow. The light flowed over Lucy and showered her skin in gold.

Without a word, Lucy reached for the hem of the tank top and pulled it up over her head, then dropped it to the floor. There she was — this woman he knew almost as well as he knew himself — and she was giving him the ultimate gift.

Her trust.

Theo sat up on the edge of the bed and let his eyes travel over Lucy. She was curvy and firm and ripe. Yes, it was obvious her body had been through a dramatic transformation, and there were marks on her skin, especially on her belly and hips, like road markers from her journey. He loved those marks. He'd been to every one of those places with her. He remembered every day.

'I've always known you were beautiful.' Theo reached out and put his palms on the front of her hips, his fingers splayed open.

She gasped.

Theo had to say his favorite part of Lucy's body was still her neck — it was elegant, perfectly designed — but now that he was allowed to do more than window-shop, there were several other specifics he appreciated as well.

He loved the delicate curve of the inside of each of her thighs and the tiny vee of space between her legs, just under her sweet pussy.

He loved the graceful curve of her strong upper arms, the faint arch of her eyebrows, the delicate twist of her wrists, the tapered strength of her ankles.

'Please turn around for me, Luce.'

She did, and he loved her gorgeous ass and the two little dimples at the base of her spine, and her shoulders — so straight and strong — and the way her waist curved in just at the flare of her hips. He loved the tender skin at the back of her knees.

He stood up from the bed and embraced her from behind, then walked with her to the floor-to-ceiling mirror in the dressing room of their suite. On the way he flipped on the overhead light.

'This is new and different,' Lucy said, smiling as she leaned her head back against his chest.

'Do you see how good we fit together? How good we look with each other?'

One of Lucy's eyebrows arched high.

'Lucy, do you see the woman I have in my arms?'

She gave him a little nod and a nervous smile.

'What do you see?'

She paused, and Theo watched her consider his question carefully. 'I see a pretty woman who is physically strong and who owns her own business and is very much in love — for the first time in her life.'

Theo nodded, and kissed the top of her head.

'Do you see a slump buster looking back at you?'

She frowned. 'I do not.'

He squeezed her tight and held her gaze in the mirror. 'You're my slump buster, Luce. My own personal slump buster.'

Her mouth fell open and he felt her body go rigid.

'And this is a very good thing — let me tell you all about it.'

In a flash, Theo had one arm under the back of her knees and one arm around her waist and he'd lifted her off the floor. Theo walked with her to the front door of their little cave retreat by the ocean. 'Can you grab the door-knob?' Lucy did, still glaring at him, and he walked with her onto the deck.

The sea breeze was warm and wet and the sun was setting behind them, and Theo was glad this haven was designed for total privacy. It's why people came here.

'You saved me from my slump, Lucy.' Theo sat down in a comfortable canvas chair and held her in his lap, stroking the smooth skin of her naked back.

'When exactly were you in this slump, Theo? I must have been napping.'

He chuckled. 'My heart was in a slump. I'd turned it off, set it aside. I was in the biggest, baddest love slump a man could be in, until you walked in my door.'

A little smile curved at her succulent lips. 'And I changed all that?'

'You absolutely did.'

'I'm glad.' Lucy nodded, her hair slipping

down over half of her face. 'I am not perfect, Theo.'

'I'm not, either.'

'Tell me about it. You have a temper. You're a work-aholic and overly responsible. You don't tell the woman you love that you actually love her. Those are all significant shortcomings.'

'Yeah. And I've got a scar over my left eyebrow, too. Someday I'll tell you how I got it. It's a pretty romantic story.'

'I bet.'

Theo cupped that beautiful face in his hands. 'I love you, Lucy Cunningham. I love you so much that sometimes I wonder if I'm dreaming, and how I got lucky enough to have you in my life, and I suppose I've avoided saying this to you because it's a little terrifying for me.'

'Terrifying? Why?'

'Because I'm afraid if I start telling you how much I love you, I'll never be able to stop.'

She gave him a little close-mouthed smile and whispered, 'I'm eating this up, you know. Please go on.'

'I love you. I want you to be my lover and my best friend and live with me and Buddy. And someday soon we'll get married.'

'We will?'

'Yes. And we'll have kids, OK?'

Lucy scooted around on his lap and puckered her lips in thought. 'I have this one nagging question . . . '

'I bet I have the answer.'

'Maybe you don't, Theo.' Lucy looked out over the water and the breeze blew into her face and she closed her eyes. He knew what was coming, and he was ready for it.

'How will I ever know for sure that it's the real me you love — not just the one-hundred-thirty-nine-pound Frankenstein of fitness?'

Theo choked and laughed simultaneously. 'Frankenstein of fitness, huh?'

'You know what I mean.' Lucy adjusted herself so she faced him, and placed her hands on his shoulders. 'You didn't love me when I weighed two hundred and thirty pounds, did you?'

'No, I did not. But that's not exactly a fair question, Lucy. I liked you back then. You intrigued me. You made me laugh. But I didn't know you well enough to love you, and you changed so fast that for me to love you at your starting weight it would have to have been love at first sight.'

'Hey, it worked for me.'

Theo chuckled and stroked her back some more. 'I was in a slump, remember?'

Lucy fiddled with his earring. 'What if I

414

gain twenty pounds? Will you still love me? Are you going to be following me around the house to make sure I don't eat any more than a half cup of cottage cheese and that it's the one-percent milk fat kind at that?'

Theo shrugged. 'You'll probably gain more than twenty pounds when you get pregnant, Lucy.'

'Oh, so you'll wait until I blow up all pregnant and *then* you'll leave me?'

'I'm trying to make a point here.'

'Then do it before I start to panic.'

'Luce, I just love you. You have to trust me on this. I mean, hey, how would it sound if I told you I was worried that you'd leave me if I started going bald? Or when hair started to grow out of my ears like with Uncle Martin?'

'That's ridiculous,' Lucy said. Then she frowned. 'That ear hair thing isn't going to happen right away, is it?'

Theo laughed. 'Look, Lucy. I've made my living as a personal trainer for the last few years, but that's not why I love you — it just happens to be how I met you.'

Lucy's eyes were beginning to sparkle again. Her hands were in his hair.

'I want to spend my life with you, Lucy, and that means we'll both change physically, but we can still keep our hearts happy and full of love. We can always stay young inside.'

'I want to believe you love me for who I am. I want that more than anything in the world.'

'Then do.'

'I'm trying.'

'Would it help if I had proof?'

'Proof?' She laughed. 'You mean like hard evidence?'

'Exactly. Wait here just a minute, baby.'

'I'm a little chilly, Theo.'

'No problem. I'll bring you something to put on.'

Theo came back to the deck a few moments later with all the tools he needed for the job at hand — the registered letter, the surprise inside, the baby pink crotchless underwear and bra. 'Here you go, Luce.'

Lucy held the slippery little pieces of satin and lace in her hand and laughed. 'Too hilarious,' she said. 'Now I know why Mary Fran was so hot for me to go to the bathroom back at the airport.'

'Yeah. She told me it was a close call. She snagged them out of the hamper on your way out of the apartment.'

Lucy slipped the panties up her thighs and snapped the bra in place, adjusting the rather skimpy cups. 'And this is supposed to be proof that you'd love me even if I wasn't a size eight?'

'No.' Theo held out the letter. 'This is.'

'What's this?'

He returned to the chair and brought her back down onto his lap. 'Why don't you open it and find out.'

Lucy sat on his lap and crossed her shapely legs, working her finger into the adhesive of the light green postal seal. 'Am I being subpoenaed?'

'Nope. You're being proposed to.'

Lucy's lips fell apart and she stared at him for a moment, then frantically tore open the envelope.

'Careful — '

First she pulled out the folded photo paper and opened it. She giggled. 'Oh my.' Lucy stared at the picture for a while, then turned to Theo. 'You really did love me that night.'

'Way before then, actually. But that night was such a nightmare — '

'No kidding.'

'I just figured I'd better start documenting things. You can never be too prepared.'

'Thank you for doing that.'

'No problem. What else did you find in there?'

Lucy pulled apart the envelope and peered inside. She removed a small jade green silk pouch no larger than a playing card, the name of an exclusive Miami jeweler on the outside.

417

Theo watched a little frown pucker her brow. 'What in the world — ?'

She unsnapped the pouch and pulled out the notecard, which Theo remembered writing that morning after the party. He'd gone in search of a ring but couldn't seem to choose. The only thing he knew for sure that morning was that he loved this woman and had to have her. He'd written:

Would you mind designing your own engagement ring? I want it to be as unique and beautiful as the woman who wears it.

I love you, Lucy.

— Theo

She was going to cry, but that was all right with him, because she'd just buried her lips against his neck and whispered, 'I thought you'd never ask.'

One year later on the Miami Herald society page . . .

Miami — Makeover celebrity Lucy Cunningham married her personal trainer in a private ceremony Sunday at the Star Island estate of supermodel Gia Altamonte.

Cunningham, 31, and University of Miami medical student Theodore Redmond, 33, exchanged vows before family and friends after a yearlong engagement, according to the couple's friend *WakeUp Miami* cohost Tyson Williams. The morning show will air footage of the nuptials Monday, Williams said.

Cunningham is owner of the trendy Miami firm Slump Buster Advertising. She lost 91 pounds in a made-for-TV makeover mission led by Redmond, then a personal trainer for the Palm Club of Miami Beach.

Throughout the yearlong publicity stunt, the couple denied rumors of romantic involvement, but they got engaged immediately after Cunningham's success with Redmond's diet and exercise regimen. Since then, they've shared a Miami Springs home but have closely guarded their privacy.

The couple's debut health and fitness book, *Put Your Money on the Fat Chick*, has already caused a buzz in the publishing world, several months before its planned April release. Williams said the couple would promote the book after they returned from their honeymoon at an undisclosed location.

'They're real happy,' said Williams, a former Palm Club trainer who briefly worked with Cunningham. 'But I should have been the one in the tux today. Redmond stole her from me.'

In a strange twist, Cunningham's former employer, Stephan Sherrod, 54, was indicted last month on tax evasion charges. Authorities found the owner of the defunct Miami advertising agency Sherrod & Thoms hiding in the Cayman Islands, where he'd been living with girlfriend Lola DiPaolo. DiPaolo, 27, was not charged. Federal prosecutors claim Sherrod owes nearly $700,000 in corporate and personal back taxes.

According to Williams, the bride wore an ivory satin wedding gown designed by Isaac Olorio, who was one of about 100 guests in attendance. The wedding cake was a four-tiered light pound cake with butter cream frosting, dotted with Milk Duds.

Contacted by telephone late Sunday night, the bride's father, Bill Cunningham, said, 'Lucy was the most beautiful bride there ever was, and the groom didn't look too shabby, either.'

We do hope that you have enjoyed reading this large print book.

Did you know that all of our titles are available for purchase?

We publish a wide range of high quality large print books including:
Romances, Mysteries, Classics
General Fiction
Non Fiction and Westerns

Special interest titles available in large print are:
The Little Oxford Dictionary
Music Book
Song Book
Hymn Book
Service Book

Also available from us courtesy of Oxford University Press:
Young Readers' Dictionary
(large print edition)
Young Readers' Thesaurus
(large print edition)

For further information or a free brochure, please contact us at:
Ulverscroft Large Print Books Ltd.,
The Green, Bradgate Road, Anstey,
Leicester, LE7 7FU, England.
Tel: (00 44) 0116 236 4325
Fax: (00 44) 0116 234 0205